D1066843

His Frozen Fingertips
by Charlotte Bowyer

© Copyright 2017 Charlotte Bowyer

ISBN 978-1-63393-345-3

All rights reserved. No part of this publication may be reproduced, stored in a retrieval system, or transmitted in any form or by any means—electronic, mechanical, photocopy, recording, or any other—except for brief quotations in printed reviews, without the prior written permission of the author.

This is a work of fiction. The characters are both actual and fictitious. With the exception of verified historical events and persons, all incidents, descriptions, dialogue, and opinions expressed are the products of the author's imagination and are not to be construed as real.

Published by

◤ köehlerbooks™

210 60th Street
Virginia Beach, VA 23451
800-435-4811
www.koehlerbooks.com

HIS
FROZEN
FINGERTIPS

CHARLOTTE BOWYER

VIRGINIA BEACH
CAPE CHARLES

*To Nessa Blackmore, for being the one person
brave enough to read the first draft.*

ONE

HE WAS NOT NEGLECTED.

Nor was he a child.

Seventeen, in Asa Hounslow's opinion, was old enough to do whatever he pleased.

Therefore, he could not be a *child*.

And neglected? When had his parents ever shown him neglect? He hadn't seen them for five years.

Asa's hands were wrapped around a mug of hot water, steam curling over the rim. He rested his elbows on the table and sipped at his drink.

"I don't see how this is my problem."

The healer caught Asa's eyes and let her gaze drop back to the table. Papers covered it, diagrams and sketches of magical shapes that seemed to shift imperceptibly in the flickering candlelight. Her hands ran over a pot filled with spiked crystals: red, blue, and golden green. They hummed softly as she stroked the sharp tips.

"I was just saying that you should have brought your guardian with you," the healer murmured. "You are not old enough to receive this diagnosis without them here."

"They're working." Asa shrugged. "I was told to come here without them."

"*Asa.*" The healer's tone was at once sharp and gentle.

"What?" he interjected.

"Where are they really?"

"I don't know," Asa enunciated, stumbling. "Working, as I said."

"I don't believe you."

"Then prove me wrong," he huffed.

The healer shook her head and wrote on a slip of paper. The weak light in the room sent shadows skittering across the ceiling in response to her careful movement. Her handwriting was cramped and slanted across the note as she signed it, sealed it, and went to hand it to Asa. He reached out for it and felt the rough sheet between his fingers before it was tugged out of his grasp.

"Forgive me. I almost forgot."

The healer grasped a green crystal from the pot on her desk. Asa tried to maintain a straight face but couldn't restrain a groan as she folded the note and placed the stone on the wax seal. She murmured some words and the room flashed blinding white for a moment before Asa blinked and the crystal was back in its pot.

"What did you do that for?" he complained.

"I bound it so that only your guardian could read it." The healer dusted her hands off. "I don't trust you, Asa Hounslow."

Asa snatched the paper, stormed from the healer's desk, and slammed the door. Night had fallen, illuminated only by the huge silver moon that hung in the sky over Brandenbury. Asa breathed a column of steam into the ice-cold sky and watched it diffuse into the dark air. The visit to the healer weighed on his mind as he strolled down deserted lanes back into the suburbs.

A fox ran ahead of him, diving from the road into the bushes that lined it. He smelled the musk of badgers as they wandered unseen through the countryside. Cows settled in the fields on either side of him, their moist breath audible even from behind the vegetation. The road was like a tangled ribbon, only a winding expanse of dusty gravel stretching ahead of him as far as his eyes could see.

Asa was so preoccupied that he didn't notice the person lying by the side of the road until he had stumbled over him, crushing the person's hand with his boot and flying head first into the hedgerow. He heard a yelp, then groan, and the unmistakable sound of someone fumbling along the ground for something. *Spectacles*, Asa assumed, pulling himself upright. The thorns caught on his loose tunic and scratched at his skin, making him swear through gritted teeth.

"What are you playing at?" he snarled at the prone figure. "Lying in the road! What did you expect?"

He groaned again and rustling indicated their movement.

"Go on," Asa instructed. "Say something."

"I was sleeping," the boy offered.

"In the road."

"Nowhere else to sleep," he intoned drily. "The pony got away."

"But the road—"

Asa paused. He recognised that voice. Creeping forwards, he placed careful hands on the boy's body, feeling him tense at the uninvited touch. His fingers sensed solid muscle under the skin, warm, vital, strong. He moved towards his head when he abruptly stood up, shaking Asa off with an incredulous laugh.

"Sorry?"

"Sorry," Asa exhaled. "Sorry. You sounded familiar, and I didn't quite know how to ask you—"

"Ask me what?"

He could feel the boy's breath in the cold air.

"Your name," Asa mumbled, embarrassed.

"Why don't you just ask then?" the stranger proposed.

"Your name?"

"Yes."

"Well, what is your name?"

"Averett," he said. "But my friends call me Avery."

Asa felt a grin pull across his face. "Knew it."

"Asa?" Avery asked. "Is that you?"

"Yes," his voice cracked as he stared into the dim figure's face. "How did you know?"

"That pleased to see me?"

"What are you doing out here?" Asa repeated, crossing his arms. "You're miles from Salatesh."

His friend sounded concerned. "Well, it's the twelfth, remember?"

"Yes." Asa tried to find the familiar face in the gloom. "I am well aware of the date."

"Check your calendar." Avery shrugged. "This is the week that I'm spending with you."

"What?" Asa spluttered. "No, no, that's next month."

"Nope," he was reminded. "This month. Don't you keep a record of stuff like this?"

"I find it to be rather a hassle," Asa muttered.

"Really? I never would've guessed." He could hear Avery smirk. "Well? Come on, then. Show me to your house!"

They meandered down the quiet road, chatting about everything and nothing at the same time. Asa kept stealing glances of the tall figure next to him, an unconscious smile playing around the edge of his mouth. He could not believe that Avery was here, in Brandenbury. Though they had exchanged letters, they had been brief; to his chagrin he had indeed forgotten that Avery was to come and stay with him this week.

The light grew brighter and highlighted the top of Avery's broad shoulders, his nose, even reflecting off his wiry blond hair. They passed house after house of the same uniform design, before entering the more unique side of the town. The streetlights illuminated the road with a flickering glow, tinted by the orange glass placed around the flame. They wandered out into the town square, passing a large fountain and some abandoned market stalls. Asa was just fumbling for his key when he heard it, dimly at first but growing louder. He strained his ears to listen, key held up to the lock.

The bell was ringing from the spire of the old Town Hall.

Other places began to pick up the pealing chime, repeating it and sending the message on. The fire service and the schoolhouse amplified it with their additions. Asa looked at Avery, who had frozen where he stood, panic written over his features. It was superstitiously bad luck to be in a public space when the bells began to ring.

"Come on," he urged. "We need to get inside."

With a gentle push, Avery stumbled along as Asa fitted the key in the lock of his apartment building. The wooden door was warped and heavy, but he slammed his body against it and let them in, pulling it shut when done. The draft extinguished several of the candles up the winding staircase. Asa gripped his friend's arm and pulled him up until the light was bright enough to illuminate them both.

"I'm fine," Avery panted.

"Good," Asa acknowledged. "You need to be."

He maintained his grip upon Avery's shoulder as they climbed the stairs to a small landing. The green paint was peeling off the walls, and the floor was carpeted in untouched dust apart from a thin path to a plain door with nothing on it but a lock. Asa slipped his key inside, turned it, and let them both into the four-room apartment with a soft click. Avery raised an eyebrow to the teenager next to him.

Asa gestured for him to sit on one of the empty stools at the table. Avery accepted the invitation without speaking, giving a wary nod. Asa then lit all of the candles on the walls using a small flint and steel, which he kept on top of the bread bin. Soon the kitchen was filled with the warm light, casting erratic shadows over their faces.

"Was that the . . .?" Avery ventured.

"Yes." Asa cleared his throat thickly before striding across the kitchen to a smouldering stove. "Tea?"

"Tea?"

"You know, the hot drink made from steeped leaves or bark."

"How can you be thinking of tea in a time like this?" his friend spluttered. "The bells are ringing."

"I know," Asa countered. "But it'll be fine. It always is."

Avery slumped onto the table with a great sigh. Asa couldn't blame him. Even though it happened annually, there was something about the urgent tolling of the bells that was taxing on a person's morale. Harm didn't usually follow the warning, but there were certain years that were fixed in the public's psyche. Years such as his fifth spring. There had been a hailstorm of rocks and ash pouring from the sky until the rivers and fields were black and scorched. He ran home to his parents, and they sought shelter in one of the deep salt mines whilst the village of Salatesh crumpled into rubble.

"Do you think Salatesh will be alright?" Avery voiced almost exactly what Asa was thinking.

"Yes," Asa asserted. "Stop worrying. Nothing will come of you moaning and groaning like that."

"I don't trust it," Avery argued. "Erebus hasn't done anything for years now. Asa, what if this year he—"

"Oh, please be quiet, Avery!" Asa snapped. "If he kills us, then we are dead. We won't even know that he has done it."

They descended into a sulky silence, filled only with quiet, uneven breathing. The apartment was drafty and Asa shivered as the temperature dropped. The only warmth in the room came from the glowing coals in the stove. He tapped his fingers on the table, wondering in spite of himself what form Erebus's wrath would take this year. The powerful sorcerer had attacked them from his walled kingdom every spring for as long as Asa could recollect. He embodied everything that Eodem didn't stand for—violence, indolence, and greed. That's why they fought across the wall. Once it fell, peace could return to Eodem. Each year, the queen chose a warrior to cross over and fight the warlock. Each year they fell.

If their luck stood out then Eodem would be safe until another hero was chosen to take their place and fight Erebus. Then the bell would ring again, and all would be peaceful. Asa wouldn't count upon it. To his knowledge, nobody had ever gone within a mile of Erebus without suffering the most painful of deaths.

Avery stood. "Is there a spare room? I need to put my stuff away."

"No," Asa mouthed.

"I'll take the sofa then." Avery pushed past his friend and went further into the flat, finding the sitting room with relative ease. Asa followed him, wiping grimy fingerprints off of his doorknobs as he went.

"This is just plain inconvenient," Asa said, scowling at his reflection in the tarnished mirror on the wall above the sofa. "You're lucky I found you when I did, before the bells rang. You'll need to leave as soon as you can though. I've got a job now, bills, responsibilities. Adult stuff."

Avery either did not notice Asa's chilly demeanour, or it did not bother him. He gave a sunny smile and jumped down onto the sofa. Asa cringed at the sound of twanging springs.

"Adult? You're barely seventeen," Avery snorted. "Come back to Salatesh. It's all been rebuilt now, not just the mines and the town. We can go boating on the lake and everything."

Asa paused. "No thanks," he sighed, sticking his hands deep in his pockets. "I'd rather not."

"Everyone misses you," his friend huffed. "You could come see all of your friends again, it's not that far. You can't escape your past, Asa. No one minds about, well, your parents."

"No," Asa shook his head. "Two days of riding to sit on a bank watching you all swim? Sounds exciting, but impossible. I'm too busy to indulge in those childish games."

"Yeah, again, seventeen. Real mature."

"Would you mind not probing, Avery? I have duties now, responsibilities," Asa repeated, feeling his ears flush hotly.

"And I don't?" Avery's face fell. "I work just as hard as you, if not harder. Yeah, drawing little maps is so tough, compared to working in the mines."

"Are you mocking me?" Asa hissed, pulling himself up to his full height.

"Yeah, maybe I am," Avery growled. "Maybe you're right. I shouldn't have come." He hoisted his bag onto his back and began to tug his shoes on, ignoring several obvious blisters on his feet. He then shoved past Asa, who stood for a moment conflicted.

"Will you please stop being such a pain, Avery?" he sounded snappier than intended.

"Says the person who dragged me out on the longest journey that I can make," Avery retorted, pulling his hood over his unruly blond hair, "only to tell me to go away."

He made to go, placing his callused hand over the doorknob. Asa started forward, catching himself on the kitchen table. Avery twisted the knob with a grunt, pulling the door towards him. He stepped over the threshold.

"No," Asa finally said, pulling at his friend's cloak as it left the apartment. "No. Wait. Don't go."

"Why?" Avery turned, looking confused. "You don't want me here."

Asa shook his head dumbly, looking at the tiled floor.

"I get lonely," he mumbled.

Avery slunk back into the kitchen. His dark eyes scanned everything in the room, from the jars of fruit preserve on the shelves to the black iron stove. Asa offered him a seat, and he took it, turning that inquiring gaze on Asa himself.

"Asa, what's wrong?" he asked, gentle all of a sudden.

"Nothing's wrong, nothing." Asa could feel his eyes glassing over but blinked tears back. "I'm just tired, is all."

"Are you sure?"

Asa could feel hazel eyes boring into his back.

"You don't look too good."

"Oh, that?" Asa laughed it off, giving himself an excuse to wipe his eyes on his sleeve. "Yeah, I reckon I'm coming down with something."

"Okay," Avery conceded. "Do you want to get to bed?"

"No, that won't be necessary," Asa insisted, swallowing some tight knot in his throat. "I'm not that tired."

"But you said—"

"I was using hyperbole," Asa pressed on. "To illustrate my point. I'm not that tired. I had a long night's sleep last night."

"Sure." Avery didn't sound convinced. "But, Asa—"

"Put your stuff down," Asa ordered in a weary voice. "And relax. I'll make us supper."

He heard Avery's footsteps clunking from the sitting room to the bathroom. Waiting until his friend was definitely out of earshot, he whisked back into the kitchen and slammed the door behind him. Nervous fingers took the note from his pocket and fingered the seal. He chuckled. Clever as his healer was, if he had no parents then he was his own guardian.

The writing was cramped and spiked all over the page, overlapping with lines above and below. He could only just distinguish each letter. Asa strained his eyes, willing the dark to be light.

To the guardians of Mr. Asa Hounslow, he read to himself, drumming the same incessant beat from earlier on the table. *We regret to inform you that after careful consideration, we have clear concerns that your ward's heart*—

"Oh, for goodness' sake," Asa blurted.

It was just as he had feared.

Asa threw the letter down on the table and raked his hands through his wavy hair, swearing once more when a few dark strands came loose in his fingers. How could this happen? He didn't feel sick. He had only gone as a precaution from these dratted headaches he'd been having lately, as well as dizziness and vomiting. It wasn't like he couldn't eat. He ate plenty, but he just had a delicate stomach—or so he had thought. He picked the letter up again, hands shaking as he scanned the contents.

"*Due to the advanced nature of his condition,*" Asa murmured to himself, "*there is no direct remedy that we can prepare for it. However, you should be able to maintain his state of being for some months more through adequate rest and medicinal teas, which should arrive in the morning post. More detailed instructions to follow. Yours sincerely, Hlr. Vanessa Fliteroy.*"

So there it was, laid down for the whole empty kitchen to see. Asa clutched at the loose material around his chest, breathing harsh and rapid. Thoughts raced through his brain so quickly that he could hardly catch a glimpse of them. He bit down any noise that he might have made, irrationally terrified of Avery hearing him. The sofa creaked in the sitting room, and Asa allowed himself to release a small sob.

"Asa?" Avery called across the apartment. "Was that you?"

Asa sprang to his feet and began to rummage frantically in the cupboards, slamming various jars onto the table as loudly as possible. "Was what me?"

"Never mind." Avery's voice quieted, and Asa froze back into an unnatural stillness.

"Food," he mumbled. "Supper. Right, okay. Uh, toast. That'll do. I'll make toast."

He fumbled some bread out of the bread bin and spiked it with two toasting forks, shoving them into the stove. The flames almost reached the crust of the slices, but merely turned them a golden brown. Asa flipped them, numb to the slight burning of his skin on the warmed metal. Soon, the smell of cooking bread filled the cramped kitchen. With an expert hand, he flipped the toast slices from the forks onto a plate and placed it on the table.

"Avery!" he called. "Food."

There was little butter left in the pot, so he spread it onto his friend's toast and split the last of the jam between them. He had meant to go to the market this week, but one thing had led to another and he had forgotten. The floorboards creaked beneath his friend's heavy boots as he entered the room.

"Thanks." Avery grabbed a slice of toast and crunched into it with relish. "You alright?"

"What?" Asa twitched. "Oh, yes. Great."

He watched his friend chew for a moment, biting his lip. All of a sudden, the apartment felt too bright, too enclosed, too loud. The beige walls made him wince as he sank onto a stool next to Avery, cradling his aching head in his hands.

"Sure about that?"

"I'm fine," he insisted.

There was a knock on the door.

"Oh, for goodness' sake!" Asa cursed, all too happy to have a distraction. "It's like a sales day market place around here! First, no one ever comes to visit, then I get two in one day. Am I spoiled or just dismally unlucky?"

He strode to the door and slapped the chain across it, opening it with such rigor that the paint cracked where the chain hit. He looked out into the hallway.

"Letter for Mr. Asa Hounslow," a stiff voice said.

"What is it this time?" Asa sighed, glancing back at his friend, who had eaten his toast. "I'm not going to buy anything from you, you know. Just go away."

"That is hardly necessary." Asa could see the person's outline. He was long and thin and wearing a strange sort of red tailcoat uniform. "Don't shoot the courier. You just need to sign for the letter. It's urgent business."

Asa ripped the letter from the spidery hand and scrawled his name on the scrap of paper with the pencil provided.

"Well, it better be urgent if you're here at this hour," he tutted, shoving it back through the crack in the door. "Are you happy now?"

"Oh, I'm effervescent." The man sniffed, filing the paper in the briefcase he carried. "See you tomorrow, sir."

"I'm sure I—wait, what does that even—?" but the man had gone, taking his signature and leaving nothing but the curiously rolled letter and a faint smell of violets. "What a strange person."

Asa returned to the table, looking curiously at the letter.

"Who was that?" Avery asked, eyeing the paper in Asa's hands. "And why did they give you an invitation?"

"No, it's not an invitation, it's a letter," Asa murmured, feeling the seal with his fingers. "Don't know who sent it to me. The seal's all official and everything."

"Interesting," Avery replied levelly, having found something to occupy his wandering attention.

Asa flipped the letter over and grabbed his paper knife, excitement running like electricity through his trembling fingers.

"The paper's so smooth," he said, feeling the texture. "So creamy. It's like silk."

"Great," his friend sounded distant, distracted. Asa looked at him, frowning.

"What's bitten you?"

"Just thinking." Avery stuffed something beneath the table, hiding it from view.

"About what?" Asa raised an eyebrow.

"Life, I guess." Avery smiled tersely. "Go on, on with the mysterious scroll."

"It's just a letter." Asa rolled his eyes but continued all the same.

The seal was easy to break; it was made of sealing wax rather than plain candle drips. Asa shivered as he remembered the thin man's words, 'I'll be seeing you tomorrow.' That was either quite ominous or exciting or both. Maybe this was his quest. Maybe it was time for him to be immortalised in literature. Maybe, his excited mind ran on, he was to be appointed as a member of the queen's court. Had someone powerful become interested in his maps? What was in the letter? Somehow, he managed to pull the leaves of paper apart and unfurl the beautiful, crested paper. Before he even read the words, he was stunned by the decadence of the pages. Gilded edges, illuminated headers—they were expensive.

"What does it say?" Avery asked, exasperated. "Go on, read it."

Asa nodded mutely, eyes flickering down to the elegant copperplate script under the letterhead. He cleared his throat, feeling his mouth go dry.

"*To Mr. Asa Hounslow, re: the State of a Nation,*" he read, feeling prickles of excitement run up his spine. "*You have been chosen out of thousands of others to lead the way to a time of peace. Your quest shall be explained in full at the Palace Royale at Jundres in three days' time. A carriage will be arriving tomorrow at first light to take you on the first part of the journey. Do not be late.*"

He reread it, and then scanned it again, eyes not processing what he was seeing. He laughed as the message sunk in. *It has happened*, he thought. He had found his quest, or it had found him. He could not believe it, and at the perfect time. Something to give his life meaning, a purpose. Asa turned to Avery, a smile stretching over his face. He waited for the blond to say something, say anything, so that Asa could re-emphasise the news.

"Well, you're not going to go, are you?" Avery asked simply, not looking at Asa.

"What?" Asa spluttered, a frown dampening his features. "No, of course I will go. Why wouldn't I?"

The blond blinked, "I just assumed that—"

"What?" Asa asked incredulously.

"That you would share my stance on this whole *adventuring* business. It's not right, able-bodied folks sacrificing their services to the community for the chance of some pitiful self-glory." Avery shrugged, tossing his fringe out of his eyes. "You shouldn't go, anyhow."

"But an adventure!" Asa exclaimed. "A chance to prove myself, to be courageous! Isn't that worth going for?"

"No." Avery shook his head. "No, it isn't. Call me old fashioned, but I like my friends un-decapitated."

"You're old fashioned," groaned Asa. "Come on, Avery. You know that this is the chance of a lifetime. You know that this is what I've always wanted. Who knows, I may decapitate myself with a pen tomorrow; cartography is just as dangerous. Why don't you come with me?"

"I'm fine, thanks." Avery raised an eyebrow. "I, personally, am aware of my physical limitations."

Asa turned his head so that he could examine his friend's face. The statement was rather foreboding—it was as if he knew. *But he can't*, Asa reminded himself. Asa had only found out recently. Avery was merely being his usual superior self, not that Asa minded about that.

"What is that supposed to mean?" he asked, trying to keep his face as open and unreadable as possible. "I am well aware of my physical limitations. I hope that I'm more aware of them than you are."

There was a pause as Avery looked to be considering his answer, and then a short bark of laughter.

"It means that you don't have the tough and well-sculpted body of a miner." He smirked, ruffling Asa's longish hair. "You're so small, Asa."

Asa laughed too, out of relief more than anything.

"I am plenty tall for my career, thank you," he mused. "You're just a giant. You must be as tall as your father by now?

You're seventeen years old! Same as me. Slow down before you hit the sun, Avery."

"I'll consider that." Avery smiled. "If you consider not going on that foolhardy quest."

Asa was quiet for a moment. "I've got to go, Avery."

"You're too young to go killing yourself on some stupid mission," the blond protested.

"I'm not a child," Asa muttered sulkily, kicking the table. "And I'm as old as you, Avery, so don't go telling me what to do. Look at me! When do you think I'll get an opportunity like this again?"

"Asa—"

"No." He held up a hand. "I just want to do this. Can't you let me do what I think is right? I know how to take care of myself. I've done it for five years now."

"Well, you obviously don't," Avery snapped, before slapping a hand over his mouth. "No, I'm sorry, that was harsh."

"Do you think?" Asa said, a twinge of something moving in his chest.

"I'm sorry," Avery repeated.

"Yeah."

They did not speak for a few moments, the silence tense and awkward. Asa could feel his stomach churning nastily in his unease. He looked down at his long, sallow fingers as they clutched the scroll, shifting microscopically in his seat. His companion noticed the movement and decided to break the silence.

"Well, it's not like you could go, even if you wanted to."

Asa refused to look at Avery. He did not know how he should feel. On one hand, he was legally an adult and he didn't have to take this from a gangly teen who still lived with his parents. On the other, Avery was his only friend. He was the only person with whom Asa had bothered to keep up correspondence. If he didn't think that Asa could do it, then maybe Asa himself should doubt it.

"I could, too." It sounded childish, even as he said it.

"No, mate, you couldn't." Avery's eyes bored into Asa's with that unfamiliar intensity. "I don't know what strange ideas you've developed since you moved in here, but they've got to stop. Face it. You aren't physically able to go on a two-day horse ride, let alone a quest of whatever extremes Queen Ria will send you on. Give up on these foolish notions and stay home. Didn't you say that you had a map-making business or something?"

"I did," Asa replied cagily. "But working is a different business. Can't you understand that I don't want to be here, to be this, for the rest of my life?"

Avery made a choked noise, like a cross between a cough and a sneeze. The muscles in his back rippled with the movement, a flicker of energy twitching across his shoulder blades. A slight look of hurt crossed his features before being reined in, and he gave a tight smile.

"Were you going to lie to me?" His voice was low and rough.

"About what? I have nothing to hide," Asa said, feeling nervous.

"How about your little . . . surprise?" Avery replied, slamming his large fist down on the table, something small clutched in it. Asa managed to tease the paper out of the strong grip, and uncrumpled it, confused. Heat began to surge through him as he scanned the familiar page for what must have been a dozen times that night.

"You've been reading my letter?" he exclaimed, pushing his chair backwards across the tiles as he stood up, shaking. The resultant screech of wood on stone made Avery flinch. "How dare you?"

"How dare you not tell me?" Avery, still sitting at the table, albeit looking stormily up at Asa, was calmer than he. "I'm your best friend."

"Wrong tense there, Avery," Asa pronounced every syllable of the other's full name, relishing the aggressiveness he could convey through doing so. "Wrong tense. You were my friend. However, *friends* don't poke into their friends' private business and they certainly don't tell them about it afterwards. For goodness' sake, you're such a complete and utter idiot. You've ruined everything."

"Watch it, there." Avery hardly seemed bothered by Asa's denouncement of their friendship. "It said not to exert yourself."

Asa grit his teeth. "That is none of your business. You wouldn't understand, anyway."

"I may not have gone to some fancy school in the town, but I still want to know," Avery asserted, raising his eyebrows. "Simplify it."

Asa glowered at him, brown eyes darkening with ire. He clenched his fists, wanting nothing more than to slam them right into Avery's mild face. His body shook, without him even intending to do so. He opened a cupboard at random, feigned interest in the contents, and then turned away for the sheer pleasure of slamming the door as hard as he physically could.

"They told me that it was the worst possible scenario," he grunted, slumping onto the table. "I was born with a dodgy heart. That's why I never did rough games when you met me. But it's been getting worse. It soon may be too weak to keep me alive."

Avery gaped before clearing his throat, his eyes wandering over the room. He seemed to be trying to look for a new topic of conversation, biting his lip.

"We're all going to die someday," he mumbled, not looking at Asa.

"Wow, thanks." Asa rolled his eyes. "This is why I didn't tell you, you know. I don't want you to coddle me. I want you to treat me the same, and in your case that means being an insufferable git."

Avery offered a weak smile. "I can work with that."

"You'd better," Asa warned, tugging his hair in anxiety.

"Don't do that," his friend protested. "You'll get hair everywhere."

"Hey!" Asa brought his hands down from his head. "One, I still haven't forgiven you for invading my privacy—"

"It was right there on the table."

"Two," he continued fluidly, ignoring the interruption, "my house, my rules. And three, who even cares if there are a few tufts of hair around my house? Gives the place character."

"Gross." Avery shuddered.

"You can have it when I'm gone," Asa said, stroking the table with a kind eye. "The house, I mean, not the hair. Of course, you'll get lots of that too. Just the few things I've owned."

"Me?" the blond asked.

"Well, I've got no one else to give it to," Asa stated. "I'm sorry if you don't want it or anything. You can sell it, if you wish. You can even have it right now. I'm leaving tomorrow."

"You're still going on that ridiculous quest?" Avery asked. "Are you mad?"

"No, I just have less time to achieve my life goals, so I figured that I should take what I can get."

"You're nuts," Avery said, shaking his head. "Barmy. You'll die before you've got halfway there."

"What a way to go." Asa shrugged, dismissing the negativity. "I'll be alone, free."

"You're actually choosing to shorten your life?" Avery sighed. "Whatever next? You're different, I grant you that, but not in a way that merits praise."

"Stars, Avery, I'll see stars. It's too bright to see them here. All we can get glimpses of are the moon, on occasion. I can hardly remember what the little things look like now. I remember that they lit up the sky, like light shining through a curtain. I want to see them again before I die."

"It won't be like the stories," his friend warned him, breaking through his reverie. "You know that it's going to be tough. Won't have a roof over your head, for a start. No warm food. No warmth. It's winter. Being out there at night when you're sick is not a good idea."

"There are villages inside the walls, Grandpa Hounslow told me so," Asa insisted.

"The walls are set up for a reason," Avery groaned. "They are put there so that we don't run the risk of running into evil things. Those villages are as crumpled as Salatesh was, all those years ago. Erebus wouldn't let intruders into his territory. You won't go through the walls anyway. Only the One Hero is able to get through, and they go through extensive training first. No, you'll be going over the Moving Mountains, freeze to death, and die."

"Sounds like a plan," Asa concluded, rubbing his hands together. "I guess I'll need a cloak though. Maybe some food?"

"You can't be thinking of doing this alone!" Avery's voice cracked. "Believe me, you can't. I don't want you to die alone and scared in some foreign place. You're too important to me. Don't go, please. Don't go."

"I'm going, Avery," Asa said finally. "I can't let this slip away from me."

"Then I'm coming with you," Avery stated.

"What?"

"You heard me," he said, hazel eyes softening. "If you won't stay safe at home, then I'll ensure that you stay safe in some other place. I'm giving you my dagger, is that what they say?"

"I have your sword," Asa said, a slow grin spreading across his face. "And believe me, Avery, there is nothing I trust more to keep me safe."

TWO

ASA WOKE EARLY THE next morning. He lay still in bed for a while, listening to the quiet sounds of a house in rest, too comfortable to move. It was still dark out; the room was shadowy and dim to his blurry vision. Asa could only just see to the end of the bed where his bare feet peeked out from under the duvet. He stretched, only letting loose a startled squeak when his flexing fingers caught on some warm figure in the dark.

"Who's there?" He pulled his arm back and crawled to the edge of the mattress, gasping for breath. It was too dark for him to discern who was in his bed. Mind racing, he ran through all of the possibilities. There was only one. "Avery?"

"Mmph," the muffled reply came. "What, Asa?"

"Why in Eodem are you in my bed?" Asa moved off the mattress, tugging down his nightshirt and staring at his friend in bewilderment. The memories of yesterday flooded back to him. "Oh for the love of Erebus! We're meeting that man from yesterday at sunrise."

"The sofa was cold." Asa saw Avery sit up in bed, dishevelled, wearing the same clothes as yesterday. "Don't worry, Asa. We've got about an hour until sunrise."

Asa threw a book at his friend, face screwed up in disgust. "Don't you dare ever climb into my bed again. Why in Eodem would you do that?"

Avery sighed and stood, the bedsprings creaking impressively as he did so. "Like I said, the sofa was cold. You can't expect your guest to freeze to death."

"Oh, I wish," Asa muttered, pulling a blanket over his shoulders and chucking another at Avery. The room was indeed colder than Asa thought. The floor in particular was frigid. He took a few shivery steps to the door and placed a pale hand on the handle. His fingers stuck to the frozen metal for a moment as he hissed. "Freezing! How, I'd like to know, is this house this cold? Winter's been and gone."

The door opened with ease and the pair of them crossed through the sitting room to the kitchen. Asa struck a small fire in the stove as Avery lit the candles in the room. In a few moments, the kitchen was filled with dancing light.

"What's for breakfast?" he asked Asa, as the latter examined the fire over his shoulder. "I'm starving."

"Whatever you can make without my help," Asa replied, rubbing his temples. "You can cook, can't you?"

"Sure," Avery said, standing to rifle through a cupboard. "Yeah, you've got bread and stuff. I'll make toast. You want some?"

"Blackened pieces of charcoal with some melted butter?" Asa scoffed. "No, thank you. I'll go without ingesting raw carbon for today."

Avery speared a rough slice of bread on a toasting fork. "Suit yourself. You not going to have anything?"

"I'll abstain from breakfast for today." Asa pulled his thin legs up to his chest and shivered. "Why do you think it's so cold?"

At this, Avery looked anxious. He shoved the bread in the fire as he looked out of the black window where he and Asa were reflected back at them. "You don't think—"

"What?" Asa huffed.

"Well, it's not happened for so many years, but what if it's . . . him?"

"'Him' being?"

"Erebus," Avery cleared his hoarse throat, toasting fork shaking as he said it. "What if it's getting bad again, Asa?"

"No, it won't be." Asa shrugged the idea off, rolling his eyes. "I can remember the last times it happened. It was all destructive and violent, not a sudden cold snap. No, some sort of imbalance in the air caused this. It'll fix itself, it always does."

"Hmm."

Asa could tell that his friend was still upset. He smiled reassuringly at him. "Don't worry. You're too young to be fretting about Erebus and all of that nonsense. Think of something more suitable, like girls or horses or something."

"Pfft, girls," scoffed Avery. "No, thank you. Anyway, you're two months older than me. That counts for nothing."

"It counts for something," Asa asserted. "I can do all sorts of stuff you can't. I'm also significantly more responsible."

"You are not!" the blond exclaimed.

"So says the child holding a fork of flaming bread," coughed Asa.

"Oh dear." Avery pulled the blackened toast out of the fire, blew on it, and took a scalding bite. It crumpled to dust in his teeth. "Don't worry, it's fine."

A few embers fell on his tunic, burning tiny holes in the fabric. Avery tried to bat them out, ripping and staining the material further. He groaned in defeat and continued eating the obliterated bread.

"As I said, charcoal," Asa reminded him. "Only you are not civilised enough to spread butter on it."

"The taste completes itself," the other affirmed. "I don't need any butter, thanks."

"Only because you're afraid that it would collapse in on itself under the weight." Asa smiled.

"Hey!" Avery chewed for a few thoughtful mouthfuls. He swallowed and made some vague gesticulations. "Oh yeah. Asa? These are my only clothes. I can't go out when they're covered in soot. I'll look absurd."

"Good for you," Asa replied, examining a mug ring on the wood and wondering where it was from. He elected to cover it with a coaster in the hopes of reversing the damage.

"I was wondering, well, could I borrow some of yours?" Avery grimaced. "I have trousers and undergarments, but do you have a spare shirt?"

"I have one that could fit you." Asa examined Avery with a critical gaze. "Yeah, I think it'll do. Come upstairs and we can see."

Avery furtively threw the toast into the fire and stood, dusting himself down. Asa shook his head in mock anger but led his friend through his cold apartment to the bedroom, still as cold and dark as when he awoke. Asa lit the single candle on his bedside table and pulled the coverlet over his messy bed. He looked to the wardrobe and opened it, one hand ready to catch any avalanche of clothing that fell upon them. None was forthcoming, so he rifled through the different colours and fabrics until he found one shapeless, rough piece of material.

"What is that?" Avery asked.

"Your tunic," Asa tutted, pulling the large tunic out of the wardrobe and examining it against Avery's body. "Yes, I think that should fit you, Avery."

"Fit me?" the taller exclaimed. "Yes, I should think so. It's enormous."

"Do you want it or not?" Asa eyed Avery's grubby clothes.

"I want it," his friend said begrudgingly. "Hand it over."

Once dressed, Asa and Avery made their way to the front door and started to pull on boots and cloaks. They were fairly quiet but were only completely silenced when there was a knock on the door. Asa glanced at Avery and leant forward to open it, not bothering with the chain. They both knew who it was going to be. The door creaked as it opened, heavy hinges protesting. There was a strong scent of violets.

The man who had given Asa the invitation the day before stepped through the doorway. "Mr. Asa Hounslow, your carriage awaits. I hope you are wearing suit—excuse me, who is this?"

"Hey, I'm Avery Hardy." Avery held forth a callused hand. The man took it in his own paper-thin one.

"Charmed, I'm sure. I am Clement Kean, of the queen's own council," he purred. "Yes, the real queen's council."

"Didn't dispute it," Avery said comfortably, ignoring the man's smugness. "So, Asa, we ready to go?"

"Hold on a moment!" Kean said. "You cannot be coming as well?"

"Yeah, what if I am?"

"I—I don't . . . This is not correct behaviour," Kean insisted. He squared himself up to Avery, and Asa could not have seen a centimetre's difference in their heights. Kean was thin and Avery was broader than him by about a third.

"We know," Asa replied, hoping for no physical violence between the two. He ushered them out of the door, locked it with a key from around his neck, and checked the handle. He replaced the golden object under his tunic, fingers almost caressing the white string. "Come on, then."

"It isn't protocol to allow more than two people at one time in the carriage," Kean argued. "If your friend wishes to ride behind us for moral support, then he is more than welcome to do so."

"I'm sure that there is enough room," Asa said. "What if I were to sit on Avery's lap?"

"It is a weight issue," the man insisted.

Asa looked exasperatedly at him. "Then why don't you ride behind us then?"

"Protocol."

"Are you having a laugh?" Avery confronted him. "Are you saying that you won't allow one extra person when the two of you are like toothpicks already?"

"Well, I guess," Kean stammered. "Fine, you may both squeeze upon the same seat. But don't blame me if the carriage falls over."

"We won't," Asa promised. "How cold is it outside?"

Kean gestured to the staircase. "Sufficiently freezing. Now please get moving."

The staircase seemed mustier than Asa remembered. The paint was still peeling, damp stains running down from the ceiling. It was like walking through a sloping green cave. The floors were uncarpeted, their heavy boots clanked satisfyingly on the wooden planks. What little light could get through the grimy windows was watery, unable to fully permeate the darkness.

Asa reached the front door first, where simple black paint was scratched and worn from many hands' paths. He struggled to lift the heavy bolts. They were thick and strong, able to withstand whatever outside threat would come their way. However, he was not an outside threat, so he should be able to open it. Surely he could manage this. Avery reached forward.

"No, Avery," Asa warned. "I can do this by myself."

He struggled for a few more moments, pulling fruitlessly at the warped metal. His fingers slipped along it as he worked the bolt loose. Kean tutted, tapping a foot on the grubby floor. Asa managed to slip it through the designated hole and the bolt made a satisfying clicking noise. He tugged on the handle and the door sprung open.

It was like they were stepping through a portal into a parallel universe. The gust of air that met their skin was freezing. A flurry of what seemed like ice fragments tumbled through the open passage, falling onto their shoes. Asa shivered in his warm clothes, and Avery shifted from side to side as the bitter wind tore through him.

"What is it?" Avery asked, rubbing his hands together. "What's wrong with the weather?"

"I don't know," Asa hummed, touching the cold, white substance that was collecting on the ground outside.

"Don't touch it!" Avery warned. "What if it is corrosive?"

"It doesn't feel corrosive," Asa mused. "It's just cold and wet."

"Oh, for goodness' sake," sniped Kean, who had been silent for some time now. "Haven't you two ever seen snow before?"

"Snow?" Asa asked curiously. "Yes, I've heard of it. Is this what it is like, then? Cold, wet mush? It doesn't feel at all as soft as it sounded in the books."

"The Moving Mountains have snow," Avery said. "You can see it capping the peaks."

"Well, yes," Kean answered Asa's question, ignoring Avery. "This is snow. I do not know why or how it is here, though. It does not usually come farther north than Tresnell."

"Tresnell's a strange place, alright." Asa raised an eyebrow. "But no wonder, if they have to combat this on a regular basis. I am rather glad that we are leaving Brandenbury. I don't know how well the locals will deal with such a situation."

They left the building, Asa shutting the door behind him. The snow was crisp and crunched underfoot, leaving a trail of footprints through the town square. Asa noted a small pony grazing through the white substance. He paused, dragging his friend to a stop next to him.

"What, Asa?"

"Isn't that your pony?" Asa inquired. "The one that got away?"

"Well, yeah," Avery said guiltily. "I should leave him, though."

"Why?"

"His owners might miss him," Avery mumbled, tanned cheeks flushing visibly.

"You didn't." Asa gaped at him. "You'd never—"

"I wanted to get here as soon as possible," his friend justified, biting his lip. "It wasn't a crime. I was just borrowing it."

"You little thief." Asa pushed him in mock aggression. "Leaving stolen goods outside my apartment? If I get arrested I will turn you in so quickly it will blow your mind."

"And you say that you've matured?" Avery rolled his eyes, but traipsed over to loosen the knot all the same.

"Come on!" Kean called over to them. "We don't have all day."

They followed Kean out of the town square and down one of the many side streets. The houses were old and covered in a layer of snow that looked like sugar. They trekked along the dark road, casting shadows on the white-dusted streets below. Asa strode ahead, hand adjusting the cowl he wore. Avery, however, was more skittish. His hazel eyes were jumping from the shadows to the dim patches of light cast by the movements of houses just waking up.

"Where is it?" he asked, flinching as a bird flew across the road. "Where is the carriage?"

"I left it in a more respectable part of Brandenbury," Kean replied, picking his way across the frozen cobblestone.

"Excuse me!" Asa protested. "This is a safe area. Security has been a lot better recently, and it has beautiful architecture."

"I will take your word for it," Kean said, gazing down at fox prints crisscrossing the road.

"Is it always this rough, Asa?" Avery asked, flinching at the scrabbling sound of some animal.

"It's not rough!" Asa said. "It's a lot more bearable than living in a village. Salatesh was too small, too stuffy. I couldn't breathe there."

"And this is better?" Avery gestured to the gutters on the sides of the road, where the small tracks of rodents could be seen. "This is a complete and utter sinkhole!"

"Oh, it's not that bad." Asa surveyed the streets with a

seasoned eye. "No rubble. No wreckage. Little violent crime. Even the thieves here are literate."

"But Salatesh is your home."

"Salatesh *was* my home," Asa corrected. "I don't have time for that place anymore. It holds no appeal to me."

Avery tripped on a loose stone, eliciting a yelp of surprise from somewhere in his throat. He straightened himself and retied the loosening rope belt around his waist.

"Your parents' house is empty now," he stated simply. "All of the windows are smashed in. The door hangs from its hinges."

"Well." Asa dismissed this with a wave of his hand. "That doesn't concern me, does it? I sold the place."

"I guess not." Avery scratched his nose.

They followed the lean man in front of them down the freezing street, the silence between them tense but not altogether uncomfortable. All had been said, the air was clear between them. The words themselves, however, lingered. Avery tried to take Asa's hand in his own warm one but the smaller man kept his limp and unresponsive, giving his friend a short scowl of dissent.

"Here we are," Kean's voice was a low purr, like a satisfied cat. Asa could see why. The carriage was stunning. His steps came to a gentle stop in front of the vehicle. The bodywork was painted white with the gold edging indicative of the royal family. Two handsome horses drew it. Asa stroked the decadent detailing with an awestruck hand. It was of more worth than anything he had ever seen in his life. Was he to ride in this?

The driver, a small, meek looking man, emerged from inside the body of the carriage. His mousy brown hair was cut to chin length, as had long been the fashion in the wealthier areas. He wore a spotless white and gold uniform to match the paintwork. Azure blue eyes raked up and down the common garments of the incomers. He tutted under his breath and spread white shawls over the velvet upholstery. This made Asa bristle against

Avery's shoulder. So, they were to dirty the seating were they?

"I can assure you, sir, that we are quite clean."

The frostiness of his tone unnerved him, sounding as chilly as the surrounding town.

"That is no way to treat *special* visitors, Grant," Kean chuckled. "Dear me, we wouldn't want your superiors to know about this, would we?"

His voice, once so mild, had turned malevolent. Avery followed Kean into the carriage, careful of the doors as if he thought that his fingerprints would sully them. Asa hopped in behind him, with Avery and him opting to take the forward-facing seats rather than the backward ones, which Kean took for himself. Grant gave them an oily smile, still unnerved by Kean's threat, and closed the door with a snap. Kean drew the white curtains over his windows and, with a wave of his hand, instructed Avery to do the same to his and Asa's. Avery's rough skin caught on the soft gilded fabric.

The carriage at that point gave a lurch forward as the horses started to move. Asa peered out of the gap between the curtain and the window as they began to move out of central Brandenbury into the surrounding farmland. His mind was lingering on goodbyes to the town that he had called his home for the past six years, which he half hoped he was never to return to. They began to travel through fields with frostbitten crops sticking their heads out of the blanket of snow. The farmers would not be able to salvage them.

Asa crossed his legs, letting loose the curtain and stroking the soft velvet seating instead. Avery laid a reassuring hand on his knee. Asa smiled at him, clasping it gratefully. He could hear his heart throbbing in his head, like the bass line of some unfortunate piano tune. Small flickers of a strange mixture of fear and excitement tormented his senses.

"It'll be okay," Avery whispered in his ear.

"Thanks," Asa said.

Kean opened his briefcase. Again came the strong odour of flowers. Asa leaned forward to investigate the contents and found a scented handkerchief placed on his lap. The thin man gestured to his sleeve. Asa frowned, looking to Avery who was examining the swatch of cloth unsurely. He tried an experimental dab of his arm and his friend gratefully followed suit. Kean laughed but attempted to cover it with a sneeze. He withdrew his own and showed them the correct way to fold the cloth so that it would fit in their sleeves.

"Don't you know how to act in court?" he asked patronisingly.

"No," Asa replied tautly. "Funnily enough, that particular situation hasn't come up yet."

"Pity," Kean tutted.

He didn't speak for a few moments, preferring instead to thumb through the interior of his case, rearranging items as he saw fit. It was rather small but packed to the top with trinkets and papers such as Asa had never seen before. He and Avery exchanged glances, waiting for further instruction. However, he did not speak more on the subject.

"Well?" Avery eventually demanded.

"Pardon?" Kean looked up, confused.

"Are you going to tell us?" Asa could feel his patience slipping as Kean tinkered idly with a small leather-bound notebook.

"Tell you what?"

"About how to act in court." He could feel his cheeks flush with shame, though there was no reason to feel it.

"It is not something that can simply be taught." Kean's face bore a predatory smile. "It comes naturally to most refined families. The arts of elegance, courtesy, eloquence, and assertive subservience are simply the products of good breeding."

Asa growled subconsciously under his breath at the slight to their heritage. Avery was grinning at his reaction. Asa scowled at both of them, wishing for a private compartment or something to kick. Preferably a cat. He hated cats.

"If we're not refined?" he spat. Forget a cat. He wanted to kick the upper-class man in front of him to Jundres and back. All of the way.

"Well, it can be instructed." Kean didn't react to the stony stares that he was being given. "If you have a good enough teacher, that is."

"And would you be such a teacher?" Asa had to admire Avery's control over his tone. He sounded sceptical, slow, bored.

"Yes, I would." Kean stretched his long limbs out intrusively in the small space. "If you are willing to learn."

"Fine," Asa muttered darkly, in time with Avery's dreary drone of the same.

The carriage trundled over the snowy landscape, wheels skidding on the uneven terrain. Asa thanked fate that it was warmer inside than out. Time wore on painfully slow as they progressed up the road, their only indicator of the time of day being the gradual darkening of the cloudy sky. Asa glanced at Averett, who was sleeping quietly in the corner and paying no heed to Kean's instructions. He sighed and steadied himself on the plush seating, eyelids growing heavier as the man rambled on and on. Eventually there came a pause in the relentless flow of information.

"So, when I am shown into the Throne Room, I have to bow and express my intent?" Asa asked, breaking the silence. "Am I to face the queen, look not to her unless spoken to, and hold myself with an air of refined elegance? I guess I can do that."

"You should be able to," Kean said snippily. "I have given you the basic instructions. I think that by now even a rock would be able to recite the rules and structure of court."

"Thank you." Asa ignored the patronisation. "I needed to learn."

He grasped Avery's shoulder. The sleeping blond shifted groggily, cracking open a wary eye to survey Asa.

"What do you want?"

"We're here, Avery." Asa grinned. "Are you ready?"

"Sure." Avery sat up, cracking his knuckles. Asa sympathised. His own shoulders and hips and all the rest of his joints were stiff to the point of being sore. He wasn't even sure how they had continued to travel so quickly for so long. Surely the horses would have had to eat, to sleep. But they had ploughed forward through the collecting snow regardless, carriage sliding on the slippery ground. Asa drew back the curtains on his side of the carriage, wide brown eyes staring at the white blanket covering the ground between the tall fir trees.

"Jundres is coming up presently." Kean withdrew a pocket comb from the case and ran it through his somewhat greasy reddish hair. "You shall receive your task from none other than HRH Queen Ria of Eodem. Look sharp; the bell has not rung yet. We shall need to step into the palace."

Asa peeked out of the window as the carriage rolled into a shadow. A wall of rock a hundred feet high was on their right. It was covered in natural grasses and mosses, blending flawlessly in with the surrounding forest. The carriage came to a sudden stop, jarring them.

"Is this it?" Avery asked, looking out of Asa's window perplexedly.

"Out!" Kean opened the door, stepping from the steps onto the icy ground. Asa ducked through the doorway, gasping in shock from the cold. Avery had exited with him, showing less distress in the snow. "We'll enter through the simplest route. Do you see that crack in the cliff face? Follow close behind me as we go through. The security is tight around here."

Kean strode through a cleared path, snow sticking to the tops of his boots. Asa and Avery followed, both daunted by the cliff next to them. The tallest of the company was walking closer to it, heels crunching. His unfathomable gaze was fixed on the opening in the rocky cliff. Asa tugged Avery forward, stomach curling as he saw the height of the rift. Avery halted at the darkness beyond, hazel eyes crinkling as he looked back to Asa. They continued towards it.

Kean reached the crevasse first. He turned to see them a few metres behind and, giving a closed smile, entered the darkness. Avery stopped. Asa continued forward, glancing back to his friend.

"Avery?"

"It's dark." Avery frowned.

"Don't worry," Asa reassured him. "It's got to be safe. Kean just went in. Hurry up, he doesn't look like he's especially patient."

"Asa." Avery fiddled with his tunic.

"What, Avery?" he replied patiently, taking a few steps backwards, towards the crack.

"How much do you trust Kean?" Avery asked.

"As much as I can," Asa said simply. He took Avery's hand, pulling him towards the cliff. "We can't go back now, Avery. Come *on*."

"Okay." His friend swallowed. He walked close to Asa as they reached the opening. Asa stepped inside first, eyes adjusting to the darkness. Avery followed, shaking the gathered snow off of his tunic with a shrug.

"It's a tunnel," Asa stated unsurely. "Where do we go?"

"I can't see." Avery sounded nervous. "Where is Kean? Why didn't he wait?"

"Okay," Asa exhaled. "Right. We'll go farther into whatever this is. He must have come through here; we'll follow the tunnel."

"Sounds like a plan," the blond laughed. "Sure, let's walk away from the light into the scary abyss. That's what real adventurers do."

"Let's go." Asa nodded. They both walked into the dark passage. The walls were sloping in on them, cold slimy substances coating the rough rock. They joined to make a ceiling a few inches above Avery's head. The path narrowed as they went forward; soon there was only enough space for them to walk single file.

"*Kean. Kean, where are you*?" Asa called in a hushed voice. A few seconds later he called out again.

"I thought you said we could trust him," Avery admonished.

"Let's keep moving. He's probably waiting for us ahead," Asa said.

Asa kept protectively in front of Avery, trying to keep up a stream of asinine chatter to distract himself from the complete blackness.

"Ouch." Avery stumbled, footsteps coming to a stop.

"What?" Asa turned in alarm, feeling forward in the dark. He found Avery's warm body and shook him, sensing for injury. "What's wrong?"

"It's getting smaller," Avery groaned. "I just whacked my head on the ceiling."

"You fool." Asa shook his head. "Way to point out the obvious, Avery."

He moved back around, a single cautionary hand bracing himself on the wall. He whistled through his teeth, trying to avoid thinking of his claustrophobic surroundings. They continued forward, Avery being forced to duck lower behind Asa. Asa's eyes were wide open, not that it made any difference. He tapped the wall, feeling the path twist to the left. It was only an inch above his head now, ebony hair grazing the rock with each step. Yet still the ceiling sloped. Asa bent his knees, keeping his breathing as even as possible.

When the two teens were fully convinced of their own entombment in the rock, the path ahead of them opened up. Asa blinked. There was light ahead. His feet hurried forward over the textured rock underneath him. He stumbled ahead, running into the opening gratefully, dilated eyes dazzled by the dim torchlight.

Something sharp pricked into his back. Asa froze, face paling as his eyes adjusted to the light. They were in a tall underground room lit by large torches, not the wax candles that Asa used at home. He glanced to his right. Avery met his eyes with a shocked stare. Simultaneously they looked behind them. Two large men were positioned behind them, swords at the ready.

His brown eyes flickered over their odd garb as he and Avery turned around, hands in the air. Asa could see the complex armour was fashioned from some form of chained fabric. With great difficulty, he lifted his eyes from his captor's chest to their masked face, seeing a pair of bright green ones staring into them.

"I'm sorry, I don't quite understand," he stuttered, moving away from the sharp blade.

"I think that you do," they said in a low, smooth voice.

"Sir, you're mistaken," he gasped, as they pressed the tip of the sword closer to his stomach. "We're not from around here."

"I realised that. But that does not make your intent any less malevolent."

"We're going to the queen," Avery pleaded, as his captor pushed him back. Asa shot him a sharp look. If they were dealing with bandits then that was the worst thing Avery could have done.

"Is that so?" Asa's captor smirked. "What business have you in Jundres, country boy?"

"A royal summons." Asa shut his eyes, waiting for the biting feel of metal cutting into him.

"Where is your guide then?" They brushed the sword over his stomach. Asa could sense the cold of the blade over his thick tunic and shivered.

"I don't know."

"Convenient." Avery's captor laughed, pushing his sword forward.

"Don't kill us," he whispered, hazel meeting brown as he and Asa exchanged glances.

"Don't trespass then," Asa's captor replied. "We don't like northerners entering our tunnels."

A chain-gloved hand gripped Asa's shoulder. He tried to

dart back, away from the formidable opponent. He locked eyes
with Avery, both of them as silent as the rock walls. He couldn't
breathe. Was he going to die now? At the hand of a masked,
sword-wielding lunatic? His captors drew their swords, bracing
their feet on the stone floor. Asa closed his eyes, hearing his
frantic pulse beating in his head.

"Stop!" a voice rang out through the cavern. Asa's eyes
flickered open. He gave a nervous chuckle in spite of the dire
circumstances. He was still alive. The captor pushed him to the
ground, his head colliding with the stone.

"Who's that?" the one pinning Avery into the same position
called out.

"Clement Kean of the queen's council." A wave of relief
washed over Asa. They had not been forsaken. "This explains
the situation. Mr. Asa Hounslow is summoned to HRH Queen
Ria's presence. As you may see, we must hasten to the Throne
Room."

"Oh, I'm sorry, Mr. Hounslow." Asa's captor helped him up
with a cautious hand. "Border control, keeping Jundres safe.
Didn't mean anything by it."

"Thanks, sir," Asa muttered. He helped Avery up, dusting
off his friend's tunic.

The tall, broad person who had been holding Avery guffawed.
"What?"

Asa's captor was removing the straps of the mask. It was
a rather heavy looking contraption, of some black metal with
bulbous insect-like eye guards and breathing apparatus.

Beneath the mask was a woman. Asa blushed, not meeting
her green eyes. The woman smiled at him, shaking her dark
hair out of its bun. She gestured to her friend, who removed
the headpiece as well, revealing a beautiful androgynous face
framed by dark Celtic tattoos.

"You can tell that someone hasn't been out of the
countryside," they laughed. Asa looked put out, frowning at his

own actions. They clapped him hard on the shoulder, causing him to baulk at the force.

"To the Throne Room," Kean ordered. "And stay close behind me, please. It's more than my job is worth to let you wander off again."

He steered Asa away from the border guards. Avery followed belatedly behind, waving goodbye to the chuckling guards. They walked to the back of the cavern, to where there was a plain door covered in wooden levers and buttons. Kean lifted a series of handles on the surface in a regimented order and then pressed the doorknob twice. The door opened, showing a well-lit corridor beyond, whitewashed and clean. Asa wondered whether or not he should take his shoes off. They carried on down the candle-lit corridor for several moments, footsteps muffled by reed mats placed on the floor. The floor felt odd to Asa's feet, it seemed to be sloping downwards. As it twisted and they passed odd little tributaries of passages to their left and right, he saw that this was indeed the case. The floor was slanted at a rather alarming angle. They were going underground.

Kean stopped at the end of the main corridor. There were no other exits, just a large pair of oak doors. He twisted the handles and pulled them open. The first thing that hit them was the smell. A putrid stench of rot and waste hit their nostrils, making Asa gag. Avery scrunched his nose, fixing the impassive Kean with a steely stare.

"Welcome to the beautiful city of Jundres. I hope that you enjoy your stay." Kean ushered them through the doorway.

They were standing on a precipice, high above the outlines of thousands of rooftops. Asa could see the stone walls stretching out for miles in either direction, a high domed ceiling of rock above their heads. A thin winding path led down to the streets below, cut straight into the side of the sheer rock face. It was warm in the cavern, stuffy and humid. Kean inhaled with relief and visibly relaxed in the close air.

"It's a lovely city, sir." Asa smiled, trying not to breathe in more of the sulfur-laden air than he had to. Kean chuckled darkly and led the way down the narrow path. As they descended, the dim light that had illuminated the city whilst they were at the top became brighter, flickering yellow gas lamps making the streets half as light as they would have been outside.

"We have been trapped down here for too long." Kean broke the silence. "The fear is what does it, I think. I am the first person in my family to have gone aboveground in many generations. Of course, one can only leave with the express permission of Queen Ria, but for the most part, people who live down here will never see sunlight."

He stepped onto the cobbled street below, tapping his foot whilst Avery and Asa walked down the final few metres of the path. Kean huffed at their slowness, turning and striding through a narrow road ahead of them, in between dark asymmetrical houses. There were many people around, though they dispersed as they saw the intruders make their way towards the centre of the city, whispering words of suspicion and interest. Doors slammed shut, tails of ragged coats disappeared around corners, and the three of them were alone in the street, their only company the blocky apartment buildings. Asa shuddered, it was as if they were being watched, observed, isolated.

"But what do the people have to fear?" he asked. "Why do they live in such a place?"

"Jundres was once a fine, terrestrial city," Kean explained impassively. "Its architecture and culture was unparalleled in all of Eodem. That was before Erebus came. His wrath destroyed buildings, withered the crops, and sent the people into hiding. They've been hidden away down here for as long as anyone can remember."

The houses were covered in a thick layer of sooty grime. They were made from different materials compared to ordinary houses—no bricks had been used. Instead, thick lumps of stone had been pushed together, sealed with only the lightest of cements. These blocks were over six foot in height, giving the impression of strange fractured walls stretching as high as the rocky ceiling.

There were no children playing in the streets, which for a large town was quite unheard of. Asa glanced from side to side. People were beginning to emerge from their houses behind them, tall, thin people, like Clement Kean himself. Their clothes were misshapen, tattered, and old. They hung off the peoples' thin frames, the thick fabrics still holding some semblance of the original wearers' shapes. Finally, the children came out, silent and wary, clinging to their parents. Now they were not alone in the street, but still being observed. Some people moved with canes, limping respectfully out of their way as they walked through. The smell was gone to their noses now, but something stifling was still thick in the air. The feeling of abandonment, the rotting of the houses, the feeling of despair.

Rubbish was piled up against the houses, decomposing and trickling into the gutter. The citizens of Jundres started to move now, making a clear attempt to go about their business without registering the incomers. There were no elderly people. Children began to move away from their parents, hobbling on thin emaciated legs, wide eyes taking in the situation. Their bare feet trembled on the cobblestones. Kean saw Asa's glance towards them.

"The lack of sunlight makes their legs weak," he explained impassively, not looking at the pitiful sight.

"Can we not help them?" Asa asked desperately. "Find them a good hospital?"

"Ha!" Kean laughed. "There are no good hospitals around here. These are the gutters of society. The only people who can leave are those who work for the queen. I have told you already, very few people ever see the sunlight. They are too afraid. The queen is too afraid. The city is always on lockdown, as we wait for the day that Erebus is defeated."

"They're so thin."

"I'm sorry, Mr. Hounslow." Kean's voice was clear now. "By this point there is nothing that anyone can do. They are too far gone to be helped by medicine."

"Oh."

Asa tried not to look at the shivering infants, a surging feeling of helpless guilt. They were so young. His childhood, which he had viewed as the worst possible affliction, had been lengths better than any of these children's. Kean steered them away from the people, gripping Asa by the wrist. The message was clear. Don't look at the citizens.

The street was long, much longer than any on the surface. The cobbles were uncomfortable to walk on, bending Asa's boots in strange angles and making him trip over his toes. Eventually, Kean bought them to a stop before another wall, this one reaching right to the roof. The doors were high and heavy. There were no windows. Asa blinked at the building in the flickering gaslight. Was it even a building? It seemed just to be a pair of doors set in the wall. Not more passages? There couldn't be more corridors. It was a physical impossibility in the confined space.

Kean knocked on the thick wood, an amplified rap echoing behind the doors. He walked close to the wall and touched it with his thin hands, pushing at a certain spot on the stone. He leant his whole weight against it, visibly perspiring with the effort before the door began to move. It swung away from them, opening into a candlelit entrance chamber.

"What's this?" Avery asked. "You expecting us to go inside, after all we've seen out there?" He gestured to the rock and stone buildings, which had been lit up in their dinginess by the light beyond the doors.

"Yes," Kean said simply, propelling Asa through them, oblivious to his struggled protests. "But it is not necessary for you."

He managed to restrain Asa within the hall, looking out at Avery standing outside. Asa saw Avery flinch and his face harden. He cringed at the weight of Kean's body supported on his shoulder and at the anger in Avery's voice.

"So, I can simply refuse?"

"It would make my job a lot easier." Kean smirked. "But, mind you, you can't just leave Jundres. Those guards are not only for keeping people out. No one can just enter or leave this city, and certainly not both. There is no tourism, and you can see why. People down here do not last long, a few decades at most. They cannot walk, you see. Their legs give out and society gives up on them. They don't ever get up after they fall. Faded flowers, dead leaves, they waste away."

Asa and Avery had been listening to this in horrified silence. When Kean's voice trailed away, Asa saw Avery square up to Kean. He opened his mouth, but Asa cut across him before he could speak.

"Avery, no! Please." He stared beseechingly at his friend.

"Asa, you don't know where you're going," Avery said cagily. "It could be a trap."

"You heard Kean, you'll never be able to leave. Is that what you want to happen?" Asa begged him. "Don't throw your life away over this. I need you."

Avery's face softened at the last three words. He gave Kean a dirty look as he stepped over the threshold, daring him to say a word about his conceding. Kean was silent, so Avery came to Asa's side, his steadfast expression not revealing that he had decided to give up his chance of leaving this place. He gave Asa a wan smile.

"Anything for you, mate."

THREE

ASA STEPPED GINGERLY INTO the intimidating hall. The walls, floors, and ceiling were made of some sort of polished rock, flecked and shiny. His shoes creaked upon the clean surface. Avery was but a step behind him, ignoring Clement Kean as the city dweller straightened his already immaculate clothes. Asa looked down at himself. He had not bathed in what seemed like forever, and his tunic was wrinkled and covered in dust and grime from the journey. He half-heartedly dusted himself down, heart not in the action. Compared to Jundres dwellers, he was sanitary.

They passed through some doors at the end of the room and entered a small chamber that seemed to serve no real purpose but to hold a crystal vase full of yellow flowers. This was soon left behind, though, as they exited through another door and found themselves in a grand sitting room filled with beautiful furniture made of some dark wood, which Asa could not name. The sofas and chairs were upholstered in luxurious navy velvet and fringed with golden beads. Kean paused, allowing them to survey their surroundings before speaking.

"I will go to see whether or not you are needed at the moment. Make yourselves comfortable. On second thought—" He paused, smirking at Avery. "Don't. Sit down, keep quiet, and don't draw attention to yourselves."

He swept from the room, not hearing Avery's low hiss of irritation. Asa kicked his friend in the shins, perching on the edge of a pouffe. Avery grinned cheekily at him, flinging his long body into the most comfortable sofa there was.

A lone foot tapped on the cold marble floor.

"Will you stop that?" Avery snapped, pinching the bridge of his nose. Asa flinched at the sudden outburst.

"Sorry."

"No, no. Sorry for snapping," Avery apologised. "This place is intimidating."

"Yeah," Asa whispered, brown eyes resting on the fixed gases of the portraits surrounding them.

"Cold, too." Avery shivered. "Wonder how they managed that? We must be hundreds of feet underground."

"It's disgusting," Asa affirmed. "That the rich get to live in such luxury, whilst the poor . . . did you even see them, Avery? They're sick. They're dirty. The people from this palace live in the same place as them, see the suffering on their doorstep, but still don't let them leave. What did Kean mean by the queen being "too afraid" to open the borders? I don't understand why she keeps her palace under such strict security. It's selfish and cowardly, if you ask me."

"Be quiet, Asa." Avery lowered his voice. "Yeah, I know. But what can we do about it? We're only two people. There are thousands of them."

"There must be something." Asa rubbed his cold hands together. "Come on, we're both intelligent people. How can there be no possible solution?"

There was a pause, and then Avery spoke, voice weary with travelling.

"Why are we here, Asa?"

"You know why," Asa replied, examining his own dirty fingernails. "Save the nation and whatnot."

"But why are we actually here, Asa?" Avery's voice was quiet now, younger. He stared at the ceiling with unseeing hazel eyes. "What do they want from you?"

"I don't know," Asa admitted.

"You can't fulfil a quest. You're not supposed to be exerting yourself!" his friend exclaimed. "You have a heart problem; you're hardly the best person that they could find. This whole thing is completely ridiculous."

"You decided to come with me," Asa said resignedly.

"Yeah," Avery sighed, kicking his legs. "It's just . . . you know."

"I didn't think it'd be so real," Asa finished his sentence. "I understand."

They sat in comfortable silence, facing each other on the sofas. Asa refrained from fidgeting, allowing restless eyes to wander around the room. His chest hitched as he tried to regulate his breathing, mind dwelling compulsively on the what-ifs. What if he wasn't good enough? What if the quest was too dangerous? He clucked his tongue and winced. What if he died?

Asa fixed his chocolate eyes on the door. His heart was thrumming in his head. As though timed by a metronome, the door snapped open with a loud clack, making Avery leap up and out of the chair in surprise. Asa chuckled breathlessly, getting to his feet. Three large bodyguards surrounded Clement Kean. He beckoned wordlessly to the two of them, a smug smile playing around the edges of his lips.

"You are wanted in the Throne Room," he stated, looking unconcerned about the large, burly men who stood by him. Asa dragged his feet as he followed Avery to the doorway. "Remember what I taught you."

Asa gulped. "I will."

Kean looked taller inside. It was like he had been moved into his natural habitat. He moved with a leonine grace—confidence making him look predatorial. He stared into Avery's hazel eyes. A strong hand caressed his jawbone, tilting the man's chin up, a clear threat.

One of the guards led the trio through some elaborate corridors, their boots leaving dusty marks on the crimson carpets. Asa blushed just that colour at the irritation on the maid's faces that they passed. He knew that he was filthy, but there was nothing that he could do about it. He tried to walk taller, to carry himself with that unconscious grace which all the members of court seemed to possess. He couldn't do it. His body would not let him do so.

They reached a door made of solid shiny wood and engraved with many curious scenes and items. Asa froze as he caught it in his gaze. It seemed to reach right to the high ceiling above them. Kean stepped forward to knock upon it. Asa wanted to reach out, to arrest the movement before he was able to tap the door. But he was too late.

There was the hollow sound of rapping upon wood. They stood in the flickering candlelight, erratic shadows dancing over their skin. The guards looked formidable in such surroundings, like golems made of stone. Asa thought that Kean was excited. His face, though impassive, was alight with a passion that Asa had not yet seen in the man. Avery merely looked bored, only the tension in his shoulders and back testament to the nerves that he surely felt as much as Asa.

"Come in," a queer, accented voice called.

Asa wiped his dirty shoes on the carpet. It would be better that they would be cleaned here, rather than upon whatever elaborate flooring was inside. Kean gave him a scathing look and Avery stuck his hands deep into his pockets, uttering a low whistle. Asa tried to grin at him, but his face was so frozen that he did not know how. He stepped forward towards the door, only just realising that he was in front. He paused before a pair of thin hands on his back pushed him in that direction. He swallowed before pushing the door open.

The room was startlingly clean. Asa blinked and gingerly stepped over the threshold, bowing his head in an act of submission to the queen. He stared at the reflection of his trudging feet in the shiny marble tiles, a queer lump in his throat. He looked to his right. Avery gave him a reassuring smile, a small wink.

"Asa Hounslow," the voice said. It was spoken in soft tones, yet held a note of undeniable authority. They were all silent, Kean and the guards sinking into elaborate bows. Asa looked up.

"My lady," he managed to say, though his fingers were quivering.

"Come forward."

He saw that the room was large, sparsely furnished and pristine. His shoes squeaked on the stone as he walked towards a huge wooden throne on a low platform at one end of the space. It was fairly insubstantial, apart from the two wide carved wings that protruded from behind the back of a bulky figure seated in it. The queen beckoned to Asa, who crept to the bottom of the platform and knelt.

"Do you know why I have called you here today?" she asked.

Asa shook his head.

She was a well-muscled woman, clad in fine velvet and silk. Her skin was milky white and free from any sun blemishes or a tan. A crown rested on top of the russet hair that was most prized by the upper classes. She wore a pair of thick, dark spectacles that covered half of her face.

She sat up, seeming to look into Asa's brown eyes through her black glasses. Asa resisted the urge to shut them, feeling as though his mind was being penetrated by the queen's intense stare. Queen Ria raised her eyebrows.

"Well, do you?" she asked.

"No, my lady," Asa mumbled.

The queen stretched luxuriously, like a well-fed cat. She seemed to examine Asa reflectively for a moment, staring right through him, before blinking and smiling.

"Yes, I guess that you'll do."

"For what?" Asa asked desperately, before reining himself in. "Sorry, my lady. That was out of line."

"It doesn't matter." Queen Ria brushed it off, the direction of her stare wandering over Asa's slight body. "You look a lot like your mother, did you know that?"

Asa started.

"You knew Mother? How so, my lady?"

"But with his father's temper," the queen said to herself. "Oh yes. That will do."

Kean stepped forward. "Your Royal Highness—"

"Quiet, Kean," the queen snapped, still looking at the dark-haired youth in front of her. "Asa, how would you like to go on an adventure?"

"I would like it more than anything." Asa breathed, a slow smile spreading over his face.

"Good." The regal figure snapped her fingers and a small boy scurried to her side, arms piled with papers and ink. "You know how to read?"

"Yes, since I was five."

Queen Ria took a sheet of fine paper from the boy and spread it on the desk next to the throne. She filled an inkpot with a practised hand, dipping a gold-nibbed pen into it and drawing what looked like a jagged circle in a single elegant stroke.

"This," the woman said, somewhat proudly, "is Eodem."

Asa nodded. "It's smaller than I thought."

The queen sketched a forest covering one side of the country to the west, and a line of mountains splitting through the trees to the east side. She then drew a sharp black curve, splitting the eastern section from the rest of the country. Asa recognised it as soon as he saw it. It was the one prominent landmark visible from Salatesh. The wall.

"Do you know what this is, Asa?"

"The wall," Asa replied.

"Good." The queen let a single blot of ink fall to the paper next to the line, on the convex side. "This is Salatesh."

She marked it with a curvy, calligraphic *S*. The blot was nestled deep in the forest, in such a precise location Asa somewhat expected the queen to have a reference picture somewhere.

"That is where your journey begins," Queen Ria stated.

"But not where it will end, I hope?" His voice rose. "We're not just going back home?"

"No," the queen said. "No, you're not going back."

She drew a dashed line from Salatesh to another ink blot, which she labelled with a swirled *B*.

"Brandenbury." Asa was sure of his answer.

The queen nodded. She continued the line until she found a sizable clearing of sketched trees and rested the nib upon the paper until it was sodden with ink. She wrote a *J*, in that same sleek, predatory hand above the ink.

"Jundres," she affirmed, forehead creasing as the line was extended through the blot, to the east. Asa exhaled as it passed through the wall, his stomach turning. Whatever was inside the wall did not bear thinking about. His voice wobbled.

"Through the wall?"

"Yes," came the response. "Through the wall."

The queen's face hardened. Asa saw her tighten her grip on the pen, knuckles whitening with the force. She dipped it into the inkpot again and slashed it across the page, drawing a jagged black line away from the wall and to the end of the country. She left a blot there, too, and labelled it with the letter *C*. "And to the concourse."

There was a moment of silence. Asa frowned at the makeshift map, wondering what it meant. It was not a short journey, not one for only two to make. No one whom he knew had ever been inside of the walls. As far as most people were concerned, the world ended there. Life was too short to go exploring in places that were not your business.

"I see." He glanced at the queen, wondering what to say next. "So, you're telling me that this is where I am to go?"

The queen nodded. "You are leaving tomorrow."

"What?" Asa exclaimed, choking on his words. "Tomorrow?"

"Yes." The queen wasn't looking at him.

"Surely not, my lady!" Asa's voice shook as he addressed the powerful woman. "It's a long route, there may even be bandits and suchlike. You cannot send us on the morrow. We're not trained warriors, my lady! We're just boys from up north. We won't survive a day. And, well, I'm sick. I have a weak heart, ma'am," he added as an afterthought.

"That's it," Queen Ria replied, looking weary.

"That's what, my lady?" Asa asked, pressing cold fingers to the bridge of his nose.

"You're dying."

"The exertion will kill me," Asa stated, looking imploringly at the woman. "It's a long way to the wall, and I was told that I have only a few months left. I'm not brave enough to go away in knowledge of my own death. I can't do this, my lady. I'm sorry, but I cannot."

"This was not an invitation." The queen shook her head. "Asa Hounslow, you have been conscripted from all of the eligible people in Eodem. You are obliged to go."

"But why Asa?" Avery pushed into the conversation, looking like he could not hold his tongue any longer. "Why him? Why a sick country boy? We know that you have warriors here. We've seen them. It makes no sense to send him out all that way. What do you want him to do anyway? That's a beach. Is he going to count shells or something? This is ridiculous."

"The concourse," Queen Ria explained, "is home to the

sorcerer whom we know as Erebus. I'm sorry, Asa. We cannot lose any more warriors."

It hit him like a swift punch to the stomach.

"Me?" Asa whispered. "You chose me?"

"Yes."

"But why, how? Many have failed before."

"Your parents put your name on a list of the eligible children to be trained for the job. Your father in particular was insistent of it. They were both high-ranking officers in the Guard. It would be natural for them to put your name down when there was such a slim chance, a hundredth of a thousandth, that it would be chosen."

A prickle of annoyance ran through Asa. "I might have known. So, my name was chosen?"

"No," the queen whispered. "No. After the death of the prince, we have decided to step back from the situation. There are more important things than this."

"You will send Erebus token fighters, but you're giving up? You're withdrawing, if in spirit rather than flesh."

"Yes." Queen Ria handed Asa the rough map. "You will be given a horse and enough food to last you there."

"Two horses," Avery corrected. "And enough food to get us there and back."

The queen barely flinched. "If that is what you so wish. One who chooses this fate cannot be relied upon to understand the complexities of the matter."

Avery bristled. "I understand well enough, thank you. You must have some sort of a device that could be of use to us. Give it to me. Give us a fighting chance."

The queen thought for a moment before nodding. With stiff hands she unhooked something from around her neck. It was a pendant, with a milky rainbow jewel dangling from the chain. She placed it over Avery's head, fingers twitching as they brushed against his hair.

"Take it, then," she told him, pain masked in her words. "For my son. It contains some of the simple magic that I am able to control. Once you have completed the quest it will shine with a brilliant light. If you touch your forefingers to it then you shall be returned here, safe to live again."

"Thank you," Avery said unsmilingly, tucking it into his tunic so that it lay flush against his chest. "I can assure you that we will."

Asa felt an odd catching sensation in his chest. He coughed, catching everyone's attention. The queen looked at him with a strange mixture of disgust and pity. Avery fell back in line with him, eyebrows knitted as though he were worried.

"That is all," Queen Ria said, eyes enigmatically cold once more. "You will go to allocated rooms for tonight. Food and clothing will be provided. You may leave now."

Avery seemed to have a sudden change of heart. "But, ma'am . . ."

"Leave," the queen ordered, raising her voice. "Before you say something to compromise my generosity."

"That can't be all—" the blond argued, before he was cut across again.

"Quiet." It was no louder than speaking volume, but Avery fell silent immediately. "Guards?"

"Yes, my lady?" one of them replied, bowing his head to the queen.

"Take the *heroes* to their room. On no account let them leave. I have no wish of seeing them again."

"Affirmative." The other grabbed hold of Avery and Asa's inner shoulders, propelling them towards the door. Kean raised an eyebrow as they were led out of the room. Asa balled his fists, having no wish of seeing that man again.

"Asa?" Avery asked, glancing at him. Their eyes met. "Are you okay?"

Asa realised that he had been clutching the makeshift map

so tightly that it had torn at the edge. He forced a smile and replied. "I'm okay."

They stumbled through the labyrinth of corridors in the palace, the clamping force still cutting into their shoulders. A dull ache was growing in Asa's legs. He just wanted to sit down. His shoes dragged and caught on the carpet, causing him to fall, but he picked his feet up again and placed them down one step at a time. They reached a door, not as beautiful as the queen's, just white panels. All of a sudden, the pressure was released. Asa swayed for a moment, readjusting to the lack of pressure. The door opened and they were ushered inside, the click of the lock testifying that they were not allowed to leave.

There was one large bed in the middle of the room, dominating the small space. A heavy blanket lay across it, with plump pillows propped at one end. There was a door in a corner leading to a bathroom, although Asa knew not where they would get the water to bathe. He huffed in resignation and threw himself forwards onto the bed, shoes still on. Avery walked around to the other side and sat down more complacently.

"Well," he started.

"What, Avery?" Asa asked, eyes shut.

"It could well be worse," his fair-haired friend reasoned. "We're inside, we have a bed to sleep on, and the prospect of going on this adventure that you yearned for so badly. We are as of this moment in reasonable health, going to bed on the eve of a life changing experience. Were it not for the death thing, this would be rather exciting."

Asa cracked an eye open incredulously. "Excuse me?"

"Don't lie, Asa, you know that you're a tiny bit excited."

"Huh," Asa snorted. "As if, Avery."

"And look at this room!" Avery exclaimed, gesturing around the small space. "Wood-panelled walls, carpet on the floor, a real bed! This is the stuff of royalty. I only wonder what we're having for dinner."

"Food," Asa replied. "As per usual. Is your mind always on different ways to fill your stomach?"

"One hundred percent," Avery conceded, bending down to remove his boots. "Not much else to think about here. You going to remove your shoes? You'll mark the covers otherwise."

Asa sighed. "In a moment."

"What's wrong, Asa?" Avery asked, exasperated.

"I don't want to die."

"But you chose this."

"I did not choose to be ill," he snapped.

"You chose to come here."

"Yes," he whispered, "I did."

"And I, fool that I am, decided to come with you," Avery continued wryly.

Asa's heart clenched in his chest. He dropped his gaze, feeling his pulse pound in his head.

"I'm sorry," he croaked, tucking his knees into himself. "It's my fault."

"Oh don't, Asa." Avery rolled his eyes. "Come on, it's fine."

"No it isn't." Asa bit his lip. "It's dangerous."

"I know," his friend replied.

"It's a long and hazardous road."

"Sure."

"You could die!"

"I am aware of that, Asa." Avery punched his shoulder. "It's okay, mate. Now take your shoes off or you're sleeping on the floor."

Asa kicked his shoes off. They slammed into the wooden panelling with a dull clunking sound. He wrapped his arms around his knees and let his mind relax. Only, it wouldn't. Like a wound string, his brain was ticking over. His thoughts rushed around his head as though propelled by some strong current. He clutched his aching head, hands clasping at his fine hair.

"I'll sleep on the floor anyway," he muttered darkly. "Not

sharing a bed with you again."

"Fusspot," Avery snorted, leaning back on the bed.

Asa had been expecting a meagre fare for their supper, bread and cheese if the palace were being kind. When the knock came on their door a few hours later, startling him from his reveries, he was not expecting to see such a feast of food as he did. Shaking his sleeping friend awake, they took hold of the wooden tray between them. No thoughts of fleeing crossed their minds as the door was propped open and the smell of warm food wafted in. Avery's stomach gave a loud rumble.

"Sorry," he apologised to his skeptical friend. "I'm just so hungry, and it all looks so good!"

Asa couldn't help but agree with this. Contrary to his usual diet of bread, rice, and vegetables, the tray was laden with every food that he had ever let himself dream about. Strange slices of golden fruit were piled on a side plate. On the other side of the tray were white doughy rolls, given with a small but ample amount of butter in a porcelain pot.

Asa had not had butter for so long. His mouth watered as he fixated upon the bread.

In the centre of the tray there were two large plates. One had a generous serving of fish upon it; the other had some sort of meat. Shredded green leaves were served with both, and red spherical fruits hidden beneath. Their supper smelt exotically of meat, oil, and indulgence. Asa grinned wolfishly at Avery.

"I could get used to this."

They each took the plate that appealed most to them. Avery dived for the fish, mumbling a fairly weak excuse about home and mother, which made Asa smile. He took the unidentified meat and tore a section off, wincing at the scalding feeling before popping it into his mouth. He closed his eyes. How he had missed this.

The meat was rich and gamey, covered in some spiced sauce. The heat from both the spices and the time that it had spent on the stove warmed his stomach. He glanced across at Avery to see that his friend had a similar look upon his face as he crumbled the fish off the bone and scooped it into his mouth.

"Mmph." Avery nodded, mouth full. The blond swallowed and grinned at Asa. "It's indescribable."

"I know the feeling." Asa looked back at his food, wiping his hands on his trousers. "I've not had meat in so long—"

His voice trailed off but he gave a small smile. He tore the meat into small bites with his fingers and started eating again.

They finished their plates, wiping grease-covered fingers rather awkwardly on their trousers, where it left stains. That never happened at home. Their usual food was more watery, but this stuck to them in a cloying fashion, smelling of fat and smoke. It was greed, plain and simple, which made this food so rich.

Their bellies were stuffed, making their heads drowsy. Both were ready for sleep, especially knowing the next day would be arduous. Avery crawled into the bed first, drunk on fruit and meat. Asa grabbed a blanket and settled on the dank floor.

The night was cold. Asa shivered in his thick clothes, clutching them to him for added warmth. His bare feet shivered against the floor, nails clicking together. Avery's breathing slowed, the man himself turning on the bed. Asa smiled at the sound and tried to relax, echoing those slow, deep breaths. The blanket didn't provide much warmth, heat escaping from all around him as he curled up in a tight ball.

Asa waited for a few beats, eyes closed. His feet and hands grew colder and colder. He huffed out a short burst of air, half expecting to see it mist before his eyes. As he sensibly expected, nothing of the sort happened. The floor dug into his right shoulder at an uncomfortable angle, forcing him to twist into several more uncomfortable positions in his search for comfort. The only sounds were the creak of the floorboards under his body and the hushed breathing of Avery in the bed. He seemed to be asleep.

Asa pursed his lips, deciding to swallow his pride. He sat up, giving the fire a final jab with the poker. In the dim light of the embers he could see his friend lying sprawled across the centre of the bed. Typical. Asa slid onto the far left side of the mattress, covering himself with a couple more unused blankets. His back relaxed in assent. Familiar warmth surged to his extremities, a rushing wave of heat enveloping him. He smiled.

"Asa." Avery turned languidly onto his stomach. Asa froze before seeing that the blond's eyelids were shut. He looked at his friend for a moment, noticing the hand that had intruded onto his part of the bed. Without thinking, his hand crept forward, palm pressing into Avery's own. Avery flinched reflexively away from the cold sensation but Asa pressed forward, interlocking their fingers and giving his hand a squeeze.

Asa eyelids were growing heavy as his vision began to fade to dark at the edges. He let his head fall back onto the pillow, half-tracking the dancing orange shadows flickering across the ceiling. He allowed himself to fully relax, feeling that strange sensation of falling that he associated with sleep. As he slipped away, his grip on Avery's hand loosened, their fingers still interlocked. He didn't notice the pair of hazel eyes staring at his relaxed face, and he didn't feel the responding squeeze from his woken friend.

FOUR

"ASA!" AVERY PUSHED INTO Asa's blurry vision. "Asa, you've got to get up."

"What?" He squinted at his friend in the dim, unfamiliar light. "Avery, you alright?"

Avery shook his head, pulling the blankets off Asa. "One, you're sleeping in my bed. Two, you need to get dressed. Three, we're going on an adventure."

"Adventure?" Asa mused.

His eyes snapped open and he threw himself out of the bed, the word *adventure* ringing in his ears. A slow grin spread across his face as he and Avery met eyes.

"You awake now?" Avery's strong accent lent a sort of teasing gravity to the words.

Asa ran his hands through his tangled hair. "We're going on an adventure."

"Yep." Avery smirked.

"It wasn't a dream? We're doing this?"

"Sure, if you're still all for it." Avery held out a bundle of maroon cloth.

"Um." Asa looked inquiringly at him. "What—"

"Uniform," Avery interrupted him. "Once again, we match."

He gave a roguish wink. Asa rolled his eyes and looked discerningly at his new wardrobe. A maroon tunic, trimmed in black fur, with an ebony badger embroidered over the chest. Loose black trousers with strange loops in them at the feet. A dark woollen cloak with a pointed hood. Tall black boots with slight heels. Lastly was a pile of linked chains. He went to lift them up.

"Oh! Those are heavy." His arm sagged with the unexpected weight and the chains clattered to the floor. "What are they for, anyhow?"

"I think it's for wearing under your tunic?" Avery suggested, picking them up. "We best get changed now, before we're tossed out in our nightwear."

Asa turned to shed his old clothes, pulling the trousers on in one swift motion. He rolled the cuffs up but found them to fit closely to his skin. His feet rested comfortably in the loops of fabric. He smiled, wondering how they knew his height. He lifted the chains with difficulty, dropping them over his head and sitting with a small thud on the bed. His first thought was of the startling cold of metal against bare skin. His second thought was that it was a vest—heavy and cumbersome.

It was like carrying a sack of money all over his body. How much use would it prove to be when travelling?

He slipped into the tunic, sighing at the delicious warmth. The fur rested on his skin, brushing his shoulders when he moved. There was no belt. It was tailored not to need one. The boots were perfect, coming up to just below his knees and hugging his legs at the curves of his ankles and calves.

A thrill ran through him as he saw the leather scabbard waiting for him—a gleaming short sword contained snugly within. Avery passed it to him, and Asa fastened the straps to his body with jubilant fingers.

"Classy," he said, smiling at his perspective of his outfit. "Reckon we look like proper adventurers yet?"

"Sure we do," Avery laughed, picking up a pillow. "Just need to wipe that vapid smile from your face and we're all set."

He hit Asa squarely around his face with the pillow, forcing him to fall onto the bed. Asa smirked at his friend, grabbing onto the end of the case as Avery pulled it back for a second blow. Avery pulled. Asa tugged. The pillow tore in two. Feathers seemed to be everywhere. The smile slid off Asa's face like water from a duck's back.

"Oh dear," he paled. "That was a feather pillow."

"Yeah." Avery stared at the carnage before them, mouth twitching.

"That would have been expensive—" Asa's voice trailed off.

"Cover for me?"

Asa shrugged. "Fine. It's what friends do, I guess."

They set about clearing up the mess of feathers that had strewn themselves over the bed and floor. There seemed to be more than could possibly be contained inside the cotton case. They swept the ones on the floor under the bed, hoping that any retribution would be useless, as they would have left by then. Finally, Asa stood straight, back cracking. There was not a misplaced feather in sight.

"Ahem."

Asa and Avery spun around. Standing in the doorway was a small boy, eight or nine years old at most. His hand was raised as though to knock on some undefined surface. A stray white feather was dislodged from somewhere and fluttered to the floor.

"Yes?" Avery inquired, eyebrow rising.

"I just wanted to inform the two guests that breakfast is ready in the central dining hall. You are to take all of your required possessions and follow me."

"Okay," Asa replied, standing from his comfortable spot on the bed. "I don't think that we will be requiring any of our older clothes anymore. Do you, Avery?"

Avery eyed the map from the previous day, which Asa had

hidden in the waistband of the trousers. Asa shook his head, willing his friend to get the message.

"I don't think so."

"That's settled then." Asa nodded at the child. "Where is breakfast?"

"If sirs would kindly follow me, then I will show you."

He leaned up on his tiptoes to unlatch the main door to the room, childish stubbornness showing as he heaved against the heavy bolt. It cracked open, rust staining the maroon robes which he wore. Tiny scratches covered his soft hands but he merely licked the blood from his skin and wiped them on his clothes. Asa was concerned.

"Where are your parents, little one?" he asked him, dusting the child's front down. "What is your name?"

"They're in the city, sir," he replied. "I'm Salley."

"Jundres?" Asa's eyes widened. "That's a long and dangerous route for you to walk at night."

"I don't walk it at night, sir," Salley said in a small voice.

"How?"

"I don't go home anymore, sir. I sleep here now."

Asa could have kicked himself. He bit his tongue, unsure of where he could take the conversation from here. Instead of speaking, he ruffled Salley's short brown hair and gave an awkward smile; his eyes directed at Avery's own shocked ones. It made sense, he supposed, to send a child to a place of safety, a position where they could possibly leave the city. But was a life of subservience truly better than what he had witnessed as he walked through Jundres? He truly did not know.

Breakfast was soon seen to be a hearty enough meal, though Avery would later complain that there was not more of it. Seven steaming cauldrons of rice were set out along each of the three thin dining tables and the chatter of voices and dishes the only sounds that could be heard as the serving class of the castle prepared for the day.

Next to the pots of rice were large bowls filled with an attractive looking red paste. Each person received a small bowl of rice with a dab of paste on top, a slice of dark bread, and a bowl of clear brown broth.

As Asa and Avery were led to their places, squeezed onto the head of the third table, they saw that they had but one item of cutlery each.

"That's called a foonif," Salley said helpfully from three seats down. "You eat with it."

It looked like a cross between a stake and a mace, with a hollowed out portion in the centre. Asa observed the people around him. Each seemed to use the foonif in an original way. Asa glanced at Avery, unsure of how to eat using such an instrument. Back at home, all they used were knives to cut into tough bits of food. Most used the spikes of the mace part to spear small pieces of fish from within their rice before ladling the white grains into the hollow part. They then deposited this into their mouth, chewed once or twice and swallowed. No one touched the broth.

Asa picked up the foonif between his thumb and forefinger, marvelling at its weight. He tried to scoop some rice, but for all of the difference it made he might as well have poured the bowl over his head. Hesitantly, he placed the foonif onto the table. He reached his fingers into the bowl of rice and ate it like that, looking around as though he were hiding a secret of sorts. Avery caught his eye and copied him, scooping rice into his mouth with clumsy hands.

"What're you doing?" the man next to Asa asked, sounding insulted. Thin-plucked eyebrows furrowed as he stared Asa down.

"I'm sorry, but I can't use the cutlery provided," Asa said, trying to sound polite.

"And why not?" The man's tone was raised so that the whole room could hear them.

"I never learned." Asa's voice was proudly steady, though he shrank backwards at the loud words.

"You don't have the right to eat in the queen's kitchens if you cannot use a simple foonif," the man growled.

"I was invited here," Asa protested, looking around for Avery, who happened to be deep in conversation with an old lady about weaving. No, he couldn't make Avery fight all of his battles for him. Besides, this may not even be a battle. "It is my right to eat here, same as the rest of you."

"Coming here from up north, are you? Such ideas from a mere northerner!"

"Are you quite finished?" Asa asked. "I've had just about enough of this."

"No, I'm not finished . . . You looking for a fight?"

"No, I'm not." Asa cracked his knuckles. "But if it comes to it then I am more than willing."

"You hold up your fists?" The older man spat on the table, leaving a glistening pool of saliva. "Fists're for the lame and the weak. You either of those, boy?"

"Yes," Asa said, after a pause. "Yes I am. Are you yet finished?"

"He may not be, but you certainly are." A dark shadow blocked the torchlight from Asa's eyes. He squinted up, seeing the haughty countenance of Clement Kean staring beadily at him. "Asa, Avery, you are to set off as soon as you are able."

They set off together out to the stables as rapidly as they could. Asa was in an odd state of mood, sensitive to the smallest of noises. Each creak and crack of the ancient palace sent a shudder of anticipation down his spine, a shot of pure adrenaline straight to his heart. Kean was more silent than usual, striding ahead so that only his coattails were visible as he rounded the sharp corners.

They passed the door through which they had exited the city of Jundres, but Kean shook his head and pulled them on. He opened one door, and another, then a third. Lastly, he fitted a large key into a wrought iron gate that divided the corridor. Through this there were stairs winding upwards into inky blackness. They were old, made from warped wood and hand-made nails of dubious quality. Avery kicked the dried body of what seemed to be a rat out from under his feet. Asa stepped gingerly over the husk and, looking upwards, began to follow Kean who had started the climb.

Climbing many stairs is a difficult endeavour at the best of times. When coupled with unusual shoes, and such darkness, Asa found it impossible. His old shoes were bulkier and these thin-soled counterparts gripped the wood much more tightly, forcing his body weight to act in odd ways. The walls were closely hugging him on either side, growing narrower the higher they climbed. Kean slipped between the close walls, as slender and graceful as an elf. Asa and Avery, however, struggled along ten steps behind, the palace not designed for their stockier bodies. After a few breaths of climbing, they reached a gap. The passage was brighter here; they could see cold light outside of the thin opening. Kean stepped through.

"I'm not going to fit," Avery said, eyeing the gap resignedly.

"Avery, you know that you must. There is no other way."

"You go first." Avery stood to the side on the stairs, letting Asa through.

Asa squeezed past his friend and reached the crevasse. It was as wide as his forearm was long. "Wish me luck."

Avery moved closer to him. They could smell the fresh air, feel it on their faces. It was thinner, colder than the Jundres air. Asa let it energise him.

"Here I go." He turned to the side and shuffled through the opening. Staggering out into the open space beyond it, a wave of freezing air cut into his body.

"Wait for me," Avery said, trying to fit himself through the gap. "No, not going to happen. This is hopeless."

"Time to lay off the pies, Avery."

"Hush." His friend rolled his eyes.

After some grunting and pushing, Avery sucked in his stomach and chest and squeezed sideways through the opening, extending his arm so Avery could pull him through.

"You nearly tore my arm out of its socket," Avery huffed, holding his shoulder.

"It was either lose an arm or remain stuck there for days until you dropped a few pounds," Asa said, laughing at his friend.

The snow outside the opening was freezing and bit at Asa's skin as he scooped up a handful. Unlike ice, it packed into the shape of his hand, giving Asa an idea. Instead of shoving it down Avery's tunic, he made a clod of the white substance and threw it at his face.

"Asa!" Avery exclaimed, covered in melting powder. "You're a real stinker, that's what you are."

Asa laughed and ducked as a similarly made missile was thrown at him. Within a few throws they were covered in ice crystals. Asa thought that the cold suited his friend. The burning ice turned his cheeks, nose, and the tips of his round ears a delicate shade of pink. He knew, though, that he looked the same. They both stood for a moment, laughing at their appearances.

"Where in Eodem have you two been?"

Kean was glaring at them from the pathway beyond the rock face that covered Jundres. Asa hid a grin as he realised that they had been scrapping on the ground like a couple of six year olds.

"Here," Avery said sanguinely.

"I can see that, thank you." The thin man's eyebrows knitted. "What I wanted to know was why you were not over there, where I was?" He pointed along the path to what seemed to be a small, snow-covered village.

"And here it begins," Asa said, surprising even himself with the prophetic sound of his words. They walked down the cleared path in the snow into the midst of the buildings. It was only once he saw the horses that Asa gave a small gasp. They were stables.

The buildings were decorated in white and gold, stall doors half open in the morning light. Asa inhaled the fresh-scented air, needing, thirsting for it. He heard the clack of hooves on stone, the sharp whinny of a well-bred horse. Stable hands shot about in their white and gold uniforms, looking harried by the stresses of a strict schedule that was painted on a sign in the middle of the yard. He could not help but think them lucky. They lived in the air and land whilst those below in Jundres dwelt in that tragic destitution.

"Excuse me?" Asa asked a passing servant, a young woman with her hair scraped back into two impossibly tight and neat buns.

"Yes?" she replied, sparing him not even the briefest of glances. "What is so important that you wish to take some valuable moments out of my already over-shared time?"

"I am from Queen Ria," Kean declared. "He deserves your time. He is the one."

Asa blushed and would have said something, but modesty stayed his tongue. She spared him a longer look this time, grey eyes catching on their maroon uniforms. Her jaw slackened a degree and she fell back a step.

"Yes." It was a statement this time, a fact. "Yes, yes of course. Follow me and I will show you to the horses."

Asa and Avery fell into step behind her as she scurried across the golden horse yard to a small side gate. She pulled it open and held it for them, urging them through and shutting the door behind Kean. The paddocks and stables were wooden here, not gold. The horses were calmer and the air held a sense of peace along with the heady scent of the grass and snow. They passed several full paddocks of grazing horses in the frost, from blanketed racing steeds to hardy plough horses. Several foals shared one pasture with their anxious mothers.

At last she paused at a small block of stables on the outskirts of the outer edge of Jundres. It was tucked into the land with six medium-sized stalls and a small meadow. Three horses were out on the snow-covered grass, coats brushed until they glistened where the watery sun fell upon them. Three stalls, however, were occupied.

The first they came to held a slender, red-coated horse. She had large, dark-lashed eyes and a striking blaze down the middle of her dished face. She wore a maroon blanket embroidered with the letters *NRB*.

"This is Neasa," the stable hand crooned, stroking the chestnut. "One of the best in our stables. She's fast, intelligent too. Not a single rider has fallen from her."

"What does her blanket say?" Asa inquired, coughing into his sleeve.

"Neasa of Royal Belonging." The servant smiled. "Most of the best horses have that affix. It is a seal of our queen's approval and shows that they are of only the best bloodlines."

She gave the horse a wistful pat, running her hands along her glossy neck. Neasa's ears perked and she moved closer to the stable hand's touch. The young woman caressed the white blaze with careful fingers. She gave Neasa a final stroke and turned away, that sad smile lingering on her lips.

"She's mine." Avery raised a hand, as they passed an empty stable. "Neasa, I mean."

Asa glared at him. "This isn't a contest. I'm sure mine will be just as splendid."

They came to one of the middle stalls, which was occupied by a beautiful black horse, in everything but coat the image of Neasa. She swished her tail and peered interestedly out at the newcomers. Her eyes were remarkably pale for a horse, a washed-out grey.

"This would have been your mount. Her name is Elizaveta,"

their guide said, looking piercingly at Asa. "But she went over on a rabbit hole last week and is currently on stable rest. A great mount, as brilliant as her sister." She gestured towards Neasa's stall.

"Pity," Asa sighed.

They approached another stable and its occupant leaned over the door and whinnied. Asa maintained his smile but his heart dropped. They weren't the most handsome of steeds.

"This is Freda." The stable hand shrugged. "She's—good."

"Is that it?" Asa joked, shaking his head.

"She is quite good. She's shy and not much of a looker, but she'll do for riding."

The skewbald nickered to her new rider, backing away from the door into the depths of her stall. There was a clatter as she kicked her food bowl. Asa noticed that her irises were different colours. One was a warm brown and the other sparkling blue. She swayed her head out of the door, glancing out onto the meadow. She was most average looking for a pony, almost ugly. Yet there was something about her, something in that dancing blue eye. Freda had fire within her. She looked as though there was more to her than one would see.

"Yes," Asa said reflectively, turning a gradual smile to the stable hand. "Thank you. She will do perfectly."

A bell was rung within the golden yard and over the next few moments, five more stable hands appeared, each clad in the white-gilded uniforms. Two of them took the horses from their stalls and two retreated to another building. The final one, a man of Kean's stature with jet-black hair, examined Asa and Avery.

"Are they—" he began, but the woman cut him off.

"Yes."

"Should I?"

"You know what to do," she said, rather waspishly.

He left, wiping his brow and giving the two of them a curious glance as he did. Asa looked at his boots, scuffing a hole in the snow. It was odd, how people avoided them now. Had they been marked for death?

Kean turned to them, something moving in his grey eyes. He smiled, for the first proper time, at Asa and nodded at Avery.

"It is time," he said.

Asa inclined his head. "Thank you. For everything."

The taller man frowned at him. "But I have done nothing."

Avery looked at Asa in astonishment. "Asa, he has literally been less than useless."

"We have got this far." Asa addressed the two of them at once. "We could not have done it without him. Useless or not, he has helped."

"Well then, thank you," Kean said sincerely. He stopped, looking like he was struggling to speak. "I hope that you make it."

Asa smiled and shook his head. He watched the stable hands saddling up his and Avery's horses. The steeds were decked in maroon uniforms, since they too were going on the mission. Their tack was clean, metal sparkling like the snow on the ground. Avery pushed Asa forward, he only then realised that they had been called over. Body numb, he managed to walk to his pony. The stable hands holding her made some semblance of conversation, but Asa did not respond. His eyes were fixed on a spot in the middle distance, ears filled with an intermittent buzzing.

"Asa."

He flinched and looked up, startled out of his reverie.

"Avery," he replied, giving his friend what he hoped was a reassuring smile. "You startled me."

"Better that than you wandering off when it matters." Avery went to stick his hands in his pockets, realised the limitations of his garments and frowned. "Useless. You'd think that they would include pockets."

"You'd think, wouldn't you?" Asa rolled his eyes as Avery made a stupid face. "Sober up!"

"Why should I?" Avery asked, yawning and stretching in the morning air.

"We're about to die." Try as he might, he could not stop the tension from creeping into his voice.

"All the more reason to mess around," Avery said cavalierly.

"Your mouth is moving but all that is coming out is nonsense." Asa took hold of Freda's reins as they were handed to him. "Looks like we're heading off."

He took her over to the mounting block and hopped onto her broad back. She looked back in surprise, as if the sensation of being ridden was new to her. Asa clucked her forwards and she wandered away from the block, allowing Avery to bring his horse to it. He vaulted onto the delicate mount, causing her to snort and skitter towards Asa and Freda.

"Careful there." It was the stable hand from earlier, eyes curiously red-rimmed. She caught Neasa's bridle and slowed the horse to a halt. "Easy, girl."

Avery looked at her. "Are you okay?"

"I'm fine," she sniffed. "Just saying goodbye."

They stood there for a moment, and then Avery nodded to Asa.

"Shall we be off?"

"Let's go." A surge of adrenaline rushed through him. Asa pulled out the basic map, and then looked at the sky. "Just follow the rising sun."

Asa kicked Freda into a fast trot, merging into a canter. He glanced back over his shoulder. Avery was hot on his heels as they disappeared into the woods that bordered Jundres. A tall, thin figure watched them vanish into the undergrowth, standing like a thin statue long after they were out of sight. The tolling of a loud bell carried with them until they were well sheltered by the trees. Jundres now knew it, as would every other town in the country. The heroes were chosen.

As the sky grew lighter, snow started to fall again. It was

finer than last time, melting when it came in contact with their warm skin. They slowed the pace to a brisk walk to save the horses' energy, exchanging few words in their sleepy morning states. Their cheeks and noses began to grow pinker, flushing in the chilly air.

Asa enjoyed watching his breath coil into the air, billowing from his mouth like smoke from a dragon's. He tried to blow a ring, or some sort of pattern, but only succeeded in making a large cloud and some strangled wheezes. Avery cast a sidelong glance at him and he coughed, trying to look nonchalant.

The sun rose high into the sky as they rode towards noon. Asa's stomach grumbled and he looked artfully towards Avery as his friend's did the same.

"Look, Asa," Avery probed, as the midday sun beat overhead. "I've got a proposal."

"Sure," Asa agreed, sitting back in the saddle. "What is it, Avery?"

"We don't have that much food," the blond said, patting his saddlebags. "We've got your bags and mine, and that's it."

Asa checked his saddlebags. "There's only the two of us."

"I think we should miss luncheon today," Avery said.

Asa blinked. "Fine."

"Are you sure?" his friend asked. "Will it hurt your heart?"

"In honesty, Avery," he said and laughed, "my heart has not bothered me since the last you saw. I'll be fine merely skipping a meal."

"Okay." Avery nodded. "Well, just tell me if it's getting bad. We lose nothing by taking precautions, but we lose you if we're careless."

"Fusspot, slow down." Asa grinned. "I'm going nowhere as of yet."

Avery laughed, bitterly this time. "Last time you said that you left the village in the middle of the night, disappeared for two years, and only let me know you weren't dead by a rather belated letter from your new home in central nowhere."

"Central nowhere?" Asa came to his home's defence. "No, mate, Salatesh was in the middle of nowhere. Brandenbury is four days away from the capital city. It is on the brink of being a rather central somewhere."

"Salatesh may not be *somewhere*," Avery said icily, "but it is our home. I thought you'd remember that, Asa. I thought that the time you spent there meant something to you."

"Why must we always fight over this?" Asa shook his head. "Avery. You know how much the time there meant to me."

"Do I?"

"You know how hard it was for me to leave. You know that I was alone. And you know, well . . ." He looked down at his cold hands.

Avery stared at him, slight confusion written over his features. "I know what?"

"That I miss home," Asa admitted, spurring his horse into a faster trot. The trees blurred as he bent over the black mane, rising and falling with her. He heard the hooves of Avery's steed behind him, speeding along the dirt track. There was no response. He wasn't sure if his friend had even heard what he had said. "Avery?"

"I heard you, Asa," Avery replied. Asa heard him kick his horse forward, and soon they were side by side. Neither spoke for a while. Asa wound the horse's coarse hair around his fingers, loosening his grip upon the reins. He opened his mouth, took a breath, and then closed it again. He couldn't quite think of what to say.

"It's cold today." It was inane, so obvious that he wanted to take it right back out of the air.

"Yeah," Avery replied, his breath steaming as he spoke. "Quite."

The snow was falling, as it had been when they'd set off that morning. However, it was heavier now, denser. Clumps of ice were sticking to Asa's fringe and frigid water was rolling like slushy tears off the tip of his nose. He could feel the weight on his eyelashes. He glanced over to Avery, who was rearranging his hood with clumsy fingers, nose a delicate shade of pink. They surely could not keep on riding in such tricky weather? But Avery kept going, Asa blindly following. His friend was a miner. He worked outdoors. He would know better than Asa when to stop.

Avery's horse had a longer stride than Freda. He pulled ahead and Asa struggled to make the small skewbald keep up. The wind was blowing in his eyes, hardly shielded by the many trees around them. Asa blinked, peering ahead. He could see nothing but white flurries and the orange-stained sky above him.

"Avery?" he called. No response came. "Avery!"

He searched the sudden white downfall in increasing desperation, eyes screwed up against the icy cold. The wind was blowing so hard now that it felt like he was alone in the world, just him and the warm animal moving beneath him. The road beneath the horse's hooves was the only scenery. He couldn't hear Avery or his horse over the sound of the wind.

Asa pushed the horse up into a canter, letting the animal choose the way, as if she could see any more than he could. The melting snow settled on his bare hands, chilling them with a vague numbness that was most disconcerting. He shivered.

His pony was jogging beneath him, tossing her plain head as her vision was obscured. Asa stroked her withers in a way which he hoped was soothing, slicking the white hair to her body. Freda raised her head, ears flat against her skull. He reassured her, winding his fingers into her discoloured mane. She glanced back at him, her one blue eye fixed upon her cold rider. He clucked and she moved forward into the snow more decisively. It came down strangely, unlike rain, in strange flurries that could be blown into their eyes. Freda stalled, refusing to go forward into the wall of unending white.

"Asa?" It was a whisper, the faintest call on the breeze.

"Avery!" Asa turned in the saddle but could see nothing but a tree line and blazing snow.

"Asa!" It was closer now. Though his fingers were like ice on the reins, lips chapped by the loaded wind, Asa felt a sudden surge of warmth in his chest. He was going in the right direction. Freda stalled again, tossing her head back and refusing to move. Asa spoke soothingly to his frightened pony, seeing her withers trembling as he tried to move her forward.

"It's okay, girl," he whispered to her. "We've got this."

She began to walk forward again, ears flat against her head. Asa clucked her up into a trot. The trees were close on either side, sheltering them from the worst of the snow.

"Asa." Asa perked up in the saddle, scanning the ground. It had not been so much a call as a statement. Avery, he was sure, could see him.

"Avery?"

"Here."

Freda pulled to a gentle halt in front of a large Eldrass tree, surrounded by fallen leaves. Asa looked to the lower branches.

"Where?" he asked, scanning the stark limbs.

"Not up there, idiot. Look down."

Asa looked, and then saw it. Between the arched roots of the tree was a gap, about as large as a small pantry, where extreme weather had worn the earth away. Inside this hollow was a dishevelled, damp Avery Hardy. He leapt to his feet and grabbed Freda's bridle, pulling the horse and its rider to a branch some distance away and tying the reins there. After kicking the snow off of a patch of grass to allow her to graze, he held out a hand and helped Asa down.

"Thank you." Asa shivered. For the first time, he truly recognised how cold he was. A sharp pain made itself apparent in his extremities. Avery took his frigid hands in his own marginally warmer ones and blew warm air onto the frozen digits.

"We better set up camp here. It's getting late."

Asa hadn't noticed. The sky was not black or blue as he was used to, but a dusky orange, like the embers of a dying fire. It was ironic, he pondered, that such a warm colour could indicate the fall of ice from the sky.

Before he had even been aware of it, Avery led him back to the small hollow under the tree. Asa's hair brushed the low ceiling as he ducked inside, pulling his legs up to his chest. It was warmer here, sheltered as they were from the snow and wind. Painful pricking warmth returned to his fingertips. He began to think more clearly, shivering slowing to a gentle tremble in his fingers until finally he was able to speak.

"That wasn't fun."

Avery laughed, opening his saddlebag and bringing out such necessities that they needed to survive the night. Some blankets, a cloth bag of food, several wrapped items, and a water skin filled with liquid. Asa looked at the snow falling outside, it wasn't as if they would have any shortage of water, wherever they were.

"It was not," Avery replied, startling Asa, who had forgotten his previous statement. "You up for some food?"

"Okay." Asa held out his hands and sighed at the meagre fare that he was given.

"Sorry," his friend apologised. "We can't waste it."

"I know." Asa's stomach rumbled. "I understand."

His supper did not even fill his cupped hands. A strip of dried meat, a small bread roll, some sort of grain cluster, and a leaf. A single leaf. He poured the food into his lap and started to tear the bread up with his chilled fingers. Maybe if he ate more bites he would feel somehow fuller. Avery sat down next to him, the same in his hands. He took a swig from the water skin and passed it to Asa, who sipped it and ate a tiny mouthful of bread.

All too soon supper was over. Asa leant against the side of their shelter, watching the snow fall as the sky grew darker. He hoped that Freda was alright. She and Neasa had proved their use a hundred times in the last day alone. Without them they would surely have become lost in the snowstorm.

"It's late," Avery remarked.

"It is," Asa responded.

"Shall we sleep now?" Avery sounded unsure. Asa smiled. Neither of them had ever slept anywhere apart from a bed. He nodded.

"Better had."

They lay down in between the roots of the Eldrass tree, sheltered from the oncoming snow. Asa curled tightly in on himself as he usually did, Avery spreading out next to him. Both of them shivered at the same time, then laughed.

"Do you want a blanket?" the blond asked, rubbing his hands together.

"Yes, please," Asa replied, catching the ragged piece of cloth that Avery threw his way. "Thank you."

"No worries." His friend smiled. "Got to keep you warm."

"Don't you have one, too?" Asa inquired, seeing Avery's face fall.

"I do, it just got completely soaked in the snow, so—"

"Share it with me."

"What?" Avery squinted at Asa. "You said you'd never willingly—"

"Avery." Asa raised an eyebrow. "How reliable has that statement been lately?"

"Fair." He shrugged, taking half of the dry blanket. Snow blew into their small shelter, brushing their feet with its sapping coldness. Asa left a courtesy space between them, though it chilled him. "Asa."

"What?"

"You can't share it like this, it defeats the point of sharing."

"Ugh, fine." Asa moved closer to Avery's intoxicating warmth. Their arms touched. Avery moved his hand into Asa's and linked their fingers, as Asa had done the night before. Asa peered at him in the near total darkness. Avery winked.

"Goodnight," he said.

"Goodnight," Asa replied.

FIVE

ASA AWOKE COLD, STIFF, and damp. He stared up for a minute in a sort of bleak daze before sitting up to stretch, cracking his joints. Avery, for once, was still asleep. Asa watched him for a moment. He looked fairly comfortable, blond hair sticking up around his head, arms and legs tangled beneath the blanket.

"Up you get, then!" Asa shoved Avery's shoulder into the ground. His friend shot up, earning a snort of laughter from him. The blond searched the hollow under the tree for the source of noise, before the meaning of the situation dawned upon him. He scowled.

"And good morning to you, too," he grumbled.

"What's for breakfast?" Asa asked. Avery dipped into the saddlebag and withdrew the cotton bag of food. Asa held out his hands.

"Remember, Asa." His friend poured a small handful of nuts and dried berries into Asa's cupped hands. He looked at his portion disappointedly, but did not complain. His stomach growled.

"I remember." Asa tried to smile, but all he wanted to do was eat. He counted the nuts— fourteen. The berries were harder to count as some had made their way into his mouth before he could stop himself.

"We're tightening our belts so that we don't die."

"Asa, don't be like that." Avery had counted out his own portion and repacked the bag before paying attention to his food. "This is the grown-up decision."

"I know." Asa chewed miserably. "I just think this would be more fun if it was warmer."

"Well, it isn't." Avery smiled, swallowing his breakfast in two rapid gulps. "And don't count on a sunny spell."

As if to affirm his point, a light flurry of snow fluttered into their shelter, covering their legs in white dust. Asa sighed and followed suit and finished his meal.

"I hope the horses are alright," he said. Several inches of snow had collected on the ground outside. He stood up and ducked out of the hollow. The sun was shining quite brightly for so early, though the sky remained orange and cloud cover was threatening the light from the east.

The horses were huddled under the same branch, shivering. Asa could have hit himself. They'd left their tack on overnight. That couldn't be good. He went over to Freda and checked under her girth. Luckily there was no sign of irritation but they'd have to be a lot more careful about it in the future. Without their horses they would be stuck, the prospects of getting home even from here would be bleak. Besides, he liked Freda.

"We are a pair of fools, aren't we?" Avery said.

"My thoughts exactly," agreed Asa, untying Freda and clambering stiltedly onto her back. Avery packed his saddlebags and hopped onto Neasa, who shifted under him. He reached forward for his reins, then realised.

"Asa, be a man and untie my horse?"

"Seeing as you asked so eloquently." Asa leant over and handed the reins to Avery. "Though I'm not sure either of us deserve a second chance with these creatures after yesterday."

"True." Avery gave his horse a hearty thump on the neck, which nearly sent the highly strung creature into a panic attack.

"Watch it," Asa reminded him, as his friend tried to calm Neasa down. She danced around on her toes for a few moments, before being soothed into a jittery halt.

Avery winked. "Still got it."

"Sure." Asa stroked Freda. She turned her head towards him and huffed a cloud of warm air onto his knees. He sat back in the saddle and picked up the reins. "Ready."

"Yes." The chestnut drew alongside Asa. Avery let her greet Freda, and then led the way down through the woods, following the sun eastward.

A light wind had picked up, swirling small dust flurries around the horses' hooves, but this was small potatoes compared to the snowstorm that had engulfed them yesterday. Asa grimaced as he thought of it, glancing upwards. They would have to be a lot more careful of the weather if they were to make it through unscathed. Their route, though, was simple. They had to ride to the east so that they could get inside the walls. This was the easier part of the journey. He did not know how they would get inside of the walls.

They soon came onto a path, more by chance than through navigation, long and straight through the trees. Asa decided to take it. It would be safer than hiking through the trees. At least if they were robbed on the road they should meet some aid. The surface was just plain dust, having been cleaned of ice sometime earlier that day. Footprints and hoof marks littered it, but they saw no sign of anyone on that section.

It was mid-morning when Asa noticed the wagon. Their road was long and fairly straight, so he saw them long before they came within earshot. There was a single dusty traveller wagon trundling towards them, clouds of dirt being scattered by the wheels. Asa cupped his hands around his mouth.

"Hello, there!" he shouted, making several birds flap in

panic out of the trees around them. "Hello!"

There was no difference in the speed of the cart. Asa urged Freda on into a canter, beckoning Avery to follow. His friend did so, and they rushed to meet the strangers on the road, regardless of their intentions towards them. The wagon stopped as they came within two hundred metres, and Avery leapt from Neasa to the ground. Asa followed, bringing his pony to a halt and jumping off. Freda scraped some ice off the roadside with her large muzzle and began to graze on the wilted grass underneath. Her masters approached the stationary vehicle. There seemed to be no driver to it, so Avery knocked on the canopy roof while Asa stroked the cart pony's neck. It was a small beast, no higher than twelve hands, with large doe eyes and the sweetest little face Asa had ever seen. It was nervous though, eyes darting from side to side as it was forced to stay attached to the weighty cart.

"Who is it?" said a quivery voice from inside the body of the wagon.

"Travellers," Avery said.

"From where?"

"Salatesh," he responded.

"Never heard of it," another, female, voice added. "Don't trust them, Mersin. They could be bandits!"

"Bandits?" The person sounded old, frail. "Oh, no, no. We don't consort with bandits. That is a terrible idea."

"We're not bandits," Avery explained. "We're travellers, just like you."

A pause.

"That sounds like a "bandit-y" thing to say." The woman pushed the canopy out where Avery was leaning on it. "Away! Away! Be gone."

"Why are you in such a hurry?" Asa asked.

"Why should we tell you?" the woman snapped.

"Now, dear," the man reasoned. "Bandit or not, he asked nicely and as of such we ought to reply. Young man, we're travelling closer to the capital."

"Why?" Asa probed curiously.

There was a scuffle from inside the wagon and cautiously an elderly couple emerged. They both were tiny, the woman's high grey bun would have barely scraped Asa's chin if she had not been standing a good long distance from the two of them. The man was bald, withered, and wore thick glasses, which reverted his eyes to blinking specks.

"There is trouble brewing at the gates," he said darkly.

The woman nodded. "We refuse to be part of such deviation from what is natural and what is right. We're going to set up somewhere new. Anywhere would be better than there."

"Where?" Avery looked at them. They had come so far, but for what?

"I keep the gates," the man said. "I am Mersin Hathor. We come from as far as you can go."

"Not us," Asa told him. "We'll go beyond the walls."

"But that's impossible, my dear boy."

"We come from the queen."

Mersin Hathor looked startled at this realisation. He took off his glasses, wiped them on a dirty sleeve, and put them back onto his nose. He blinked mole-ishly at them both, assessing their uniforms.

"So you do," he said. "So you do."

"Who will be there when we arrive," Avery asked. "To open the gates?"

"I have failed." It seemed as if Mersin had forgotten that they were there. He stared into the middle distance and sighed. "I have failed indeed."

"But why, sir?" Asa was intrigued. "What task were you entrusted with?"

"Two," the elderly man said. "Every year, my first job is to open the gates. I do this but once every year. It is a one-way journey for most who venture past the walls. I have done it for fifty years now, and my father before I—generations of Hathrows allowed people to travel between in and out. But my second duty, only by leaving my post did I fail that. I have a message that I have told those who passed through every year. I have failed as a gatekeeper. The borders of Eodem rested upon me, but I decided to shift the burden onto someone else. No one shall get through those gates again! For only I have the keys, and I shall do with them what I see fit."

"We need passage," Asa told him.

"Excuse me?" His little eyes widened behind the spectacles. "Oh, indeed no! That I cannot have upon my conscience. Not again."

"You must," he insisted, drawing closer to the little man. "If, as so you insist, the fate of Eodem rested upon you, then you shall do no more damage by letting us in."

"In," Mersin Hathor scoffed. "Ah, yes. Indeed, being let in would be the worst thing to ever happen to you. Of course. No, you come from the queen, correct? Of course she would tell you to go *in*."

"What in Eodem do you mean by that?" Asa exclaimed. "We mean to gain passage through the walls, and through some means of wit or luck defeat the monster which lurks within. We just require this of you."

"I have been too far," the old man declared, throwing up his hands. "No more I will travel. No more!"

"Well then, give us the keys." Avery simplified their request, if somewhat roughly.

"I cannot entrust you with them."

"I'm sorry." Asa cast a sidelong glance at Avery, who nodded at him meaningfully. "But if you do not give us the keys then we will have to take them by force. We do not wish to do so."

Mersin squinted at him. He looked at his steely wife, who at that moment was wearing a murderous expression on her pinched face. Her mouth was so far folded in on itself that it became a single line of wrath. He sighed.

"Fine." From his pocket he withdrew a large ring of keys, which he handed to Asa. "Do not blame me, I beg of you. I tried to warn you."

"Mind repeating it?" Avery said. "I didn't quite catch it the first time."

Mersin Hathor shook his head.

"What would a canary know of the world outside?" He held his hand out to his wife and they climbed unsteadily back into the wagon. "We are off."

"Goodbye, Mr. Hathor," Asa said.

"Goodbye, young canary. Be watchful for cats."

Asa jumped at the sharp crack of a whip and the cart pony began once more to trot down the path. They stood there, quite still, until even the dust on the road had settled behind the disruptive wheels.

Asa looked at the keys in his hands. There were an inordinate number of them, but he assumed that the single huge key would be the one to the gate. The rest were merely surplus. He trudged back to his pony and tugged on her bridle to bring her away from the grass back onto the path. He stuck a boot into the stirrup and hoisted himself into the saddle.

"Should've asked them for some food," he conceded to Avery, who had managed to control his horse for the first time.

"Yeah," Avery said. "However, he seemed convinced of our impending demise. Not sure if that would be taking advantage or not."

They rode off once more, the snow on either side of the path crisp and clear. Asa's head felt woolly and odd from lack of sleep and food. As if to answer this thought, his stomach gave a twisty rumble, which made Freda's ears perk up. To his great irritation, they did not stop for lunch. A stream ran close to the road, ice chunks caught in the stream like lumpy boats. They let their horses take a short drink at noon before setting off at the same brisk walk. Asa sighed, loosening his hold on the reins. Travelling was a lot more boring than he had assumed.

As the day drew to a close they passed more people, great groups of them, travelling west down the road. They walked barefoot, carrying the essentials for survival. Women held children's hands, muttering condolences in their ears. All around were the same frightened, gaunt faces that had seen more than anything Asa had ever experienced before. They whispered and muttered as they saw the direction that the two were taking.

"Are you sure that you wish to go to the east?" a young woman asked them, a sword strapped to her waist in its scabbard. Her dress was a functional brown one, with a leather vest over the top. She had wide, expressive eyes and a flower tucked into her plaited hair.

"Yes," Avery replied, halting Neasa so that they could talk. "Yes, we are."

"But, sirs," she said curiously. "The way is long. We have been walking for some time now. It is unsafe for just two of you to go such a way."

"We have little choice in the matter." Asa shrugged. "We must travel where we must travel."

"We were told that we would find safety in Jundres." She smiled contentedly, straightening her back. "That is where we will seek asylum. What is it that you ride for?"

Asa frowned at her mention of the underground city, but decided that he would not speak. He looked straight into her eyes.

"We ride for the queen," he declared. "We ride for the concourse."

"The concourse?" she exclaimed. Instantly, a hush fell over the halted group. Whispers of excitement and fear flashed around like quicksilver. The two of them were gazed at reverently, as though they were deities of some unknown amount of power. The girl tossed her flower at Avery, who caught it, blushing.

"You're going there?" a child asked. "You're a hero?"

"I'm not a hero until it is done," chuckled Asa. "But yes, that is our goal."

The girl rested a hand upon her sword. "My name is Lili Brandon. Would you like to rest with us tonight? We will celebrate now that we are out of danger from the snowfall. I would like to become better acquainted with you."

"That sounds brilliant." Avery was grinning foolishly.

Asa smiled. "Yes, I am sure that that would be nice."

If it had seemed that stopping in early afternoon was too long a rest, Asa realised soon that he was wrong. Once he and Avery had tied their horses to a low-hanging tree, several men had brushed a route through the snow to a small clearing one hundred paces into the treeline. The villagers brought a huge cloth, which they spread across the ground. Two ancient trees were felled, their broad stumps used as tables. A huge fire was lit with the wood—fiery tongues of flame dancing in the brisk wintery breeze.

The food was bland but sufficient. It reminded Asa of what he had eaten in Salatesh when he was young. A huge stew pot was suspended over the fire, the cooks of the town piling in mountains of root vegetables and salted meat and topping it off with handfuls of melted snow. They stirred the spitting pot until steam whisked around their heads and wetted their brows. Filling, homely smells drifted throughout the clearing. It was late afternoon now. The air was calm and close, humid. It stuck to Asa's skin and felt as though it would burn him with the cold of it.

Wooden bowls were passed around, hundreds of them. Everyone joined a line, just waiting for their turn for a splash of stew and, if they were lucky, a lump of bread. Asa and Avery stayed at the back of the queue, out of place with these eastern people. They were friendly, but Asa felt distrustful as wary eyes bore into his spine. Finally, it was their turn. They were each served the same measured bowlful of stew, the bread having disappeared long ago. Asa lifted the bowl to his lips.

"Smells good." He nodded to one of the younger cooks, who eyed him in apprehension and nodded back.

He took a sip. It certainly tasted good. Surrounding the meat and vegetables was a thick, glutinous gravy. Asa licked his lips. *What is it?* That powder that his mother had added to her own soups and stews. Brown powder, acrid and salty if eaten on its own kept in that little earthenware pot above their stove. The bowl warmed his hands as he sipped it, trying to find that secret ingredient. He remembered being given it when he was sick, mixed into a mug of warm milk. *Salt-kidney powder; that's it!* Asa made a mental note to keep that recipe in mind, if in some merciful coincidence he did survive.

A middle-aged woman dressed in a skirt and bodice of forest green was playing with something in a corner. Asa watched her curiously. She unclasped a leather case and withdrew a beautiful wooden instrument, a fiddle. She took the bow to the strings and played a long, mournful note. There were a few snatches of conversation, but the clearing quieted to a gentle murmur. One word was repeated time and time again, dancing.

The bowls were discarded to the sides of the huge cloth, left for a group of sullen-faced teenage boys to clear away. The elders of the village congregated in the middle, the dying light of the sun giving their silver heads a warm glow, putting colour back into the grey strands. The fiddler increased her pace, jumping from note to note and string to string with remarkable speed. The clump of elders split down the centre, beginning the first steps of a dance that Asa knew all too well. For people who had no ability to read, dancing was an all too necessary skill. He felt a rush of remembrance. He and Avery had been to many dances such as these.

A huddle of young women approached them, dressed in pastel coloured pinafores over their functional work dresses.

The leader, a girl wearing a light-blue dress, extended her hand and walked up to them.

"Would you like to dance the next dance with us?" she offered to them both, no hint of nervousness in her tone. "We have no male partners."

Avery perked up at this, but Asa shook his head, stamping on his friend's foot.

"I'm sorry," he declined. "Much as I would love to, we must save our energy. Thank you, though."

He watched with growing relief as the small group wandered away, not looking disheartened. He turned to continue his and Avery's conversation, to find his friend looking exasperated.

"Oh, get a grip, Asa!" Avery exclaimed. "Some of those girls were lovely."

"I'm terribly sorry, but I didn't notice," Asa replied.

A tall girl with chestnut hair approached them. Avery nudged Asa with his elbow. She smiled at them, winding a glossy strand round her fingers. Asa sighed. He could see that she was nervous so he tried to smile back, offering his hand. She put her own in his and he raised it to his lips in a stiff kiss. Having had her offer accepted, the young woman led him out onto the cleared area, where there were many other couples dancing. Asa shot a panicked glance back at Avery, who winked at him.

The pace of the fiddle seemed to slow as it entered his ears. Asa moved stiltedly, though he knew the steps. The girl was taller than him. Her hair fell across both of their shoulders in its luscious volume, untainted by the dust track which she had walked. Their hands were linked in a strange mockery of intimacy as they stepped forward, drew back, and spun in time with the frantic tune of the fiddler ringing in their ears. Asa stared at the darkening sky blankly, registering the uncomfortable sensation of small, soft hands encased in his own.

After what seemed to be an eternity of formal twists and paces, the music stopped. Asa's hands flicked open and he turned to run away from the brunette, not bothering to ask for her name or even another dance. He returned to his best friend in ill grace, half-scowling with anxiety.

"Asa!" Avery chastised him. "That wasn't polite. She's looking so confused now. How hard was it for you to simply say goodbye?"

"Impossible," Asa said simply.

"Every other man on the floor would have given their right hands for a girl as beautiful as that," Avery snorted.

"Well, every other man on the floor can have her, and keep their right hands too," Asa replied. "Why should I dance with her? I know nothing of her, she nothing of me. Why should we be forced together by aesthetics and situation? It's horrible."

"Something wrong with you there, mate." Avery eyed the dancers. "Hey, do you think I could ask that girl from earlier to dance? Lili? She's all alone over there."

"Sure." Asa shrugged.

"You don't mind?"

"'Course I don't." In fact, he minded a lot.

He watched the dancers, muddling through his convoluted thoughts. He watched Avery move across the dance floor, swinging the light girl as if she was a child. They laughed and joked as they span, too close, way too close. Their chests were pressed together as close as lovers. He only just managed to stifle an annoyed yelp as Avery leaned down, whispered in her ear, and kissed Lili on the lips.

"Alright, time to go." He crossed the dance floor and grabbed Avery's arm, wrenching him bodily away from Lili, who looked up admiringly at his friend with her dark eyes. Avery mouthed something at her, and she mouthed it back, but Asa pulled them both out of the clearing with nothing more than a mumbled expression of gratitude to the woman who stood at the entrance.

Avery was fuming. "Asa, what in Eodem was that about?"

He ripped his arm away from Asa's clenched fingers but Asa

held fast. They could hear the noises of the people, the music, and the clatter of feet on ground. Outside, the air was colder and emptier. Asa looked in confusion at Avery.

"Avery, the real question is, what that was about?" he asked in disbelief. "You're not together romantically, and you never will be. That was foolish. You don't even love her!"

"Hmm." Avery made a small sound in the back of his throat, though he walked away from the party to climb onto his horse. Asa sprung up onto his pony's back, peering curiously at Avery, whose shoulders were hunched as though he was in some sort of awful discomfort.

He nudged Freda into walking and beckoned Avery to follow. His friend waved a wistful hand and they together trotted down the road, hearing the cheers of the people for some time after they were unable to see them. Asa buzzed as he sat on his horse, hands shaking from pent up excitement.

"They know about me now, Avery!" Asa grinned, bouncing up and down in the saddle. "I'm famous!"

"Great." Avery twiddled the flower that Lili had given him.

"They knew you too." Asa turned to him, anxious that he knew of his importance. "It's not just about me."

"Thanks."

"What's wrong?" Asa asked, surprised and hurt by his friend's lack of interest. "What's eating you?"

"Nothing much." Avery placed the flower in his saddlebag. Asa caught this and a small smile crept onto his face.

"Oh," he said incredulously. "Oh, I see."

"See what?" snapped Avery.

"Mister "I don't go in for girls" Avery Hardy has a crush? That's why you kissed her! You plan on finding her when this is over. I see that now! Oh, I was blind not to!"

"What?" Avery snorted. "No. Of course not. She just had pretty eyes. I got caught up in the moment, that's all."

"Nice eyes, a cute laugh, and thought you were a hero?" Asa

counted on his fingers. "Can't see the attraction, personally."

"Ah, shut it." Avery shook his head. "She's one in millions. I'll never see her again."

"But you want to?" Asa said suggestively.

"I might do," his friend conceded, chuckling. "Did you think she was cute?"

"As you said, one in millions of others like her." Asa shrugged. "But her face was tolerable enough, I suppose."

"Tolerable?" Avery gaped. "You miserable old git! She was an absolute stunner. And clever, too. She said that she's always studying, even now on their migration. She likes me, too. Asa, I think that she's the one."

"You got all of that from a kiss?"

Asa raised an eyebrow, which reduced the blond to a stony silence, occasionally breaking out into a tut or a shake of the head as Asa's statement repeated itself. Asa ran a hand through his hair, breaking the wild order that it had been in. It stuck up about his head as if it were a dark brown mane. He laughed at the still-irked expression written clearly over Avery's features. His friend, no doubt about it, was sulking.

Freda trundled along, occasionally stopping for a snatch of grass or a cheeky leaf from a low-hanging branch. Asa noticed but didn't have the heart to reprimand her. She was only a pony and was allowed to have something to eat occasionally. Neasa just looked miserable. Her head hung low as she trudged along the road, Avery slumped in the saddle.

"Sulking, much?" he teased. Avery glared at him. "Oh, come on, Avery."

"You shouldn't tease so much," he scowled.

"It was just a joke," Asa apologised. "I'm sorry that you did not find it amusing."

"Well, it wasn't funny," his friend scowled.

"But," Asa started, then stopped. "Seriously, maybe you've got a chance?"

"Asa, I'll never see her again."

"And why not?"

"Because she's travelling to a reclusive underground city and we're going ever-so-nicely to our certain deaths." Avery kicked his heels into Neasa's sides. "Gee up, you. Stop dawdling."

Asa sat silent for a minute.

"Avery?"

"Yeah?"

"Who says that we're going to die?" he asked. "I say that our prospects are good—"

"Asa, you're an idiot."

"Don't you dare interrupt me," Asa chastised him. "Anyway. We're going to survive and then go back to Jundres to meet the queen. The crowds of people, they will be ten rows deep and all of them chanting our names. We'll use our influence to change their lives. We'll tell them that. They'll have hope yet, Avery. Then you'll see them, a pair of large eyes staring into your own. You'll get off your pony, handing the reins to me, and you'll walk to her. 'How are the studies going?' You'll say 'I trust you have been expanding your knowledge.' And she'll laugh and tell you, and you'll arrange a time to meet again and all shall be wonderful."

"Ha. Wonderful," Avery mocked.

"Hush you. It shall be perfect. Now, onwards to victory and a meal that will fill our poor empty bellies."

"No use pining, I suppose," Avery sighed. "She'll still be there when I get back."

A cloud drifted over the weak sun, blocking out its light. Asa shivered. He pulled his sleeves down over his wrists. A definite chill came over the pair of them, sitting close together on their horses. Asa scowled and Avery swore as, one by one, tiny fragments of ice began to fall once again from the sky. The novelty was lost on them by now. Asa checked his saddlebags were fastened and sped Freda up into as fast a walk as she could comfortably maintain. They were doing this on distance, after all. If they completed this part of the journey then maybe they could sleep earlier. Asa could only hope. He wiped some sleep from his eyes and focused his vision on the road ahead.

They passed over another icy river, faster and deeper this time, the road narrowing to not much more than a plank of wood. Freda took the few steps with ease, ears pricked forwards. Avery was having more trouble with his horse. She was wanting for some serious exercise, not just their simple walking. The racing blood that ran so clearly within her veins made her antsy, skittish, and unreliable. Asa could tell by his friend's envious looks at his own pony that Avery was jealous of Asa's "misfortune" in receiving such a boring mount. Neasa tugged at her reins, dancing on the spot as Avery tried to get her to cross. He kicked her, resulting only in her performing a sort of half-rear and whinnying to Freda, whose plain face displayed only mild concern for her comrade. Avery grimaced and snapped a small switch from a branch. He gave Neasa a light tap upon her shoulder, softer than he could even nudge with his heels.

Instantly, the horse flinched away from the unwelcome contact. She shied backwards, slipped on some ice, and gave an almighty buck. Avery was sent head over heels into the freezing waters that he had been trying to cross. Asa caught not much more than an expression of almighty surprise. He yelped and dismounted hurriedly, not caring as to where Freda wandered in the intensity of his panic. Asa rushed over to where Avery had fallen in, groping about in the dark river despite the undeniable fact that the current would have carried him off had he been unconscious. He called his friend's name, voice higher than usual. No response was forthcoming. Asa had been starting to suspect the worst when, all of a sudden, there was a splash and a hand gripped onto the bank of the river. Knuckles whitening, it strained and Avery's face came into view under the water. Asa plunged his hand deep into the icy depths, feeling a surge of relief as Avery grasped it in his, pulling his torso up and onto the bank where he floundered desperately until his legs were free of the sucking undercurrents.

"I just lost my horse," he whispered. "I literally lost my horse."

"Ditto." Asa whistled through his teeth. "But, hey, at least you didn't die?"

"Indeed." Avery was soaking; voice disappearing into chatter as he fully registered what had happened. Asa wiped at his dripping clothes with his hand but soon denounced that as pointless. He asked if Avery was cold, but his friend either could not or did not want to hear as he just looked blankly at him. Asa checked over his shoulder. As he had suspected, Freda was gone, having bounded over the primitive bridge in pursuit of the bolting horse. He swore darkly under his breath. It would be harder going from now on, make no mistake.

"Well," Avery said distantly. "The road goes on, let us now do so too."

"Can you walk it?" Asa asked.

"Sure I can." A flush of slight pink returned to Avery's cheeks in indignation. He strode forward, casting a supercilious glance at Asa. "Can you?"

"Certainly." Asa followed Avery for a moment, before seeing the pools of water. "You're dripping."

"It was my intended look," he replied, before breaking into a short laugh. "Who doesn't look better when dripping wet and frozen to the bone?"

They started to walk down the path, not knowing what else to do. Asa sighed. If only he had thought to restrain Freda! One pony was better than none at all. But no, he had been too intent upon saving someone a lot stronger and more powerful than him, someone who didn't even need saving. He had let her go.

Avery fell silent after a short while of attempting to describe the surrounding countryside. His comments had turned to shivery breaths, clouding in the cold air. Asa wrapped a supportive arm around his waist and tried to warm his cold skin. He was the temperature of a stone. Asa tried not to worry as the blond's lips turned blue-grey. He felt for a pulse, only a languid thud every few moments in response. Avery stumbled over his own feet, body succumbing to the ice that seemed to spread through his every breath.

Asa checked the sky above, noticing dusky shades of pink beginning to streak over it from the west. They couldn't go much farther, not like this. He half dragged his friend off the path and into the surrounding trees, sitting him on a fallen trunk as he surveyed their options. Firstly, the trees here were thin and spindly. They were set too close to be of any use to him as a source of shelter. Secondly, there was a lot of snow on the ground. This was his only material to work with. Thirdly, the temperature was set to drop the darker it got. Avery would not survive the wind chill if he was not sheltered. Asa contemplated his surroundings, trying to understand how it would all fit together. The snow was key. There was no sudden rush of coherency, but gradual ideas began to float around his head. The snow was the key; there was no doubt in his mind. *Look to the snow.*

He piled up a mound of the fluffy, unmarred snow, marvelling at the texture and crumbliness of it. His hands chilled as he smoothed it down, piling more on top. It was only when he had collected a huge pile of it, rounded at the top, that he stopped to decide what to do. He checked Avery, who was dozing on the log, eyelids twitching as he dreamed. He must move fast. A biting wind had started up as the sun sank below the horizon, turning Asa's nose pink with cold. Avery's face was an odd, drawn shade of grey.

Asa glared at the pile of snow. He could not move it—it was as tall as he was. He could not build a house. He had no physical skills in this sense. It was Avery who was good at this, he was a miner.

An idea occurred to him, brightening his previously gloomy

demeanour. Reckless of the cold, Asa dug his fingers straight into the pile of snow. It resisted his entrance, which made him smile all the more. The wind and his hands had frozen it until the surface had turned to solid ice. He managed to carve out a considerable cavern in the pile of snow, digging down until his fingers met limp blades of grass. When the shelter was big enough for two people to huddle in, Asa started to smooth it down. The water on his hands began to freeze as he stroked the ceiling into one plane, a few inches all that was left between him and outside. It was warmer in the ice shelter, away from the wind outside.

Once it was finished, Asa jogged outside to get Avery. The blond's teeth were chattering, even in his sleep. Asa shook him awake.

His hazel eyes opened, and Asa's heart sank at their general fogginess. He took one of Avery's limp hands and tugged him into a sitting position. From there he pulled his friend up until he was standing. Lurching with the extra mass he was carrying, Asa helped Avery through the snow. Avery tried to assist him by moving his feet, but this was for the most part useless and for the other unhelpful as he occasionally caught Asa's limbs in his feeble kicks. Eventually they had staggered the few metres to the shelter, and Asa manoeuvred his friend inside and laid him down on the grass floor. It was at this moment that he had a horrible realisation. Their blankets and food were in the saddle bags attached to their absent horses. Asa looked down at the frozen form of his best friend, shivering in their icy shelter, and made up his mind.

As quickly as he possibly could, Asa pulled his tunic over his head. The close material seemed to take all of its warmth with it. As he leant against the snow wall, metal clad back aching in protest of the temperatures, he draped his item of clothing over Avery's prone form, watching his friend's shaking slow and hearing the teeth chattering grow softer. He took off the protective metallic vest, knowing that it would freeze to his skin if they were to sleep that night. He lowered himself onto the ground, hissing as the cold spread all over his body. He left a minute amount of distance between Avery and himself, courtesy still ruling over his mannerisms. The blond moved closer to him, until they were nose to nose. Asa looked closely at Avery. There was so much that he had never noticed about him. How sharp the line of his jaw was, how defined his nose seemed in the dim, wintery light, how long his eyelashes were. If they ever got through this situation, Asa would definitely tease his friend about being such a girl.

He curled in on himself, bare chest warm to his cold fingers. Unsure of what he would wake up to, Asa allowed himself to drift off into a fitful sleep of sorts.

"You've made a rather bad mess of things again, haven't you, Avery?"

Asa woke quietly in the morning to the sound of his friend muttering to himself. He kept still, closing his eyes to a crack so that he could just see the outline of Avery sitting up in their small shelter. He moved slowly to get a better view, feeling goose bumps on his bare chest. Avery was looking in his general direction, eyes not quite focused upon Asa's sleeping form.

"He's just gone and given you his own clothes because you managed to lose both your horses and your dignity. What a noble adventurer you are, indeed. He must be so cold."

"Not half so much as you were," Asa replied flippantly, before clapping a hand over his mouth. Avery blushed scarlet, and then turned a mottled puce colour. He gaped wide-eyed at Asa.

"You were listening?" he asked desperately, as though the answer could be no.

Asa stretched leisurely, the cold feeling dissipating as he pulled his tunic roughly over his head. "Only for the last few moments, mate. Nothing too scandalous, I can assure you."

The purple receded from his friend's cheeks, and he smiled in what looked to be extreme relief.

"Well then, good morning." He nodded at the snow roof above his head. "You were excellent last night. Thank you."

"No problem." Asa was about to ask about breakfast but then remembered. "How does the morning greet you?"

Avery frowned. "I feel as though I have run to the moon and back and then drunk my own body weight in alcohol. Otherwise, I'm great. Bring on more adventuring."

"Good for you," Asa said wearily. He touched the metal vest cautiously, fingers shrinking back from the cold material. He stripped his tunic off again and dropped the armour-like garment on underneath before redressing. As he crawled out of the narrow opening which he had made the day previously, there was a curious jump in his chest, as though something flipped within him. It was not altogether painful but did not feel pleasant either.

"You okay?" Avery asked from inside their shelter.

"Fine," Asa gasped.

He shuffled away from the opening and lay down on the fluffy snow.

Avery stuck his head out curiously. "You sure?"

Asa sat up, slightly incredulously. "I think my heart literally skipped a beat."

"Seriously?" His friend pulled his body through the gap and stood up stiffly, cracking his back. "That doesn't sound good. You okay now, though?"

"Fine." Asa stood up with him. "Let's go. We need to make the most of this light with no horses."

Avery twitched. "You're right. Eastwards, then."

"Until we drop off the very surface of the world itself," Asa finished wryly. He walked past the shelter and stood on the path through the trees, waiting for his friend. The blond joined him then and together they walked off down the dirt track.

It struck Asa then how very large the trees were. They towered over them both, casting grim shadows on the ground in front of their feet. The mists gave the woods a nasty chill, nothing too definite, just a sting on the end of each breath, a bitterness to the sweet morning air. The road crunched satisfyingly under their boots as they strode out the distance, feeling dampened yet still optimistic.

However, Asa soon felt a sharp pang of hunger shoot through his stomach. He paused for a moment, hitting the offending organ with a bunched fist. Avery cocked his head to one side as he surveyed his self-injuring friend, but Asa muttered something about stomach trouble and they continued forward. The ache in his belly was growing with every breath he took in the cold wintery air, like it was caving in on itself. Never had Asa ever felt this kind of all-consuming hunger before in his life, not even when he had left Salatesh. He plodded miserably on, shoulders drooping with every dragged step. Avery checked him out, concerned.

"You sure that you're alright?" he asked Asa. "You look all peaky."

Asa rolled his eyes irritably. "I'm hungry."

"I'm sorry."

"Yeah, you should be." He closed his eyes briefly, before blowing on his frozen fingertips and glancing up. "Don't worry. I'll be fine."

A little while later the path narrowed to go through some trees. People had been here recently; many makeshift shelters had been created. They were now covered in thick layers of snow. Unlike Asa's ice cave, these were made from fallen boughs of trees, packed tightly around a tree in a cone shape. They were like little temples among the towering trees.

A flicker of movement caught Asa's eye. A white squirrel was scurrying over the frozen snow, carrying what seemed to be a nut of some sort. How odd, nuts were scarce at that time of the year, and only such sophisticated creatures as themselves would possibly be able to store food for the winter. He looked past the squirrel and saw another shelter, this one seemingly made from sticks and some sort of cloth. Sticking out into the snow were two pairs of tanned bare feet.

"Look!" Asa exclaimed. "Travellers! Avery, we're not the only people going east."

He squinted, still just about able to make out the two figures hunched inside their shelter about two hundred steps away.

"Careful at it, Asa," Avery warned. "You don't know where the ground is under all that there snow."

"Pfft," Asa scoffed. "I'll be fine. They're alright, aren't they?"

He started to make his way, albeit a bit more carefully this time, towards the shelter in front of him. Avery stood still a moment, and then followed.

"So we'd hope," he muttered darkly, so quiet that Asa only just heard it.

He rolled his eyes, tramping through the inches of white cold. It stuck to his boots, cooling his feet inside. He could see the people up ahead. They appeared to be sleeping. That would explain their lack of response to their noise. Asa kicked a flurry up petulantly, waiting for Avery.

"Hello?" Asa ducked under the collapsing structure, shaking a woman's cold shoulder. The woman's form was stiff and sinewy, skin stretched tight across bone. Her eyes were closed but there was no gentle swell under her lids. The long hair caught on Asa's fingers, coming loose as easily as cobwebs. Asa shot backwards, hitting Avery roundly in the chest. Hastily, he spun around, eyes wide with horror. He retched at the sight before him, but he had not eaten in a while and so he could not force himself to be sick.

"Asa?" his friend asked, concern ringing clear in his voice. "What's wrong?"

Asa struggled to speak for a few moments, the words leaden on his tongue.

"They're bodies."

"Oh, goodness. Are you alright?"

"You're asking if I'm alright?" Asa exclaimed, voice hollow from shock. "They're dead!"

"Yes." Avery stepped towards them sadly, hazel eyes darting around the scene. "And they have been for quite some time, probably."

He respectfully removed the thin blanket that linked the two bodies, a man and a woman, and laid it aside. Asa let out a choked cry. The two figures were clad in loosely hanging uniforms of a fading maroon fabric. The same one of which they were wearing. Only not. These were articles for a much drier time. They were loose and light—a cotton shift for the lady and trousers and a jacket of the same stuff for the man. Avery looked through their two odd satchels to find many of the same things that they themselves had been given. Dried fruit, nuts, and strips of desiccated meat. He took one bag and held out the blanket for Asa to stuff into the other one.

"Tell me they're not—" Asa whispered.

"Not all heroes live to be legends, Asa," Avery said wearily. "Take the blanket."

"Avery!" Asa was appalled. "No!"

"And suffer the same fate as them?" Avery snapped at Asa, a rare occurrence. "Take the blanket."

"But respect?"

"Asa Hounslow, I will be damned if I let us both die for want of respect for a dead body. We can give them that through making sure that we are the last people who ever have to do this again." Avery's voice held such gravity that Asa took the blanket, and their tattered satchel. "This is the least which we can do. For us. For them. For the rest of our kind."

Asa swung the bag over his shoulders. He couldn't argue that. His eyes caught upon the woman's wasted face, heart sinking.

"Avery?" he asked quietly.

"We're going, Asa," Avery said stonily, voice and manner so unlike his usual mild self.

"Shan't we do something?"

"Like what?" Asa heard his friend grit his teeth.

"Bury them? Say something?" He kept his gaze on their skeletal forms. "We can't just leave them here. We're better than that."

"Are we?"

"Yes," Asa asserted. "We are."

He picked up a handful of snow and started to cover the bodies, as if he were dusting them with sugar. Avery raised an eyebrow, but Asa kept going. The snow stuck to his hands in a wet, cloying manner and dampened his sleeves in a way that made his arms all the more cold. Eventually, he had amassed a large mound of snow, which fully covered the couple. He briskly cleared the remains of their shelter, what was left. It had worn away so much that it was really not more than a few sticks and some cloth.

Their minds a lot heavier for what they had seen, they followed their footsteps away from the camp and continued as quickly as they could on their way.

"That upset you, didn't it?" Avery asked his friend gently.

Asa tried to stop his hands from shaking. "What if that is what happened to my parents? Doomed to eternity on this forsaken roadside. It's not a pleasant thought, is it?"

"I would embrace you but I assume that you would prefer not to." Avery looked at a loss for words.

"You are correct in that assumption." Asa almost laughed.

"How about a nice professional handshake?" His friend held out a hand in offering.

"Well," Asa pretended to debate the matter. "I guess that could be okay. As long as it's professional."

"All business, Asa."

They shook hands twice, Avery almost squashing Asa's fingers beneath his. Asa withdrew his hand as though it had been burnt.

"I believe that I detected some sentiment there, Mr. Hardy!" He laughed sadly. "I don't want any pity shaking, thank you very much."

"It wasn't in pity!" his friend protested. "I merely wanted to flatten your white, ladylike hands."

Asa just laughed.

SIX

THEY HAD LAIN FOR hours by a frozen lake, drinking mouthfuls of the water with cupped hands, too tired to even consider going forward. Both of them drifted in and out of consciousness even beneath the blankets that they had taken.

"Are we going to die?" Asa asked.

The water was thinner than that at home, sharper, airier. It seemed to be more fluid somehow. Frost burned their fingers and turned their throats to ice. Still, it filled their empty bellies, and Asa could not complain of being thirsty.

After they had found the bodies, with the supply bags that they had so desperately needed, they had continued determinedly forward, one goal in mind. They had made careful shelters each day, piling snow into windbreaks or stacking branches into primitive roofs. They had gone on for two days in this manner. It had been a stressed time, yet an amicable one. They had sung songs and eaten their supplies in proper meals. Asa had been optimistic of finding the walls soon enough. If they carried along this path, dubbed The Great Eastern Trail by Avery, who was more romantic than he would admit, then they surely had to meet the wall at some point. It was in the east, they couldn't miss it.

Then another snowstorm had hit. They had been convinced of their imminent demise. Together this time, Asa and Avery had crawled into a ditch, huddling under a threadbare blanket. The snow had piled up around them, and they had fallen asleep for what seemed to be the last time ever. However, when they woke the next morning, they were under a small snowdrift and seemed none the worse for the experience. Asa had laughed in sheer relief. The situation was not hopeless. The snow had soon been brushed off and they had clambered out of the ditch to stand upon the white-covered ground once again.

Their food supplies had lasted another day. Without complaining, Asa had eaten the last nut. The evening was relatively balmy and they had slept outside, staring up at the orange-tinted sky above. Asa's legs twitched with exhaustion, and he kicked out a cramp in the muscles with an irritated groan. Avery turned onto his front, blinking bemusedly at Asa.

"What time is it?" he croaked.

"Mid to late afternoon," Asa replied.

"Oh."

"Problem?"

"Nah," the blond sighed. "I just don't know."

"Yeah," Asa's voice cracked. "Neither."

Avery dug his fingers into the thawing mud beneath his body. He returned the expression somewhat mutely. Then his face changed. He looked down in surprise, pulling mud-coated fingers towards his body. Then he dug them back in, pulling back a browny, orange root.

"Look what I found."

"What is it?" Asa asked.

"A root of some description."

Asa shook his head. "Funnily enough, I got that."

"I'm going to eat it," Avery said reflectively.

"Are you off your rocker?" Asa exclaimed. "What, if anything, are you even thinking?"

"I'm starving," Avery snorted, wiping the root on his clothes before popping it into his mouth and chewing reflectively. "Mm."

"You're going to die," Asa stated.

"Stop being so morbid," Avery mumbled, mouth full. He gave a gargantuan swallow. "It appears to be fine. It may be a carrot."

"A carrot." Asa's muscles tensed.

"Maybe not a real one. A carrot of sorts. It sure tasted like it." Asa hit him on the back of his head. "Ow!"

"Don't make me worry like that," Asa hissed.

"Fine." Avery dug up another. "You want one?"

Asa glared at the offending vegetable. "Of course."

They turned the smooth turf up as efficiently as the most experienced ploughers, scrabbling fingers grabbing the round roots in handfuls at a time. When at last they seemed to have exhausted the earth's supply, they both sat back to observe their food with dirt smeared all over their faces. Their stomachs made low sounds, not in protest, but due to their being full. Asa lay down in satisfaction, wiping muddy fingers on his clothes.

"We've got so many." Avery smiled.

"Enough to last us a lifetime." Asa was sleepy. He lay down on the ground, pulling his blanket around him. He heard Avery counting the roots under his breath and then lie down next to him, cuddling under his own blanket.

"Let's hope not." Avery yawned. "We're getting home, remember?"

"True." Asa let himself relax, feeling warm and impossibly sleepy. He closed his eyes, aware of his eyelashes brushing his flushed cheeks. Avery moved closer to him, their backs brushing. He couldn't quite pinpoint when he fell asleep, muddled thoughts merging with confused dreams.

They ate a good breakfast that morning, washed down with the thin water. It was surreal to Asa. Yesterday they were on the brink of death, yet now they were preparing to move forward again. Camping drained their high spirits, though, and the two of them struggled with the straps of their satchels as they lifted them over their heads. Asa's breaths were lighter than usual, shallow and rather sore. It felt as if he was coming down with something, without the actual symptom of being sick. He checked that they had packed everything, pacing the site where they had laid with a restless fervour.

"Give it in," Avery told him. "You look like a nutter."

Asa kicked the dirt, anxious to leave as soon as it was possible. Avery rose, stretched his arms out and then led their way back onto the road that they had assumed they would never walk upon again. They followed it in morning silence for a few moments, each deep in their own contemplations.

"We are going to reach the wall today," Asa announced. "I can feel it."

"You say that every day." His companion yawned. "And yet here we are."

"We're going to make it." There was a sudden upsurge in his spirits. "There's nothing that you can say to stop me believing that."

"Sure."

The sun rose as they walked towards it. Asa's mind was filled with whimsical, nonsensical things. Was it rising, or was the world moving? He shook his head. No one had time for such restless nonsense. A hand pressed at his temple, rubbing away the beginnings of a headache. He smiled at his friend, who averted his gaze.

"Thank you, Avery dear."

He froze.

"No problem, you just—" Avery stared blankly at him, eyes wide.

Asa swallowed. "Yes, indeed. Thank you."

He flushed scarlet and pulled his satchel over his shoulder, striding ahead. His breaths came in shallow gasps as the full weight of what he had said dawned upon him. He shuddered. Why had he used such an intimate term?

He was walking in such a strained fashion, eyes somewhere in front of his feet, that he did not notice at all the rather large tree root sticking out onto the path. By the time Avery had shouted, Asa was dragged to the floor. He coughed as the wind was knocked out of his body.

"You're going to be feeling an idiot now, aren't you?" Avery smirked.

"Yes," Asa replied in distraction, heart racing at ten thousand beats per minute, shaking his chest as he gasped for air.

"Oh, fine, I'll help you up." Avery held out a hand and somehow managed to haul Asa unsteadily to his feet. Asa swayed, then straightened himself.

"Thank you," he muttered yet again.

"No problem, *love.*" Avery stressed the last word triumphantly.

"I'm sorry." Asa looked down. "I didn't mean anything by it, promise. It's not as if I love you or anything. It was stupid. It came out quite wrong."

"What?" Avery's eyes darted over Asa. "What did you say?"

Asa looked imploringly at his friend. "I didn't mean to call you *dear*. It was an inappropriate pet name, and I feel dreadful about it, honest. I didn't mean to imply love between us."

Avery frowned, eyes downcast.

"What?" Asa asked.

"You don't feel anything for me?"

"No, no, I like you plenty, Avery!" Asa exclaimed in relief. "Erebus, I thought that you meant—"

"That's it?"

"There should be more?"

"I have travelled around half the country for you, Asa

Hounslow. Just for that sake, I should hope that there is more."

Asa looked around him desperately, panicking. "I—I don't know."

"Don't you feel anything for me?" Avery shook his head, bending down to look into his eyes. "I should have known."

"I do, Avery," Asa affirmed. "You know I do. You're my friend."

"But what do you feel for friends?" Avery demanded.

Asa was silent, confused. "You like them, don't you? It's a mutually beneficial relationship."

"I should have known," Avery swore, tearing at his hair in frustration. "No, Asa, that's not what you should feel for friends. You should love your friends."

"Avery, it's not like I'm . . . I'm not gay," Asa laughed, disbelief washing over him. "I can't love you."

"You don't need to be gay," his friend pleaded. "It's platonic, like a sort of chosen brotherhood. Look into your heart, Asa."

"I don't know what I can say." Asa swallowed. "But I can't say that. You're my friend. Loving you would be weird."

Avery was silent, and his hazel eyes filled with some sort of emotion that Asa thought that he could never, not if he lived to see eighty years, fully understand. He shrugged and set off again ahead of Asa, feet stamping with what seemed to be undue force on the ground. Fragments of frozen dirt flew up and sprayed out behind him as he vented his frustration on the dusty road. Asa's face flickered with a look of consternation, before he flew to his friend's side. He grabbed Avery's shoulder, fingers lingering for maybe longer than they should.

"Avery."

"Huh." Avery turned green-gold eyes on him. "What?"

"It wasn't my intention to offend you," Asa said mutely, voice trailing off and dying. Avery looked at him with a scathing glint behind his blank face.

"Maybe it was my intention to be offended, then," he snarled.

"Oh, Avery," Asa sighed, raking his hands through his hair. "Can't we just move on?"

"You don't get it, do you?" Avery looked more desolate than Asa had ever seen him.

"No," Asa said, words tumbling out of his mouth. "I don't. Why don't you help me understand, then?"

The blond nodded. "Maybe that would be for the best."

"Well?" Asa asked, speeding up his gait to match Avery's longer one.

"I left my family for you, Asa," he said in response, face shadowing over. "They loved me. I had assumed that you did, too. Otherwise I would have let you go on alone."

"You're not leaving me, are you?" Asa's mouth was dry.

Avery contemplated it for a moment. "No."

"No?"

"No," his friend said. "I may not agree with what you think, but I cannot stop my own feelings from getting involved. I will continue and maybe, just maybe, you'll come around to my way of thinking."

Asa exhaled in relief. "Maybe."

"Thank you, Asa." His eyes, so different in shape and colour to Asa's, seemed to melt. He gave his friend an awkward smile, the corners of his mouth pulling upwards. Avery shrugged. "Do you want a carrot?"

Asa chuckled. "Yes, I would like that. Toss me one?"

A scramble around in his bag and Avery threw Asa a round orange root. Asa bit into it, rejoicing inwardly at its resonating crunch. He finished it in three large mouthfuls. Avery swallowed his whole, merely biting it once when it was in his mouth. Asa looked at him in astonishment, which made the blond grin.

Lunch over, and the sun shining dimmer than it had ever seemed to have done farther down the road, the two of them stepped in time on their way. Asa peered ahead, anticipation building in his stomach as they approached a tall line of trees.

These were giants, even for the oldest trees in the oldest forests in the world. Their branches were as thick as the path was, their trunks wider than both he and Avery lying in line. He looked into the darkness ahead of him with strange excitement. Something was due to happen now. He could feel it. The sunlight grew weaker as they entered the shadows of the trees.

Asa shivered from the illusion of warmth that the light had given him being stripped away. Avery, however, looked complacent, even bored. The trees were set close together, closer than was surely natural for such huge species to grow. It was as if they were entering a tunnel of dim, unsteady light. Avery glanced at Asa's look of apprehension and chuckled.

"It's fine, Asa."

Asa's voice was higher than usual. "It's dark."

"The dark is good," Avery's deep, accented voice calmed Asa. "The shadows are where you should be careful."

"But doesn't "dark" mean everywhere is in shadow?" Asa swallowed.

"No, Asa," his friend replied. "The dark is the absence of light. Shadows are where something or someone is blocking it out."

There was the sound of leaves rustling in the trees behind them, which made Asa wheel around, looking about to see where the disturbance had come from. Avery placed a firm hand upon his shoulder and tugged him along the path without a word. Asa's breathing was erratic, heart racing in his ears. Avery did not mind Asa's weight being placed upon him as they trudged along the path together.

Everything was quiet for a few long moments, their breathing the only sound in the otherwise silent forest. It was eerie. Asa had begun to wonder if he had been imagining it, when the sound came again. And again. Something was tracking them through the undergrowth. Asa's hand whipped up to grasp Avery's arm.

"Avery!"

"No, it's fine, Asa," Avery muttered. There was a low growl from somewhere to their right, and the muscles in his friend's arm tensed as the blond made for his sword. "There are no wolves in Eodem. We're quite safe."

Another growl. Asa's hand snaked to the gleaming blade hanging unused in its scabbard. He had no idea what he was to do with it, but felt better for having a sharp poky thing than not. They could hear something else breathing near them, but the darkness of the forest was so near complete that they could not see more than two feet around them.

"I feel so safe," Asa said, more to reassure himself than anything.

"As well you should." Avery nodded. "Because there is nothing to worry about just so long as we keep moving."

Asa stiffened and stopped as he heard a snarl. His legs froze and he found that nothing that he could do could get them to move. Avery tugged him but he just swayed, stuck to the ground in dumb fear. His friend took a double take and tried to pull him forward but Asa just couldn't. He shook with fear as near-silent paw treads approached.

"I'm sorry," he whispered. "I'm so sorry."

"We have swords." Avery peered through the darkness with attuned eyes picking up what Asa could not. He withdrew his sword with a theatrical flourish and held it steady, waiting. He braced his feet as the silence grew. Then the creature pounced.

Avery swung his sword upwards in an arc with remarkable aim and strength, considering his inexpertise in the subject. There was a dull thwack of metal hitting flesh, and something large collided with Asa, claws scrabbling. Asa yelped and pulled his sword out, holding it with both hands and trying desperately to hit the struggling creature. The volley of shrieks and growls were human-like, yet the thick black fur covering it told a different story. It batted at them with its broad paws, claws tearing into the ground around them but never quite reaching their limbs.

Avery kept pushing himself protectively in front of Asa, inflicting a well-executed slash down the creature's stomach. It yelped and hissed at him in a feline way, trying to bite and scratch at them both. They shouted incoherent commands and encouragements at each other as sweat beaded on their foreheads and in their hair. Their attacker was bigger than the largest bear that Asa had ever seen. When it drew itself up from the floor, its shoulder was on a level with Asa's own. He stabbed at it with his sword, his erratic movements much less effective than Avery's strong, easy swings. A thick, long tail whipped at their legs as the animal turned in a cornered circle, yowling at them. It attempted to floor Asa with a nasty shove of its front paws. Asa yelled out at it in fear, and in the mild hope of scaring it away. It swiped at him again. Asa plunged his sword in terror into the beast's chest just as Avery slit its throat.

They didn't know who delivered the final strike, but the cries gurgled to a halting stop, the creature stilling. Asa bent down in the dark, reaching out to stroke the black fur. It was like velvet beneath his cold fingers. Warmth not having deserted the body of the creature, he petted it as if it had been a yard cat in his own home. That was what it was, he concluded, feeling pointed ears under his fingers. A cat. But what cat reached such proportions? What cat was content to kill people who crossed their path?

He stood up. "It feels late."

Avery's head turned towards him. "It's not yet evening."

"Are you sure?" Asa looked up to the dark canopy of trees above him. "It surely must be night at the earliest?"

His friend wiped his sword along the bark of a tree, removing most of the blood. Asa copied him, movements slowing to match his. They stood over the body of the huge cat for a moment, both silent in their disbelief and awe that such an animal could exist.

"It can't be," Avery assured him. "It's just dark."

"Dark?" Asa shivered. "No, this place is more than just dark."

"It's so quiet," Avery said distantly.

"Yeah." Asa nodded. "Shall we . . . you know?"

"What?" Avery laughed, in his old spirits again. "Go on?"

"Yes," he replied. "Shall we?"

"Certainly." Avery picked up a thick stick and leant on it as they stepped over the dead cat. He kept hold of it as they walked, tapping it on the ground as the forest grew darker. Asa stayed close behind him, heart fluttering in his chest. Every creak of the living forest was danger to his ears. There was a snap behind him, and he wheeled around. A small rodent dashed across their path in a couple of fast bounds. Avery snorted, earning himself a clip on the ear for his troubles. Asa huffed in irritation, pulling his satchel close to him. The low thuds of the stick on the ground were all to be heard. Asa didn't have to wonder why there were no birds in this forest.

It was strange. As they walked along there was a strange illusion of being watched. The trees seemed to lean in conspiratorially as they passed, boughs creaking without any wind. Avery quickened the pace, and Asa followed at an anxious trot, palms sweating as he balled them into tense fists. It should not be that quiet, something was amiss. Their footsteps disturbed rocks on the path, the stones rolling away from their feet. Asa looked around as they hurried on, both of them wishing nothing more than to leave the forest. They reached a particularly large tree, which Avery circled reflectively, examining it. When he saw nowhere to shelter, he cursed and kicked it with a despondent boot.

"It must be late," Asa said.

"It feels it," Avery pondered sceptically. "But how? Where did the time go?"

"I don't know," he said unsurely.

Avery tried to hoist himself up onto a tree branch. It didn't work. The branch was too high for him to do more than just hook his hands around it. He glanced at Asa, and then shook his head. Asa only caught the motion because he was looking at Avery's dim form. He squared his shoulders and walked determinedly up to his friend.

"What, Asa?" Avery tried to lift himself up onto the branch but dropped down onto the ground in frustration.

"Lift me," Asa demanded. "I'll climb the tree."

"No," he laughed. "You don't have the strength."

"Try me." Asa could feel his lean muscles tensing under his skin.

"Asa."

"Try it," he ordered. "Lift me."

"Fine," Avery conceded. "Don't . . . don't die. Okay?"

"Sure." Asa grinned, rubbing his hands. "So, I get to the top and just peek out, see what time it is and then climb down? Easy."

"Be careful," Avery warned.

"Will do." Asa walked up to him and leapt like a squirrel onto his back. Avery stumbled forward a few paces, then trudged Asa to the tree. "Thank you."

Asa gripped the first branch with his hands and moved his weight onto the wood. The tree held firm. Confidence boosted, he moved to a kneeling position on the wide branch, getting to his feet. He wobbled for a moment, steadied himself on the limb above, and walked down towards the trunk. When his shoulder grazed the bark of the tree trunk, he placed his hands around a small offshoot and put his foot on the branch above him. He closed his eyes, wished, and opened them again. Asa steeled his nerves and clambered onto the second layer. He exhaled in relief. Success.

He glanced up. His eyes widened as he fully comprehended the climb before him. The tree reached right up into the canopy of branches hundreds of feet above their heads. Avery stood worriedly below him, hand placed supportively on the trunk of the huge tree.

"You alright, Asa?"

"Grand." Asa's voice trembled. "Just grand, thanks."

He managed, through luck more than anything, to twist his way through four more layers of branches and twigs. The tree was sticky, sap clinging to his hands like a second skin. It stung as he tore blisters on the delicate pad of his palm. The fifth layer was more of a challenge. Asa tried and tried, but it was much too high for him. He sat down on the branch, legs swinging, and thought about his situation. Avery he could not see, but he knew that his friend was down there, waiting for him to return. He would not do so empty handed.

Vines hung down to this level. It was some sort of thick climbing plant with round green leaves and garish orange flowers. Asa tested one for strength. It held for a moment, and then snapped off in his hand, plummeting the not inconsiderable distance to the ground below.

He tried again on another thicker one. It held for a good few moments before succumbing to the same fate as the last. The last vine seemed to be the same thickness as the one previously. Asa swallowed. It would have to do.

He placed his hands as far as he could on the vine above his head, trying to steady his butterfly hands. He waited a beat, and then transferred his weight onto the vine, pulling himself up as hard as he could, willing his arms to be strong. He was in reach of the next sturdy, tall branch. The vine began to stretch, close to tearing. Asa swung his weight away from the tree, buying time. He was in luck. The momentum brought him close enough to wrap both arms around the next branch up, clinging to it with a vice-like grip. The vine snapped, but he managed to swing himself onto the next branch up.

The tree limbs grew thinner as Asa climbed higher. He was through the canopy now. The leaves arched up in a huge grey-green arc over his head. He breathed in the sharp cold air and gripped up on the next set of branches. Nuts were growing in clusters around the leaves. Asa took hold of a cluster in curiosity and smelled it. He thought for a moment then started stripping the branches around him of their odd fruit and dropping them down to Avery below. He only hoped that his friend knew what he was trying to do.

Asa could feel the bitterness of the fresh air on his skin. He was on the top few branches now, ready to reach up and look out. There was a thick white blanket capping the top of the tree, blocking out what he assumed must be sunlight. He sat himself down on one of the precarious thin limbs and pushed up into a wall of icy coldness.

The snow filled his mouth, nose and ears. Asa coughed and blinked, trying to clear his blocked vision. He opened his eyes, and struggled not to fall off of his precarious perch.

It was a clear, cold evening, the rays of the setting sun behind him illuminating the landscape. Asa could see for miles around, across a vast area that seemed to be blanketed in green foliage. He looked forward to the east. The trees broke down into separate clumps, then sporadic dots, then wide open field. If he squinted, he could see a grey line along the horizon. It must be the wall.

He drew himself back down onto the branch that he was sitting on, buzzing with sudden energy. Body numb, he dropped down onto the branch below, descending quickly to share the news with Avery. His feet hit the ground with a thud.

"Asa!" Avery embraced him, examining his demeanour. "What's wrong? Are you okay? What took you so long? What time is it?"

"Night," Asa gasped, as Avery squeezed the breath out of his lungs. "Avery—let go."

"Oh, sorry." Avery released him. "How was it?"

"Cold," Asa complained. "And sore."

He showed Avery his torn hands. His friend gasped and winced.

"Oh my, Asa. What have you done to yourself?"

"The tree did it to me." Asa grimaced.

"I see that." Avery plucked a splinter of wood from Asa's cut hand, watching the blood from the minute puncture drip down the sides of the wound. Asa didn't even blink. Compared to the fire burning the rest of his hand, that pinprick was negligible. Avery licked his thumb and dabbed the blood from the palm, stemming the flow.

"Spit stops the wound from getting an infection."

"I still could've done it myself." Asa smiled.

"Well done." Avery looked upwards. "You were throwing stuff at me?" He held out a handful of rather battered nuts out to Asa.

"Yeah." Asa took one and cracked the shell open with his knuckles, demolishing the rich meat inside in one mouthful. "I thought that they could be useful."

The nut was bitter, like tea which had fallen to the bottom of the cup and been left to rot. Despite this, it was a welcome break from the boring fare that they had subsisted on so far. Asa would have murdered anyone for some hot food, even a plate of Avery's burnt toast. He yawned and his eyes twitched with tiredness. His friend looked at him in concern.

"How far to the end of this forest?"

"I don't know," Asa replied. "A few miles? It shouldn't be too far. Oh, Avery? I saw the wall."

Avery's face lifted in that one sentence. "The wall?"

"I assume so." Asa shrugged.

"Thank you!" the blond exclaimed. "The wall! We're almost there."

Asa withdrew the battered map that the queen had drawn from within his belt. He surveyed it for a moment, then refolded the paper down the worn creases and stuffed it back where it had come from. Avery inclined his head, but Asa made no comment. His friend asked him what was wrong but he just replied with a noncommittal answer.

"Just tired, I guess."

Avery's face fell. "How far is it, then?"

Asa frowned. "The wall is fairly close."

"What's the problem, then?"

"It's not far enough along the way." He patted where the paper lay against his body. "Roughly a third of the way there, if that. This is going to take so much time."

Avery grabbed Asa's shoulders and pulled him off the tree and onto the path so that they were facing the way that they had to go. It was rather cold as night drew in, however unprecedented the change of time had felt. He gestured up the dirt track.

"Somewhere up there is your destiny, Asa Hounslow," he said. "Don't be so impatient. It will come when it will come; it would be well that it would come quickly but that may not happen. You just have to keep going. Each step we take is closer there. I suggest we start by leaving this terrifying forest before it eats us or something."

Asa laughed. "You know how to make a guy feel good about his life prospects, don't you?"

"Sure, that is my job." Avery winked. "You know, aside from acting as a nanny for a seventeen year old who cannot even tie his own bootlaces without crying—"

"Hey!" Asa exclaimed. They both grinned at each other before restarting their fragmented journey along the dusty road.

The trees started to thin out as they continued forwards through the forest. Asa was struggling to keep up with Avery's rolling gait, swearing at his unfazed friend under his breath as his own numb limbs caught on the trees around him and sent him staggering all over the path. His breathing was as light and erratic as usual but more desperate, as if he had a fly on the back of his throat that he was longing to cough out. He paused for a moment, leaning on a tree, and coughed like a cat with a hairball. Avery walked a few steps further, then turned back to see his friend. Asa waved a hand, wheezing out a weak complaint. Avery rolled his eyes in response and beckoned for him to follow.

Asa shook his head, feeling all at once the sensation of the world spinning around him. He couldn't go on, he just couldn't. One lapse of coordination on his part would send him scattering into who-knows-where. He opened his mouth to tell Avery this, but instead choked and vomited on the ground. This sent him to his knees, and to his horror he managed to fall straight into the acrid puddle on the ground. He heard Avery hurry towards him.

"Oh Asa." He looked up. The blond's hazel eyes were concerned and sad. He was pulled to his feet and only had time to vaguely wonder what was happening before Avery lifted him over his shoulder as though he had been a sack of salt. Asa protested, but his friend held him fast and continued out of the forest as fast as his long legs could carry them. Asa breathed a sigh of relief as green foliage gave way to patches of dark grey, and eventually large areas of sky. It was colder, sure, but he felt warmer inside for knowing that he was out of the shadows of those vast trees.

They were standing in a huge wilderness, covered in shrubs and sporadic lonesome trees. The ground was less dusty here; sand having been frozen into a convoluted mess of a surface with the footprints of the passers-by imprisoned in a layer of frozen water. Avery saw a raised rock and Asa felt his body being placed on the stone numbly, as though he was dreaming. Nothing seemed to be real. Everything was once again covered in snow.

A few moments passed without occurrence, then Asa winced as his friend cleaned his clothes and cuts with melted slush water. This was far too real. It could not be a dream. He pulled his hands away from Avery's, batting away his caring touch. He just wanted to sleep. He pulled his legs and arms in on himself and settled down for a distracted, queasy rest. The world around him seemed to spin on its axis, the only steadies in it being the rock upon which he lay and the calming voice of his friend beside him.

Birds were singing as he opened his eyes. Asa sat up. His tunic was freezing cold and sticky? He touched it. The water with which Avery had cleaned him yesterday had frozen solid into the material he was wearing. He truly had the best of luck. Asa grimaced as he remembered what had passed yesterday. The taste of vomit rushed into his mouth, and he leapt from his stone seat to rinse his mouth out with ice water. He spat it out into the snow before him, flushing it from his lips so violently that a froth of pink blood joined the snow with his saliva. He crushed it with a boot, revolted.

Avery was asleep, breath misting in the cold. He didn't wake as Asa crept towards him, announcing with a foghorn voice, "Avery! The mines are awaiting!"

The teenager leapt out of his skin, standing up in one swift movement and searching over the ground for his uniform. He looked quizzically at the snow, saw Asa, and then the penny dropped. He raised a well-trained eyebrow.

"You are the worst friend ever to exist."

"Noted." Asa smiled.

"Feeling better?" Avery's face changed to one of genuine interest and sympathy. Asa did not like the combination one bit.

"Fine," he replied, loathing the pitying look. "I feel heaps better."

"That's good." Avery did not look convinced. "Breakfast?"

Asa's stomach lurched. "I don't think that that would be a good idea, thanks."

"Suit yourself." Avery was already crunching away on a root or two. "They're in my satchel if you want one."

"I'll bear that in mind."

SEVEN

THE ROAD GREW WIDER as they travelled to the east and soon they were able to walk side by side. The birds flitted across the sky like coloured darts, singing their noisy songs. It was not quite warm, but the air lacked the chill that they had felt near Jundres. As they walked closer to the thin grey line on the horizon, houses appeared on the sides of the path and fields of cultivated crops swayed next to them in the light winds. The area was so quiet it was as if they were the only people there.

They reached a deserted town square. Flagstones were overgrown and covered in mud-filled cracks. The hairs upon the back of Asa's neck stood on end. It was eerie, this silent place. No one called out to them, no one chattered, nothing moved. Even the trees appeared to be dead. He was walking around the shell of a shattered and desolate fountain, when a voice cried out from somewhere on his left.

"Hey! What are you even doing here?"

Asa spun around, grabbing his sword from his scabbard in one movement. Avery looked less astonished. They stood back to back, scanning the row of rickety houses in front of them, their swords held protectively out. The voice had come from the upper floor on the left-hand side. They waited for more information, but for a few tense moments it seemed like none was forthcoming. Asa exhaled and allowed his sword to drop before a ball of light shot to the ground in front of his feet and exploded, smashing the flagstone as though it was glass.

Asa yelped and leapt backwards, heart in his mouth. He held his sword out in front of him; Avery was saying something, but another explosion caused him to step backwards.

"Stop!" Asa shouted. "You could kill us, you fool!"

A thick cloud of smoke from the explosions was around their feet. It was dark grey in colour and acrid smelling, the sort of pungent odour that made Asa feel sick and dizzy. Balls of energy smashed into the ground, white hot at the moment before impact. One of these hitting either of them could be disastrous. Asa swiped at them in futility with his sword, having no idea as to how to tackle the burning hot rain of what seemed to be fiery orbs. They hit the flagstones with a sharp bang, a crack like that of a whip. They were coming too thickly, too fast. He wasn't sure how much longer the volley of bangs and smashing could continue.

"Spawn of Erebus, you shall not be suffered to pillage our town anymore. Begone!"

Asa saw someone bent over the sill of a window clutching a long pipe in his hands. He had tangled greying brown hair and matte black eyes that seemed to gaze at them with ferocity. He dropped his sword to the ground. Any fight on their part would be hopeless and in vain. Avery refused to drop his sword, hazel eyes narrowing.

"Avery." Asa locked eyes with his friend. "We can't."

"You always say that, Asa," Avery growled, glaring up at the stranger, who had pointed the pipe at him. "When is it time to say that we can?"

A crack and the flagstone to his right was demolished. Asa pulled Avery to the side, begging him to not be so foolish. Avery sniped back something inaudible, choking on the smoke that was now thick in the air.

"You idiot," Asa hissed in his ear. "Do you want to get us both killed?"

"No." Avery stared at the grizzled man in the window, making stony eye contact. The man raised the weapon in his hands. Avery, with a great effort, dropped his sword to the smashed flagstones. It clattered for a moment, and then fell to stillness.

"What're you doing in these parts?" the man asked, black irises surveying them. "I thought that all of the people here had gone west."

"They have," Asa said.

The man nodded appraisingly, finally lowering the weapon to both of their immense relief.

"I'm Parlan."

"I'm Asa." He kicked Avery, who had been silent for their short introduction. The blond rolled his eyes but complied without too much obvious aggression.

"I'm Avery," he said.

"You may take your swords." Parlan gestured towards the weapons and they picked them up gratefully. The elder man strung his strange system of pipes onto his back and invited them inside the house. Asa accepted for both of them, feeling that Avery's forgiveness would not stretch so far as to enter the house of his attacker.

Avery stopped short of the doorway and pointed to the contraption that they had only recently been acquainted with. "What's that?"

"What's what?" their benefactor asked.

"The weapon," Asa supplied curiously. "What in the world was it?"

"This?" Parlan turned back to them. "It's something I picked up last time I left the walls. I got powers. This just directs and focuses. It makes me powerful. I swear I could take down a bear with this in my hand."

"What about cats?" Asa inquired. Seeing Parlan's confused expression, he clarified, "Not like normal little cats, I was talking about huge ones. Like black wolves."

Parlan smiled. "Oh, I daresay it could indeed take down a large cat."

Parlan entered the dark building without another word and Asa, mouth dry, followed him. He did not glance behind for Avery. His companion's steady breaths the only testament he needed to his presence. They ducked through the low doorway and into the house itself.

Candles were lit at periodic intervals down the damp bare walls of the corridor they walked down. Paintings and weapons hung in equal measures on every surface imaginable. Asa followed close to Parlan's heels, examining everything. They went through another doorway and entered a small kitchen thick with steam, a huge log stove taking up an entire side of the room. Parlan sat in a chair at the head of a small wooden table, and gestured for Asa and Avery to draw up two more.

"Do you want a drink?" he asked.

"Water please," Avery said.

"Do you have any tea?" Asa responded at the same time. The elder man smiled at them, not with his mouth, but with the corners of his eyes. They crinkled in such a way that he might have been laughing, had his mouth not been an interminable straight line. He nodded at them both.

"Aye, I have tea, and thusly water too," he croaked, pulling his chair back and stepping towards the kettle on the stove. It was already piping hot, so he poured it into a metal cup and made tea. For Avery, he went to the corner of the room and poured a small amount of cold water from a water skin into another metal cup. He gave them the beverages. "Here you go, then."

"Thank you," they both murmured, manners they had been taught together as children kicking in.

"So," Parlan grunted. "What is your business so far east?"

"We—" Asa's voice died off. He decided to change the subject. "What did you mean when you said that you got your powers from outside of the walls?"

"Don't change the subject," the man snapped. "Answer the question. Are you the police? The army? Why are you in my territory?"

Asa looked at him. His moods had changed so quickly. All was not as it should be in this house. The place was covered in a layer of thick dust, cobwebs trailing their threadlike strands from object to object. Asa caught sight of a spider the size of his fist crouching in a teacup on the dark stovetop. He swore he could hear its pincers click.

The tea was harsh. Asa managed not to spit it over the table out of sheer grit and courtesy. Dust congealed on the surface of the hot beverage, thick clumps spinning in the dark water. It tasted as though the tea had been used and reused. He gave an approving smile and pretended to drink more, tongue not suffering to touch the tea again. Avery laughed at Asa's reaction, his expression changing as he sipped his water. Asa smirked, despite his unease. The water in the tin cup smelled like pondweed and algae.

Parlan had been looking at their reactions with a queer flicker of some emotion. A grey eyebrow twitched as the elder man glared at them.

"We are here on orders from the queen," Avery explained, replacing his cup, too.

"The queen? Queen Ria? Worse than all of the special forces in herself, I'd say, and you her humble servants! I should've stuck the both of you when I had the chance."

Avery watched him cagily, but Asa stared down at the table, ignoring the rant. He should not feed this man's anger any more than he already had. He saw his friend sigh, stand, and walk over to the unstable man.

"Avery?"

"Don't worry," Avery mouthed, before continuing in a louder tone. "Well, you did not "stick" us, did you? There must have been a reason for that."

"Aye, there was a reason," Parlan reckoned.

"You see," Avery explained surely. "You didn't kill us because you knew that we weren't going to hurt you. You're a good person, Parlan, aren't you?"

"Aye."

Avery's tone was steady and soothing, but his eyes belied his tongue. He looked at Asa and then back to the now-quaking older man. His constructed mask of composure was slipping. Asa saw him bite his tongue as Parlan fell against him, quivering.

Avery's voice was controlled. "You weren't going to kill us."

"No." The man's grey head snapped up. "Yes."

"Avery, back off," Asa warned.

Avery retreated to where Asa was sitting, and they both backed away from Parlan, moving into a corner. The man let loose a low growl, as feral as that of the cat they had killed. He was drooling, with flecks of spit running down his grimy, stubbled chin and dripping slickly off onto his clothes. His eyes rolled back in his head so that none of the black was visible. All Asa could see was bloodshot off-white. A deadly silence overtook the room, wrapping itself around them both that neither could think to utter a single word. Parlan was curled over as he panted, the spine of his back showing through his thin shirt. He whined in apparent pain.

"What's wrong with him?" Asa asked, spooked by the odd mannerisms.

"More like what isn't wrong with him," Avery muttered darkly. "Have you seen this house?"

"What do we do?"

"Get away from him, Asa! Good, to your right. You're clear. We'll make a break for it. We run."

"We can't just leave him. He's clearly sick."

"Sick in the head." Avery shook his hair out of his face. "We can't help him. On three, okay? One . . . two . . . Asa!"

Asa had stopped. He frowned in consternation, thoughts dashing between the man convulsing next to him and his companion's apparent ire. He paused for a breath. Avery repeated his name again, more forcefully now. Asa sighed.

"Coming, Avery."

"Go." They both ran at once for the door. Parlan turned, dark irises huge in the dim lighting. He smiled, and Asa realised that the dim light in the room had come from the old man's colour-changing eyes. His drawn face was thin, the skin sticking to the bones of his skull. It gave him an odd, skeletal look, translucence and opacity merging in the sharp angles. Asa stumbled once, grabbed onto the door handle, and pulled himself through the thin gap before Avery slammed it shut behind him. They paused for a single breath before retreating down the narrow corridor.

They burst into dazzling sunshine, eyes shrinking back at the bright light. The dust was settled now, trickling into the cracks left by the weapon that Parlan had used. Everything was still. Asa lead the way over the broken fountain, feet gripping to the smashed stone, and found the road that they had been taking, slipping from a jog into a full-out run when his mind had fully comprehended what he had seen. That man, that ordinary man, had possessed powers that he had never seen before. He had shrunk in on himself and had become something condensed, strong, something altogether darker than a mere human.

The streets were as empty and as quiet as Asa had ever seen a town. Snow capped the roofs of the houses and left a thin layer underfoot, just enough to make the stones slippery and uneven. A thin, balding rat scurried down a gutter and into a hole. He eventually slowed to a walk, out of breath and tiring of the fast pace. It didn't feel as dangerous here. The demonic creature that had lured them into his house surely would not go out during the middle of the day, he thought. It would be dangerous at night, to be sure, but by then they would both be long gone.

"I'm sorry," he apologised breathlessly.

Avery squinted at him, dodging a tree root. "What are you going on about?"

"I keep on doing this." Asa swore. "I wish that I was as talented as you."

"At what?" Avery snorted.

"At this, Avery," he scowled, kicking a stone out of his way. "This was my idea, okay, and I thought that I would be better at it than you. I wanted to be the calm, confident one. I wanted to be the best for once. And yet again, I am the damsel in distress. I lead us into danger. And you just follow me into trouble then get us both out."

"But you're the one who knows what we're doing," Avery mumbled confusedly. "I have done nothing but swing a sword about, and Erebus knows that isn't helpful."

"I hate this," he whispered. "I hate it."

"We're doing it now." Avery shrugged. "Nothing can change that."

The houses finally thinned out, leading to a single swelling hill. It wasn't high, or even steep. Still, their feet and calves ached as they ambled towards it. Asa frowned. He didn't want to walk anymore. The boots rubbed his feet raw, blistering his lower legs and ankles. He limped, licking dry lips.

Avery coughed, bringing Asa back to the present. His legs burned as they mounted the peak in a few long strides and were able to look out on the landscape below.

At once, the low rolling hills of the countryside had given way to a length of flat snow-strewn land. Stretching up, grazing the clouds themselves, was an immense stone wall. They stopped to look at the landmark. It was dark against the light grey of the sky, a silhouette of a giant's plaything. Asa had a stirring, odd sensation deep in his stomach. It was the feeling of being out of scale, a tiny speck on the infinite world. It pressed down on his shoulders, and he could do nothing in that moment but stare up at the plane of stone, mouth open.

Avery walked jerkily forward, Asa following in his wake. The grasses were scratchy and dry beneath their blanket of snow, suffocated. They trailed down the hill as slowly as they possibly could, relieved at the lack of stress to their sore limbs. It could have been Asa's imagination but the way down was miles shorter than the upwards ascent. Soon their feet met the clear snow-covered flat. The ground was darker here, under the shadow of the great wall.

The two of them crossed in complete silence, a sort of reverential awe in their muffled footsteps. The shadow was ice cold, a feeling of being soaked by a bucket of dry water.

"A house," Avery choked out in front of him.

A small cottage, a tiny snuffbox to their perspective, was propped against the stone ahead. Asa squinted at it, unsure whether or not he was imagining things. Avery voiced his thoughts.

"Is that the gate?" Their eyes met.

"Gatekeeper's cottage," Asa said. Avery smiled and withdrew the loop of keys from around his belt. They exchanged a victorious smirk before racing as fast as their tired legs could carry them towards the wall.

Predictably, Avery reached the cottage first. He hit it with his fists and waited for Asa to get there, panting. Asa stumbled the last few steps and flopped face first into the snow, dizzy as anything and so very cold. Avery let him lie there, then grabbed his arm and heaved him to his feet.

"Come on, get up." He chucked Asa under the chin and kept one hand on the back of his neck in case he fell over again. Asa leant into the warmth.

Avery pulled him to the door of the rickety wooden cottage, supporting a good proportion of his friend's weight with one arm. He searched on the loop of keys for the one that might open the front door. Asa watched him, leaning against the wood. He let out a startled cry, like a baby chick, as the door swung open under his bodyweight. He crashed to the doormat and stayed still for a moment, blinking up at his friend, whose arm was outstretched as if to grab him. Avery exhaled, a breathless laugh.

"Seems to me that this is all I ever to do as of late." He smiled. He offered a hand but Asa refused it, pulling himself peevishly up on the doorframe.

"Depend on it, this is not my fault." He scowled, stamping his feet as he entered the small cottage.

It was remarkably clean inside, neat and ordered. Asa remembered the withered old man whom they had taken the keys from. He and his wife must have spent their whole lives here. Mats lined the cold floors and a huge patchwork quilt covered the double bed, what seemed to be a lifetime of scraps weaved into a vast tapestry. Asa trailed his cold fingers over the soft fabric, catching his breath. It was so still, so perfect—like a house in a fairy tale.

Avery followed him, looking injured. He slunk off into the other side of the two-room apartment, off on his own devices. Asa sat comfortably on the hard bed, wrapping the coverlet around him. It smelled of must, old furniture, polish, and smoke. He inhaled the scent, rolling his mind around it giddily. It smelled like home.

There was a victorious shout from the kitchen and Asa jumped up, startled. Before he was able to inquire as to why Avery was creating such a racket, the blond sped into the room, clutching boxes and bags of something Asa could not quite read. He dumped them on the bed in front of him and grinned.

"Not too shabby, eh?"

It was food. Boxes and boxes of food. Asa's mouth watered. He reached out for a box. Dried peas. The rest of the fare was of the same sort. None of it was luxurious, but it was food nonetheless, and food was what they needed. He laughed with his friend, forgetting their heavy journey in this flash of fortune. The words rushed to his lips.

"Oh thanks," he said gratefully.

"Thank what?" Avery cheekily inquired.

Asa chuckled. "I don't even know. Thank luck, I guess."

"Thanks, indeed." Avery started to bundle the food back into his arms. He came to the door in-between the rooms and paused, looking back. "And, Asa?"

"Yeah?"

"We'll feast tonight." The blond winked, retreating into what Asa assumed to be the kitchen.

Asa rolled his eyes, leaping from the bed. He crossed the room to the fireplace and reached across the high mantelpiece until he had found what he was looking for—a small flint and steel. A large woven basket stood next to the hearth, piled with logs of all kinds and a small faggot of kindling. Asa piled a few into the fireplace and set about lighting a small blaze, just enough to warm them. The flames burst into life, a mockery of any other one that they had seen on the entire journey. The crackling of the logs burning and the soothing smell of smoke comforted Asa's soul like nothing else had. For the first time he had an overwhelming feeling that everything would be alright.

He heard Avery banging around in the kitchen, the dim clanking of pots and pans being thrown onto the stove reminiscent of his childhood. He stared into the flickering light for a few moments, lost in his thoughts. It was only when he heard his friend calling his name that he turned, stood, and went to investigate the delicious smells coming from the other room.

A thick cloud of steam greeted him as he came into the room, clouding his vision until it dispersed. Avery was bent over an archaic stove, stoking a fire beneath it with a cautious boot whilst stirring a pot with one hand and toasting bread with the other. He gestured Asa over to a small table with a flick of his head, a single bead of sweat running down his cheek. He pulled the toast out of the fire with his left hand and dropped the charred pieces onto rustic wooden plates with a skilful aim. He stopped stoking the fire and stirred the steaming pot a couple more times, smelling the cloud that had gathered above it with relish. He lifted the pan up with care and carried the water across the room.

"What's on?" Asa asked.

"Mushrooms on toast," Avery said distractedly, draining the water out of the open window.

He used a wooden spoon to ladle out the brown lumps onto the blackened bread, wincing as the scalding metal brushed against his skin. "Ah, hot!"

"You okay?" Asa inquired.

"Fine." Avery carried the plates gingerly over to the table, depositing the pan on the stove.

"Codswallop," Asa snorted. "Let me see."

His friend put down their supper and held out his hand. Asa took hold of the callused fingers in his cold ones and examined the small blister that had formed on the palm, on the soft pad beneath the thumb. Angry red lines surrounded it.

"Don't touch!" Avery exclaimed as Asa reached out a tentative index finger.

"Wasn't going to," Asa lied. The blond raised an eyebrow. "What?"

"Do you take me for a complete fool, Asa Hounslow?"

"Not a complete one, Avery," Asa mumbled, before continuing in a more enthusiastic tone. "What are we even waiting for? Food!"

"Food indeed." Avery picked up his slice of burnt bread. "At last."

Asa bit into the warm meal, his mouth relishing the way it filled it with heat and food. His stomach grumbled, and Asa patted it like one would a dog. Soon, he thought to himself, soon I will be full. He continued eating the crisp toast, flavours from the aromatic mushrooms seeping into the plain bread. He leant back on his stool and smiled at anything, anyone. The ceiling would even do.

The moment of fullness came sooner than even he had expected. In less than half a slice of bread and vegetables, Asa found he was too stuffed to continue eating. He fought against the feeling, loathe to waste any of the rare meal, but found that the idea of more food had become simply nauseating. He put the remainder of his food down in surprise, hoping that a short break would aid his digestion. Across the table, Avery stopped chewing and looked down, dropping a crust to his plate.

"I'm full," Asa stated blankly.

"As am I." Avery looked at the solitary crust incredulously. "Is that normal?"

"I don't know." Aware as ever of wastage, Avery collected their half-eaten meals and put a bowl upside-down over both of them to stop them from going bad in the warm house.

They made a brief excursion out of the front door and into the snow, rinsing their hands in the clean ice. The sky was less clouded here, blackness merely washed with a tint of grey. If he squinted, Asa could swear that he saw pinpricks of light shining through the cover. Stars. He searched the darkness for any clearer but saw nothing, not even the moon. He had always been able to see the moon, even in the town. When did it leave the sky?

Aware of his breath forming clouds in the cold air, Asa retreated back inside the house, rubbing his chilled hands. The fire seemed ever warmer as the night drew in, wrapping the house in a shield of light and safety. Asa relaxed. He was trying to remember when the last time he had been able to do so was. It couldn't have been for over a week at least. Two maybe. Not since they started their adventure. He thought back, struggling to recollect how many sunrises he had seen since their departure from Brandenbury in the white carriage.

He couldn't remember. The days all seemed to have blurred into one long string of snow and sun and arguments. He shivered, despite his warmth. It was not at all how he had imagined it. Not at all. As an amateur cartographer, he had always dreamt of going on an expedition, mapping isolated regions of the country's most extreme environments. He had read about this snow. He had imagined it. The soft, crunchy feel of it under his fingertips, the coldness and the stark beauty. Nothing could have prepared him for the reality of it—the icy damp sensation of it seeping through waterproofed clothes. He was an idealist, a dreamer. The romance that had tainted his decisions made real life a pale comparison of what he had thought it would be.

Avery was stoking the hot fire with a stick of ivory when Asa had mustered the willpower to move from the doorway. He nodded to him as he wandered in, collapsing in a soft chair behind the blond's back.

"Thanks for the fire," Asa said, taking his boots off for the first time since they had received the clothes. His feet looked strange in the fire's half-light, alien and ethereal. They were pale, covered in sharp wounds and gashes from the abuse that his legs had received on their journey. He reached forward and touched them with a gentle forefinger. They were less delicate than they had seemed, hard callused skin meeting his careful touch.

"No problem." Avery dusted his hands off over the hearth and stood up, dumping himself in the chair next to Asa. "You started it."

"And you finished it," Asa said wryly. "As ever."

"Mm."

They sat in silence, relishing in the warmth and light that their situation afforded. Asa stayed still, too tired and sore to consider moving. Avery was the opposite, cracking his joints loudly and stretching his long limbs out of the chair. As a hand smacked his face, Asa directed a weak glare at his friend, not even bothering to turn his head. Avery stopped instantly.

"I'm thirsty," Asa remarked idly, looking at the ceiling.

"Me too."

"Is there anything to drink?"

"Well,"—Avery flushed—"there is some mead."

"Mead?" Asa was intrigued.

"Like a sort of honey wine," his companion explained. "I saw it in the pantry."

"Honey wine sounds great," he reflected. "Would you mind fetching it?"

Avery sighed and heaved himself out of the chair, stomping to the kitchen and rummaging around in the cupboards. Asa heard the thud of cups on the table, a pop of a cork, then the gurgling of liquid. Avery returned to the room with two old-fashioned wooden cups filled to the brim with an amber substance. He shoved a cup at Asa.

"Here's his majesty's beverage."

Asa smirked. "Without the insubordination, if you please."

He sipped at the liquid. It had a sweet taste, only marred by a strong alcoholic smell that overwhelmed it. He stuck his tongue in experimentally. It burned in the mead, forcing him to conclude that it was some strong home-brewed stuff. Avery gulped his drink down in three mouthfuls, not seeming to even taste it. He glanced at Asa.

"You going to try it?"

"I have tried it," Asa said, scowling when Avery raised an eyebrow. "Don't do that!"

"Do what?"

"Ugh." Pinching his nose, Asa tipped the cup back into his mouth and poured the fiery liquid down his throat. He gasped at the burning sensation it induced, eyes watering despite his efforts to stay strong.

Avery clapped, laughing obnoxiously. "That's more like it."

The room around Asa spun once, then came to a stalling halt. He stuck his tongue out, trying to get rid of the taste. Avery was still grinning moronically. Asa shrank back down in his chair, wanting to disappear. Why were they even on this adventure?

He just wanted to go home.

"What do you want to do?" he asked. "This evening, I mean."

"Nothing, I guess," Avery said.

"Sounds like a plan." He massaged his temples. "Nothing is better than nothing."

"Bit boring, though," Avery said, after a pause of roughly three breaths.

Asa smiled at him, mocking him. "And quiet."

"Too quiet," Avery agreed, missing the sarcasm.

The room was growing warmer and seemingly smaller. He relaxed into the soft chair, hearing his friend's breaths rise and fall melodiously. Asa closed his eyes, feeling some unknown force pulling him towards unconsciousness. A pair of warm hands touched his shoulders. Someone murmured his name. He lay in a foggy stupor as he was lifted a few feet to a soft and warm surface, a heavy quilt piled on top.

The surface sagged to the other side as a warm presence clambered on next to him. Asa moved towards the warmth, mindlessly reaching out. His hand was caught in another and he squeezed it, happiness showing through every movement.

Asa's nostrils twitched as he flopped over onto his front, legs tangled together in the quilt. He huffed contentedly, blowing a strand of brown hair from his nose. He couldn't quite remember, but something nagged at the back of his mind. Something big. But what big happenings occurred inside Brandenbury? He cracked open an eye, greeted with weak, dewy light. It was so early in the morning. Why was he even up?

There was a thud somewhere close by. Asa shot up, blinking in the direction of the noise. If he squinted then the light wouldn't sting his eyes so badly. The room swam more clearly into view, disorientating Asa for a good few moments as he struggled to regain his bearings. For some reason his head ached badly and his mouth was as dry as sand. He smacked his lips and wiped some sleep from his eyes. Then it all came back to him.

"Well," he groaned, clutching his head. "I won't be trying that again. Honey wine, honestly!"

He peeled himself off the soft mattress, wincing at the bright obnoxiousness of the sunlight. His footsteps were muffled on the floor mats, and he padded into the kitchen to see what Avery was making for breakfast. The blond wasn't there. Asa checked one, twice, just to make sure. No Avery.

He lifted a flap on the woodwork and peered out. Nothing to be seen. He frowned, worried. Had his friend just been going to relieve himself, he would have been back by now. Surely something had not happened?

"Avery?" he called uncertainly, worriedly, as though his companion was within the house. "Are you here?"

No response greeted him, confirming his troubles. Filled with dread, Asa dropped backwards into one of the soft chairs. He bunched up the material of his trousers in his hands and pulled in anxiety. He could hear his heartbeat in his head, thrumming a tattoo against his mind. He ran his fingers through his hair, taken back to the time when he was younger and this same thing had happened.

He stroked the surface of the chair therapeutically, waiting for something, anything that could tell him what was happening. The sunlight grew brighter, spilling through the windows and alighting on the floor and surfaces in the room. As still as if he had been carved from stone, Asa waited.

After what seemed like an infinite amount of time, there was a loud crash on the front door of the cottage. Asa did not startle, as he once would have, but stared at the wood, a small knot of worry in his stomach. This was either Avery, injured from some unknown injury, or it was the being that had managed to subdue the powerful man. Needless to say, neither option looked good.

Asa got up out of his chair with cat-like stealth and took hold of the ivory poker. The door creaked open.

"Avery!" Asa dropped the poker, surveying his panting friend concernedly. "What's wrong? Are you okay? Where were you? What happened?"

Avery looked surprised. "Asa. I didn't think that you would be up until at least noon time."

"What?" Asa shook his head. "Where even were you? You've been gone for ages."

"I went on a run," the blond explained, running a hand through his curly, sweaty hair. "You know, a quick check of the location of the gates in the wall. I can't have been gone for more than an hour or two."

"Why didn't you tell me?" Asa demanded.

"I'm sorry," his friend apologised. "I thought that you would be asleep. You were out of it last night. I wanted to find out where we are going today."

Asa's curiosity got the better of him.

"Where?" he asked in a light, offhand tone.

"Only bit farther." Avery grinned. "I think we should leave as soon as we can. The snowstorm is only going to get worse, and the wall should provide us with some shelter."

Asa stepped forward, pressing a hand to the embroidered badger on Avery's maroon clad chest. He leant into his companion's torso, biting his tongue.

"You precocious brat," he muttered. "Don't make me worry like that, okay?"

The warm weight of Avery's hand landed on his shoulder. His friend smiled apologetically at him, bashful.

"Fine, old man," he said, moving away into the kitchen part of the cottage. "Right! I've been up since before the birds so we're all packed. Just need to eat breakfast and then we'll get going. Sound good?"

Asa followed him in, stomach protesting. "I'm fine."

Avery checked him out, eyebrow raised. "You're hungover, that's what you are."

"Am not," Asa huffed, seating himself on a wooden stool.

"And you're grumpy."

"I'm not grumpy, you fool!" Asa snapped, before realising the tone of his words. He lowered his gaze embarrassedly and blushed. "Pardon. I guess I might be a bit hungry."

"Knew it." Avery pried open the lid of a half-empty crate that he had been fiddling with and withdrew two gleaming red apples from inside. "Breakfast."

He tossed one to Asa, who caught it and bit into it, too fatigued to argue with his friend. The apple was deliciously light and crisp to his worn mouth. Sweet juices ran over his lips and chin. The inside was as white and ripe as any he had ever eaten. He picked a strand of straw off the skin and continued biting around the outside of the fruit, wiping his mouth on his grubby sleeve. When he was at last left with the core, he broke it in two, pouring a stream of the tiny bitter seeds into his mouth, before crunching up the remaining fruit in two large bites. He held up the stem, in better spirits.

"You want my stem?"

"Gross, Asa." Avery scrunched up his nose. "No, no one eats the stem."

"I remember that boy in Salatesh who would eat your stem if you gave him another apple," Asa said reminiscently. "Do you? His name was . . . Oh, I can't remember. It was so long ago."

"Nori Legh," Avery said.

"That's it." Asa nodded. "Knew it. How's he doing nowadays?"

"I don't know." Avery shrugged. "He works in the mine."

"You work in the mine."

"My dad never gives me dangerous jobs." Avery's face darkened. He stared down at the table, dropping his own stem to the ring-marked wood. "The others have noticed. Legh especially."

"Oh." Asa flicked the two delicate twigs reflectively off the table. He stood up, watching Avery for any sign of distress. The blond followed him stiltedly, going to the door and taking their chained vests off the hook. Asa frowned. He couldn't remember taking off his vest.

"You couldn't sleep in it," his friend explained. "I removed it."

Trying not to dwell on the thought of his handsome friend undressing him, Asa slipped the vest on beneath his tunic, grimacing at the cold against his skin. He put on his boots, flinching at the pricks of pain from his blisters, and stood up. Avery opened the door, pulling up his hood. Asa mimicked the action unsurely, looking out and taking the filled satchel, which Avery handed to him. A cold blast of air and snow hit with all the gentleness of sandpaper.

Exhaling his last shred of warmth as he exited the homely cottage, Asa pushed his way into the torrential snowfall, his only guide the maroon line of Avery's back ahead.

Avery flung his arms over his face, pulling his hood closed around his face. Asa only had time to notice this when a gust of wind hit his body like a physical wall. He covered his face as best he could, pushing against the cold air with a sense of increasing strain. Avery turned, grasping his hand in his own calloused one, and they somehow managed to pull themselves to the other side of the gust. They glanced worriedly at each other as they stumbled across the snowy land. How much more could the snow build? It was already past Asa's knees on level ground. The prospect of fathoms-deep snow drifts was not inviting.

Avery called something indistinct, gesturing at the goliath wall just paces from their feet. Asa followed his line of sight, heart leaping when he saw in front of them, carved into the stone itself, an ornate wooden gate. It was huge, as tall as at least three men, and twice as wide. Elaborate symbols were carved into the surface of the gates, criss-crossing like angry scars over the beautiful wood. Asa walked over to it, touching the complex runes. They were dangerous looking, making him want to turn away, to leave. But still he stayed there, frozen to his spot, touching the angry marks on the gate.

His friend approached him curiously, wiping away the slushy ice from the crevasses of his clothes as he did so. "You okay, Asa?"

"I'm fine," Asa said distantly, before wrenching himself away from the gate. "I'm sorry, what?"

Avery looked spooked. "I said, are you alright?"

"What? Oh, yes, I'm fine." Asa, against his instincts, turned his back on the gate to look earnestly into Avery's eyes.

"I know, you just said that." Avery frowned.

"Did I?" Asa asked, humouring him.

"Asa, are you sure that you're feeling alright? You look pale."

"I'm sure," Asa reiterated. "It's just—"

"Just what?"

"Don't you feel it?" He moved back against the gate, feeling the warm wood under his frozen fingertips.

"What, Asa?" Avery just sounded tired. He pushed his friend out of the way and withdrew the ring of keys from his satchel. He found the largest key and fitted it into the lock. His hands were steady even with his shivering.

"The energy."

"No, I don't feel it," Avery replied.

Asa's shoulders dropped but he resumed his normal composure and smiled as Avery turned the key. "No worries, then. I guess I'm being too imaginative, eh?"

"You think?" Avery winked, before twisting the handle of the gate door to the right. Some mechanism inside clicked like a huge insect's talons, and the gate opened a tiny crack. Avery gave the wood a small push and slipped through it, pulling Asa along after him. Asa's satchel stuck for a moment but soon he was through, stepping under the gate into a whole new world.

EIGHT

AVERY SHUT THE GATE behind them with a resonating bang. Asa kept his gaze forwards, marvelling at the change that a human made structure could create in terms of dividing a country. Inside the walls was warmer than not and no snow fell here. The sun was high in the sky above them, but if Asa looked back, he could clearly see a thick line of cloud cover stretching along the wall. A sharp divide was present from the ground to the skies.

"We made it." Asa breathed, and then louder, excited, he said, "Avery! We did it."

"It's so different." Avery grinned at Asa's exuberance. "Like another world."

The grass was crisp and green underfoot, and the sky was a clear turquoise. If Asa had not experienced the bitterness of the cold on the other side of the door, hadn't still had the ice in his hair, he would have assumed his entire life before to have been some sort of dream. This was too perfect not to be real. Energy surged through his body. He felt well again, fully well. Nobody could be ill here.

They were on a hill, looking down over a rolling green landscape of small clutches of low houses and penned-in fields. At first this confused Asa. Why would anyone live on that side of the wall? But then he understood that no one would do so out of choice, they must be natives to the land. He breathed in the fresh air with thirsty lungs, heart aching with the beauty of the landscape below. He stepped forward, staring around him as if his eyes could not get enough of the scenery.

"We going to go?" he asked, bobbing on the balls of his feet.

Avery lingered by the gate for an imperceptible pause, hand resting on it.

"Sure," he said, looking out into the middle distance ahead of them. "World's awaiting."

"You're sad," Asa stated in what he hoped was a sympathetic tone of voice.

"Not sad," Avery corrected him in a soft tone. "Just homesick."

"Already?"

"We're in a new place, with new weather and a huge wall separating myself from my family." Avery paused. "I think that it's natural to feel homesick."

"I guess so." Asa paused before laughing. "I hadn't thought about it."

He started to walk down the tall hill, but his feet felt lighter on the grass than they had in months and soon he found himself breaking into a bounding run. The light breeze caressed his skin as he ran, winding his hair into untameable knots. He reached the bottom of the slope in a matter of moments, eyes watering from the sudden exercise. Avery stopped dead next to him and his breathing sounded disapproving.

"Where're we going?" Avery asked.

Asa fished the scrappy map out from his belt, trying to decipher the markings upon its surface. He frowned, humming lowly under his breath as he squinted at what seemed to be a huge smudged black line. It was spiked, running right through the centre of the map, even passing through the wall. If the directions were correct then it should appear in the north if they walked far enough; they couldn't exactly miss it.

"Oh." It dawned on him, as he looked up to scan the distant skyline. "The mountains."

"The Moving Mountains?" Avery glanced at him. "What about them?"

Asa traced the line on the map, figuring their journey out. "We have to pass through them."

Avery scoffed. "Not happening."

Asa checked his directions, running over the dog-eared sheet of paper with a cartographer's eye. He shook his head, trying to figure out some other way. There was none. He explained this to Avery, who repeated his aforesaid statement with a pedantic expression.

"Well, how do you plan on getting there?" Asa asked.

"I don't know," Avery replied. "But my father says that you can't go through, under, or around those mountains. They're too close together for you to do anything but go over, and too high for you to do much of that. They're not an easy obstacle, that's for sure."

It could have been a trick of the light, but if he squinted, Asa thought that he could see the vague outlines of the jagged peaks in the distance. He shifted his heavy bag and looked Avery in the face, sizing him up. Avery stood his ground, staring levelly back.

"Are you doubting our ability to make it across those mountains, Avery Hardy?"

"Maybe I am," his companion replied, folding his arms. "Problem?"

"Only with that attitude," Asa asserted. "Avery, we are going to do this. We have to do this. You may not have realised it, but whilst you were whining about how hard it is to cross the mountains, the snow is still falling outside of the walls. How long until people start dying? Their lives are with us. We have to make it count."

Avery smirked. "And yet the tale grows more fraught."

Asa clipped him around the back of the head, tugging his friend towards a strange road that was a few paces away from them. It was made of a matte grey substance, like liquefied stone had been poured along a path. He stopped before pressing a cautious foot to the grey surface. He waited for his leg to sink into nothingness, to become stuck, to reach some untimely end. It did not. Asa stepped onto the smooth road, shoes clicking as he stood in the middle. They faced down to what Asa assumed was north, or at least, where the road went. Avery started to saunter down, his object a strange metallic structure stuck into the ground a little way from them. Asa examined it from afar, and then joined his friend.

It was a signpost. Rather underwhelmed, Asa peered curiously up at the large arrows pointing up and down the road. To his great astonishment, he found that the writing was illegible. He could not read the cramped letters—or even work out their basic shapes. He blinked. Surely he was just tired, imagining things. But the sign remained incomprehensible.

"You seeing this?"

"More like not seeing." Avery cricked his neck and winced. "And I thought that the pretentious signs near your house were bad."

"Shall we go down this way?" He pointed what he assumed was north. "Get to those impossible mountains. And maybe find some locals? We need all the help we can get if all of the signs are like this."

Avery nodded, plodding away from the sign without complaint. Asa gave it another puzzled look, and then moved on, trying to decipher it. As the lush surroundings changed, he found that he could not quite remember how it looked, eventually giving the whole lot up as a bad job. It wasn't worth his thought power.

A rattle sounded ahead. They both simultaneously looked up to see a small horse and trap trundling over a bridge in front of them. The driver was short, squatted low on the seat as the cob pulling it chomped on the bit and tossed its head up. Asa nudged Avery and stood on the side of the road and held out his left arm, flagging down the cart.

The driver looked up, saw Asa's outstretched hand, and tugged on the reins as he tried to bring the chunky horse to a satisfactory stop. His hat and low-cut fringe obscured all but his mouth and the tip of his nose. Asa crinkled his nose and tried to look polite.

"Hello, sir," he said. "Would you know where the nearest village to the mountains is?"

The driver stuck his chin out as he surveyed the pair of them. Asa noticed his clothes. They were odd—to say the least. He wore tight brown trousers and a green jerkin over a dirty white shirt. Asa decided not to mention it, clamming up as the silent man nodded. He waited. Still he was not offered directions.

"Can you tell us?" Avery asked.

The man remained as still as stone. Asa was struck by a sudden thought. He looked exactly as he had done many years ago when his tutor had tried to teach him to master the Ancient Tongues.

"Can you understand me?" he asked.

The man in the cart shook his head, and then nodded. After what seemed like an age, he managed to put words together and speak, in an accented tone.

"We don't speak your language here," he said. "It is not for us to know."

"Please take us north," Asa pleaded.

"I am not going north," the man refused.

"But, sir!"

"I am going to market," the man stated. "I'm late."

"Take us, please," Avery persuaded.

"We need to get to the mountains," Asa supplied.

The man did not respond. Asa was about to brush the infuriatingly long hair out of the driver's eyes, when he drew the horse around in a slow circle, turning to face up the road. He pointed a thumb to the bed of the cart.

"I can take you to town," he said dismissively.

"Oh, thank you, sir!" Asa scrabbled over the sides of the cart and seated himself on the wooden floor. Crates of miscellaneous fruits and vegetables were scattered to every side. Avery pulled himself over as well, leaning back against the side of the cart as he sat.

"We're so lucky," he mouthed disbelievingly at Asa, who smirked, giving him a wink.

The man shouted a harsh encouragement to the cobby horse, who broke into a jumbly trot as a whip was cracked on its flank.

The countryside around them was neat with short grasses trimmed cleanly by grazing deer, which scattered as they trundled past. As the man in the front cracked the whip again, the cart began to climb up a steep slope, wheels spinning and sliding beneath them. Asa stared out of their vehicle in awe. The warmth of the sun caressed his back, heating him both inside and out for the first time in the last month. The fruits around him gave off the sweet, cloying scent of summer or early spring, as it should have been on the other side of the wall. Flies bothered them, bumbling dreamily over their heads and landing in their hair.

The journey took only a fraction of the time they had expected. Within a few whispered words of mounting the hill, the area around them became more developed. Houses sprang up—not normal houses, such as the ones in Salatesh or Brandenbury, but strange dwellings. They were low on the ground, white-washed huts that were cuboid in shape. Instead of windows, they had open gaps in the walls over which people had hung gauzy fabrics in a multitude of shades of brown. The man stopped his beast with an angry *hup* and the cart jerked before Asa and Avery were able to dismount.

"Thank you, sir," Asa told him, shifting on achy feet.

"Goodbye," the driver droned as he wheeled the tired animal around. For a moment, Asa could have sworn that he could see something strange as the small man's long fringe fluttered in the wind, something in the glazed quality of his rather milky eyes.

"Thanks," Averett said.

There was a clacking sound as the cart's wheels struggled to catch traction on the road surface. Eventually, it was able to get a grip and their driver sped off down the road, as though he was being chased by some invisible foe.

Asa turned confusedly to Avery, who was examining the world around him with a dreamy sort of curiosity. He tapped his friend bracingly on the small of the back, laughing as Avery blinked and started in surprise.

"Oh. We going to go through the town?" he asked.

"I don't have a plan," Asa admitted, rubbing the back of his neck.

"Sounds like a good idea, then." His friend made to walk down the firm road, but Asa wasn't certain.

"What if they don't want us here?" he asked.

"Then we'll leave," said Avery simply.

"They don't speak our language, Avery," Asa elaborated, fiddling with the somewhat worn hem of his tunic. "What if they don't understand us? I don't want to be butchered."

"Don't be so derogatory," the blond chided him. "Honestly, just because they don't speak like us, you'll avoid them? That's not how the world works, Asa. Brush up on your charm and get some personal awareness about you."

Asa sniffed, refusing to refute or acknowledge Avery's point of view. He hitched his satchel up on his shoulder and walked away from his companion, waiting for the idealistic youth to follow him. He did, eventually, but only after an exasperated sigh and loud footsteps stamping up until they were side by side.

They entered the small town, shoulder to shoulder. The houses were not close together, and they were so unlike their home in looks that it did not register to either of them that they were walking down a street. There were no doors to the houses on either side but bead curtains swayed with soft clicks in the drafts from the steady footfall of people in the street. Unlike their entry to Jundres, this was muted, relaxed. No one seemed to notice them as they wound their way through the quiet street, looking up to where the sharp peaks of the mountains ahead grew more defined. They were only a short walk from the foothills, and those would take them on their way well enough.

The people around them were shorter than any they had seen before. Asa was a good few inches taller than even the biggest of the men, though they seemed to make up for it in sheer mass. They were lumpy and stocky with thick arms and legs that seemed to be packed with nothing but muscle. Their gait was mechanical and stilted, as though they were puppets on the end of a master string.

One of them bumbled into Asa as they weaved through the ordered lines of people. He gazed up at him with a vague sort of anxiety in his eyes, as though he was going to be punished. He mumbled an apology in some lilting, musical tongue. Asa shrugged in response and the man's head snapped forward, his feet moving back in perfect time with the person's in front of him. His eyes held the same qualities as the driver from before. Dazed and unfocused. Creepy dolls' eyes in sculpted faces.

Asa stiffened involuntarily and Avery's hand on his back pushed him forwards in a frightened sort of shuffle. Everyone around him, he realised, had that same look on their face. They were moving in time with each other. Together. He glanced to the side to see Avery's calm, hazel eyes looking perturbed. With a great effort, he heaved his weight forward and supported himself as they moved through the silent crowd. The only sound was the shuffling of many pairs of synchronised feet.

They weaved forwards, avoiding the fixed stares of the townspeople. The air was close, humidity beading on Asa's forehead and making the palms of his hands prickle with sweat. The sun was still high in the sky when the two of them rested up against a wall, relaxing in the shade that a tree cast over the ground. Avery withdrew a water skin and took a measured sip before passing it over to Asa, who was careful to drink the exact same amount as his friend. The water was sweet and cool as it ran down his throat. Liquid life.

"Excuse me." A man stepped out of the flow into their resting shade. "Why are you not in line?"

He was taller than anyone else in this town, and that was the most Asa could see as he stood in the dazzling sun. His hands rested on his hips, one swift flick away from grasping the handle of the sword that lay in its scabbard against his leg.

"We are not from around here," Avery replied. "We are travellers."

"Who said that you could travel here?" the man inquired nastily.

"No one," the blond asserted. "We took free passage."

"That is unfortunate." The tall man shrugged. "Nothing is free in these parts, let alone passage. You'll be coming with me now."

"And what if we—" Avery began, but a sack was pulled over Asa's head before he could finish and his friend's words were blurred with the sudden darkness. He smelled something strange, sweetly acidic, and his body was pulled into a wretched sort of non-sleep. He let himself be dragged down, eyes finally closing.

Asa cracked his eyes open drowsily, squinting in the bright light. He blinked for a few moments before the tightness across his wrists and ankles became all too apparent. His stomach lurched in that familiar way that happened when he tripped or missed a step walking downstairs. Something was wrong. Incredibly wrong. There was a strange smell in the air, he couldn't move, and the light was sharp and clear. Worse of all, there was a ceiling above his head. He hadn't gone to sleep inside. In fact, he remembered with increasing alarm, he hadn't gone to sleep at all.

"Avery?" he called, voice higher than usual. "Avery? Anyone? Where am I?"

There was a bang to his right. Asa's head snapped to that side, brown eyes darting around the space. It was all white, the walls, the floors, even the small wooden door was painted matte white. His breathing quickened as the handle began to turn, mind making impossible bargains for his own safety. He kept still, only the flickering of his irises testament to show he was alive. The door opened.

A tall man entered, taller than Asa had ever thought possible. He was at least a head over Asa's, with lean muscle and strange, fitted garments. He carried a thin board with paper attached to it. Asa flinched back, straining to get away from his restraints. The man looked at him, gaze curious and somewhat clinical. His eyes were black. They were dangerous, cold, and scientific. He moved some of Asa's hair out of the way and examined his face shape, cold fingers tracing over Asa's forehead.

"Who are you?" Asa stammered, flinching away. "Where's my friend?"

The man looked astonished. He wrote something on the paper and squinted at Asa, a small smile creeping onto his face. He opened his mouth and a noise came out, but Asa didn't understand. It was all one stream of undecipherable gibberish. He tried to move away from the dangerous looking man, muscles aching at the strain. He just wanted to sit up, to back away, just do anything but be forced to lie here.

The man shrugged. Asa assumed he was some sort of doctor.

"Where is my friend?" he asked clearly, voice steadier now. "What do you want?"

The man peered at him again, alight with some sort of repressed excitement. He started spewing the same sounds again, slower this time, making confusing hand gestures. Asa rolled his eyes, tutting. Instead of looking put off, the doctor looked delighted. He moved so that he was standing over Asa, casting a shadow down on him. Asa moved his hands desperately, trying to have something to defend himself with. The bonds held fast. The doctor tightened them, just a bit, but enough to make Asa hiss with pain.

"No!" He tried to pull his hands free, the skin caught in the ties. "Loosen them!"

The doctor barked a short laugh, those black eyes glittering behind the glasses that he had slammed onto his nose. These were different to the ones back home, less bulky, with leather straps that tied around his head. His long brown hair was scraped back into a knot at the back of his head. Asa saw the stark difference in colour between their skins. Whilst his was a dirty pale beige colour, the doctor's was dark tan. Asa blinked back a couple of tears that threatened to fall from his eyes, promising that for Avery's sake he would be brave. His vision blurred and he let his head fall to the side, biting his lip hard and tasting metal. Immediately, the doctor's hands were examining his features, curiously probing at his eyes and mouth. Asa grimaced at the gentle wiping sensation across one of his eyelids, forcing saline tears to go down his cheek. What was wrong with the other? Had he never seen tears before?

Sweaty fingers were stuck inside his mouth, running over his teeth. Asa tasted salt and oil, and all manner of things that he would have rather not known about on those fingers. He resisted the urge to bite, to snap his jaw shut as hard as possible. That would only get him hurt. This was painless and relatively unobtrusive. He let it be, sighing around the doctor's clumsy hands.

The doctor ceased the scrabbling around Asa's mouth, wiping his hands dismissively on his strange clothes—thin, fitted trousers, in dark brown, a linen shirt, useless for warmth and scooped at the neck, and a snug leather waistcoat over the top. Asa felt dirty, primitive. He frowned at the doctor, stilling for the first time and meeting the man's eyes. The man spoke to him again, and turned his back on Asa. The door slammed shut as he breezed through it.

"No," Asa murmured, alone once more. "No."

The bindings around his hands and feet were so tight he could not even twist his joints. He licked his lips, mouth rather dry. Where was he? What had he done wrong? He made an effort to lift his chest up from the surface upon which he was lying, straining as hard as he could. His back cracked. Asa gave up and shed a few bitter tears. He couldn't do it. He couldn't even save himself. He tugged in futility at his wrists again. A small cut opened on his right arm and he growled at it. Useless skin, his body couldn't even keep his own blood in.

"Avery?" he called, in a small voice. "Avery? Can you hear me?"

His ears strained to hear a voice, anything. The room seemed as though it was buzzing. He heard the strange mutters of that same person as before outside the door. He turned his head to look clearly at the doctor as he entered the room, brown eyes hardening in anxiety. A tiny figure followed behind, looking at the floor. By the angle of their back, and their stature, Asa assumed that they were female, but he could not be certain.

The doctor said something in that strange tongue as his black eyes stared into Asa's. Asa averted his gaze.

"I'm sorry, but I don't understand you," he apologised resignedly.

The doctor said something in that quick, sharp voice, glancing at the person next to them. They stepped towards Asa. She was a small child. His first impression was of her striking beauty. She was wealthy looking, plump and smooth skinned, with doe-like brown eyes, unclouded but filled with fear. Her skin was that same shade of beautiful brown. Her mouth moved, and the man snarled at whatever comment she made. She looked hurt, and gestured to her wrists.

The child muttered something rebellious under her breath, or at least it sounded that way to Asa. He waited for her to poke at him in that bold childish way but instead she shook her head determinedly and set forward towards his face.

He was seized with a sudden, irrational fear of her.

The doctor snapped at the girl, clipping her around the back of the head. She was propelled forward a few stumbling steps but shrugged it off, as though she were used to it. Asa froze as still as he possibly could, a silent statue, as she came up next to him and set about completely undoing his wrist bonds. Blood rushed to his aching hands. Asa pulled them reflexively back to his body, a gradual smile coming to his dry lips for the first time. He fixed his eyes on the girl, who was looking at him.

"Thank you," he croaked, blood from his wrists running down onto his tunic. "Thank you."

She nodded at him. He waited for a moment, and then mimicked the action, trying to convey his gratitude. The doctor made furious notes on the paper, a sinister smile upon his face. As soon as it appeared though, it was replaced by a frown. He snapped at her, making her flinch and recoil from Asa's side. She left the room in a hurry, sparing not one kind glance back to the prisoner that she had unshackled.

Asa kept his hands glued to his lap, sitting up so that he could look the doctor in the eyes. The doctor reached out and took one of Asa's hands, prizing his grip from the cloth of his trousers. Asa winced at the feeling of the hot, dark skin touching his cuts, muttering a curse at the odd man under his breath. The doctor took a cloth bag from a pouch around his neck and from it withdrew a pinch of dark powder. It had the appearance of something that you would smoke. Asa's hand still held in the vice-like grip, he rubbed the powder into the cuts.

It was as if fire was being poured over his skin.

Asa screamed, tugging backwards with his feet still restrained. The leather bonds strained and broke, sending him head-over-heels off the hard surface and onto the harder floor. He lay still there, the fingers of his left hand clawing desperately at his right wrist. Odd mixtures of profanities and pleads to some unknown person spewed from his lips. He heard the light, pleasant laughter of the doctor and knew it, just knew inside. He was going to die here.

Strong hands gripped his shoulders and held him still. He shivered, closing his eyes for what he assumed to be the last time. Instead, blood rushed into his feet, sending strange a pins-and-needles sensation through them. The doctor rubbed the tense muscles on his back, making Asa hiss with relief. His feet and hands were warm again, more like his own. For the first time in hours, he stood.

"How are you?" The black-eyed man spoke for the first time to Asa. His voice was accentless and soft.

"Fine," Asa said automatically, and then paused. "Wait."

"What?" The doctor looked penetratingly at him with his deep eyes.

"You speak my language?"

"We're not *speaking* anymore, child." An ancient wisdom trickled into his words. "We're not speaking any language either you or I know. Though you only know your language, and me mine, we are surpassing the boundaries of speech. Surprising, as it does not often happen, in one as young as you."

"Then what tongue are we conversing in?" Asa inquired.

"As for that, I have no idea." The doctor pulled him up and sat him squarely on the surface, peering closely at him. "I think that this is a necessary bridge that we have been able to cross."

"What are you?" Asa's voice grew bolder. "Why am I here?"

"That is a long story." The doctor smiled a secretive smile and started to pace in front of Asa, whose concerned gaze followed the unfamiliar man as he seemed to rack his brains. "And not one for this day, I'm afraid."

"It must be one for this day," he said darkly at the dark-eyed doctor. "I must be gone as soon as possible. As for whatever evil ideas you have planned for me . . . they are futile. I will find a way to escape."

"I am not the one you should fear, Asa," the doctor sighed.

Asa stared at him. "Did I tell you my name?"

"No," the stranger told him. "I knew it because you told it to my brother."

"Your brother?"

"I am not the only one of my kind whom you have met, Asa," the doctor explained. "There are two others you encountered before you escaped from inside the walls."

"Parlan!" Asa exclaimed. "The madman. But no, what do you mean? Inside the walls? I don't understand you, sir."

"You must be confused," the man stated.

"Explain, then."

"It started long, long ago." The doctor gazed out into the air for a moment, as though wondering where to go next. "There were five of us back then, you see. Five had seemed like a good number. Three would be too few, seven ridiculous—and no one would ever entrust anything to an even number. There would be no majority among six or four, and we needed to have a clear vote on our actions. Two girls and three boys. We were chosen, created, to do one thing. We were to control Eodem. The country was already filled with those such as you, such ordinary and primitive peoples, yet quarrelsome and warlike. We were only young, and we were so eager to help. It was our purpose. But people were afraid of our strange, white eyes."

"White?" Asa interrupted. "Your eyes are black."

"I said white, and white is what I meant," the man snapped, before shaking his head and resuming his steady tone. "Anyway, where was I? Oh yes, white eyes. Our creator, who has been gone for many moons now, sent us away from her with the greatest power and the whitest eyes of any ever seen. People were besotted by us. They worshipped us as gods. Silly, but that was what happened. Though we started out so similar, we soon grew apart. My elder siblings began to fight."

He sighed, a hand combing through his long brown hair, which was strained looking and dull. His tanned skin looked a warm caramel in the darkening light.

"And?" Asa prompted.

"They fought for some time." The doctor looked weary. "Thousands of years. Indeed, they still fight today. I am the youngest of them in some ways, but in maturity I am the eldest. Parlan and Gil fought first. They taught us all why we should not do so. The stress of the matter brought them both close to death. Gil never touched her weapons again and Parlan, he was driven mad. He was never completely sane to start with. Then came the next pair. I have not heard from Ria in many a century, but all I know is that she was forced to flee from her area of the country as my second eldest brother, Erebus, threw her out. Erebus is terrible in anger, his power far surpasses all of us."

"Erebus?" Asa's voice cracked and died. "You're his brother?"

"Why should that surprise you?" the man asked. "Even the most powerful have family. I cannot say that I am on his side, though. It is most prudent for me to be neutral. Erebus took the Southwest of the country and my younger sister took Parlan and created her own separate nation in the Northeast. She built a tall wall around it, fencing in the population and telling them that they were freed. I don't know what to feel about my sister, Ria."

Asa's mouth slackened. "Queen Ria?"

"The same." The doctor nodded.

"Ria. *Queen Ria*?"

"Are you alright?" the man asked with static sympathy. Asa nodded mutely. "I'm sorry for being insensitive. I have lived too long to have time to take things at anything less than this pace, if you see what I mean? Good, thank you. Erebus is winning the fight. Now it has come to what could be called cold warfare. He was always good at those kinds of spells. And now you two civilians come bouncing through the walls, for all the world looking as though you were going to bop him on the head with one of your toothpick swords! Wearing the badger, too, Ria's favourite animal. Has Ria given up, then?"

"Her son was killed." Asa swallowed.

The doctor stilled. "She had a son?"

"Yes," Asa replied. "Prince Edmund. He was killed by Erebus."

"Erebus killed his own nephew." The black eyes showed little to no emotion, and his words were considered and steady. "That is terrible."

"Same flesh and blood," Asa snorted, crossing his arms.

"He's mad." The doctor shook as he stood. "They're as bad as each other. Oh fortune! It's all gone bad now, that's for certain."

"Why?" Asa asked.

"He killed my nephew. He killed his own nephew. That child would have been a demi-mortal, and our own law forbids the slaughter of our kin. Ethereals do not kill their own."

"That's what you are, then?" Asa probed, eyes narrowing. "An *ethereal*?"

"I am one, yes," the man said, closing his eyes. "But that is not all I am. My name is Kaspar."

"What are you going to do to me?" Asa voiced this question for the first time.

Kaspar looked as though he was making an immense decision. He eventually met Asa's gaze and gave him a reassuring smile. "I cannot stay neutral on this. I will help you. Stay where you are and I shall retrieve your angry friend. He has not been quiet on the subject of your capture."

He left the room, feet light upon the hard floors. Asa lowered himself gingerly off his perch and down where he could sit.

His head fell forward into his hands as he thought about what Kaspar had said. His world had been a lie. People he knew had lived and died at the whims of these immoral beings. And for what?

"Where in Eodem have you put him? Tell me or I'll run you through myself!" A ferocious roar echoed through Asa's ears. "Answer me, you demon!"

"I am taking you to see him," a calm voice murmured in response.

"As if I would be stupid enough to believe that!"

The door of the room burst open, and Avery stormed inside, his eyes a flaming amber. He turned his back to the room and stared down Kaspar with a wild reckless bravery that Asa had never seen before. He stood there taut, like an arrow ready to be let loose from a bow.

"Well, he was here." Kaspar sounded surprised, if concerned.

"I knew that you were lying to me, you black-eyed ghoul," spat Avery.

Asa rose off the floor and pulled himself up on the surface that he had been sitting on. Avery cleared his throat.

"Avery, I'm fine. I swear it."

His friend spun around, eyes locking with his in a moment that Asa could only describe as one of sheer relief. His face broke from a cross scowl into a smile. Avery walked the few steps across the small room and crushed Asa in a hug, causing him to cough as his lungs were crushed.

"You had me scared back there," he admitted.

"And you continue to frighten me every day of our luck-lacking lives," Asa jested.

"Ahem." Kaspar cleared his throat. "When you two have finished your little reunion, I would like to explain the situation to your companion here . . ."

He ran through the same details that he had told Asa earlier, skipping over some particulars but filling the general outline in for him. Avery was mostly silent, occasionally asking a curious question or fiddling as he sat down on the floor with Asa, as though they were infants in their first schools.

Asa leant back against Avery, exhausted. His friend jerked as his weight was transferred but made no complaint. Asa exhaled, trying to find some place of inner calm inside him, but to no avail. His heart jolted in his chest.

"Are you in pain?" Avery muttered in his ear. "Can I help?"

Asa shook his head with a wince. He stared up at the ceiling.

"No pain, as of yet," he replied. "Don't worry, you are."

His eyes locked with his friend's and a small smile crept onto his face. Avery wrapped his arms around him, but Asa unpeeled himself after only a few moments. He raised an eyebrow.

"What?" Avery looked hurt.

"No offense intended, but you haven't bathed in six or seven days, mate. You don't smell all that good."

"Hey!" Avery sniffed. "You don't smell of roses either."

Kaspar clicked his fingers in an authoritative manner and the same young girl from before appeared in the room. She was dressed in simple but neat clothes, a grey pinafore tied around her brown dress. She fiddled with her collar as the tall man spoke to her, full eyes fixed on her bare feet. She nodded before retreating away from him as quickly as she could, stifling a half-skip on her way out.

Kaspar sighed. "I have told her not to do that."

"What?" Asa asked, bemused. "She was just skipping. She's little. Children like to dance."

"She annoys me," the ethereal said simply. "The sounds that she fills this house with . . . I have been most merciful in my self-restraint."

He shuddered, fingers curling. Asa shifted and sat up, away from Avery. When the little girl re-entered the room, scraping an enormous silver basin along behind her, he tried to catch her eye. When she looked at him she flushed and giggled, hiding her face in her hands. Deep-brown irises peered through her fingers curiously.

"Then why is she here?" Asa demanded. "Why is she not brainwashed like everyone else in this town?"

"She was the princess," Kaspar said. "It would not have been proper. Anyway, those in the town are not brainwashed. I merely subdued them. It would not be kind to make them witness the instability of our nation."

"They're asleep in their shoes!" Asa exclaimed. "They wouldn't know what they wanted."

"Who rules here?" Kaspar grew still, radiating a fury of such proportions that Asa could swear that he felt it brush against his skin, a physical barrier. "You know nothing."

"Fine," Asa conceded, backing down despite himself.

The child had brought a large jug of steaming water to the basin and was filling it with shaking hands. She left the room again and again, returning each time with the same heavy weight clutched in her small arms. It seemed that in that moment time slowed down to Asa, he saw her struggling with her burden alone but the bath could never be filled. However, with a few stumbled journeys back and forth, she managed to complete her task. She approached the ethereal with a wary expression, mouth moving.

Kaspar ignored her with a practised patience, gesturing to the steaming tub of water as he walked towards the door. His hand cupped possessively around the child's head, pulling her along close to his side.

"Bathe," he ordered, not altogether harshly. "I will find some suitable clothes for you to wear. Your garments are falling off your backs."

The door closed with a muffled tap, but the bolt passed through it and when Avery tried it, the handle would not turn. His shoulders dropped as he returned to the centre of the room, emotion stirring in his hazel eyes. Asa tried his hardest to smile, to cheer him up, but could not find the energy. He pushed himself over to the tub on his hands and knees, sticking a cold hand into the depths. It was only then that he realised how filthy both of them were. Avery's blond hair was far from its usual straw colour, instead having become a light brunette, flecked with dark specks of dirt and dead leaves that had tangled in there. He reached up incredulously to touch his own and found it dry, as brittle as fresh hay.

His skin was not much better. Black mud billowed out into the water where he touched it; the skin beneath it scarred and more tanned than it had ever been before. He touched his fingers gingerly, patting the discoloured skin until it turned yellow white. Jaundiced. Sick. Avery started to wash his hands as well, the water ripping skin from his sore palms. Asa winced for him and turned his attention away from him and onto scrubbing the dirt from his forearms and face. Rivulets of liquid dirt trickled down his face and splashed into the basin. Asa reached deeper into it and found a rag, which he used to dab at the grime that coated his neck and behind his ears.

Avery poured water from his cupped hands over his hair. As the brown tinted liquid fell to join the main body, the original golden colour of his hair showed through. It was like rubbing dust off an old object, Asa mused, pausing his own washing to reflect on his friend. As he raked his fingers through his short hair, Avery was just cleaning the accumulated dust off himself. Like spring cleaning in a way.

Asa pulled his tunic over his head, surprised at how loose the material was. Whether it was weight loss or fabric strain was unclear, but he wondered how it had come to pass that he had not noticed the excess of clothing. He looked down at his pale chest, unused to seeing it in the light. He had only taken his shirt off once since they began their journey. This was not unusual, as a child he had been sewn into his undergarments when a particularly cold winter struck, but older Asa was fastidious and did not leave his house often before he had last gone. He could see his bottom ribs with a disgusting clarity, his hipbones jutting out over the loose band of his trousers. Whatever muscle he had prided himself on having built was gone, replaced by this farcical look of skin on bone. He caught Avery looking at him, shocked into silence. Asa shook his head and rubbed his thin frame raw with the rags, hating it. Without him even fully realising it, a hand stopped his own, removing the rough cloth from his fingers.

"Stop," Avery said, and it was enough. Asa relinquished the rags without complaint, face emotionless but mind reeling.

Stop, Avery had told him. What did that even mean? Asa did not know whether it was his thoughts or his actions that his friend had taken offense to. It could have been neither. It could have been both. Avery might not have spoken. Quick, shallow breaths rose in Asa's throat as he stared dumbly at Avery's clever face. *Stop*, he had said. *Stop*. His head ached with the light and the sounds that amplified as though he was in a magnifying glass. He could not stop this. *Stop*. Asa lifted his head. He was stronger than this. He fixed his gaze on Avery, copying his even breaths. He could do this. He was in control now.

NINE

ASA FIDDLED UNCOMFORTABLY WITH the red neckerchief that was tied around his neck. His clothes were rubbing in unusual places and he found himself pining for the tunics and loose trousers that he was able to wear at home. Though these were of comfortable material, they were too light and in a strange style. He was by one of those gauze-covered windows, looking at the dark streets lightening as the orange rays of the morning sun started to filter onto the road.

"I'm hungry," Avery groaned.

Avery was dressed differently to Asa, though they both wore their metal vests from Jundres as Kaspar had proclaimed them to be good enough to protect them. His scarf was blue, a swatch of material taken from the off-cuts of Asa's cerulean shirt. Their swords were suspended from slender leather straps that wrapped around their thighs, trapping the blade close to their legs. Their edges had been sharpened and were razor thin and gleaming. Avery's sword glittered as he moved over to the window also, beams of sunlight being scattered by the small amount of metal that could be seen on the top edge of the scabbard.

"Too bad."

Asa wasn't interested. He shivered, snakes writhing in his stomach as he waited for the ethereal to come to them. He had told them that he was *sorting something out*, whatever that meant. He rubbed his hands along his too-tight trousers with a worried glance out at the silent streets. They both heard the front door slam shut. Brown and hazel eyes fixed on the door to their room. Asa's stomach growled, and he reached up to rub the pain away. Avery glanced at him.

"When was the last time that you ate?" he asked.

Asa frowned. "I can't quite remember. Where's your bag? I'll have something."

Avery paled as he searched his body for the missing item, eyes darting to the floor and skirting around the walls. His expression grew stonier and colder as no bag miraculously appeared. Finally, he straightened his back with an inaudible click and turned to Asa, livid.

"First," he growled, "we had to sleep on the cold floor with no blankets, now this! That bag was in this room, Asa, when we went to sleep."

"Maybe they washed it?" Asa dismissed. "It's fine."

"Maybe, indeed," Avery huffed. "Don't worry about us, then. It's "fine" because they are "washing" our only possessions."

"Shh." Asa slid down the wall and sat on the floor, holding his head. "Let's both just be quiet."

"But—"

"Inside voices, Avery!" he snapped.

A pause. Asa shut his eyes, the white room being replaced with the warm orange glow from behind his eyelids. His knobbly spine hit the wall at a thousand uncomfortable angles, yet he could not summon the energy required to move. He breathed in and out. It was a slow, comfortable rhythm, sending him into a strange half-sleep. Asa could hear the movements of his friend next to him but his hands were numb, a cosy apathy taking over his body. He heard the door swing open.

Shoes clattered upon the hard floor, forcing Asa's eyelids open. The entrant was tall, with longish chestnut hair that sat on his shoulders. Asa blinked. It was just Kaspar. What did he want? Were they to be sent off again, now that they knew exactly what they were to face? He pulled himself up on the wall and faced the taller man. The calm black eyes frightened Asa to some extent, powerful as he knew they were.

He was wearing a brown coat over his strange clothes, a neat black cane in one hand. Asa nodded at him, and he returned the gesture with a stiff smile. He stepped towards them and handed Avery two battered satchels.

"They have been washed," he said melodiously.

"Thanks," Avery grunted, looking in the bags, before glancing up. "You changed our food."

"We replenished it for you," Kaspar replied. "Fresh food would just go off."

"Okay."

Avery handed Asa the lighter satchel. Asa rolled his eyes at the gesture but shrugged the strap over his head anyway, dropping the small weight onto his shoulder with a small wince. Kaspar lifted his chin and held the door open, beckoning them both to follow him. Asa led the way, face calm despite the discomfort caused by the fitted clothes.

"Breakfast," the ethereal announced, leading them down a short passage to another room that was wood panelled and contained nothing but a large wooden table. "I will fetch the servants. They will serve us."

Avery's eyebrow twitched at the mention of servants. He drew a chair for himself with a loud clatter and sat relaxed. Asa lifted his chair over the floor and placed it a foot or so away from the table. He sat up upon his seat bones, a strange shiver going up his spine as he saw Kaspar firstly ring a bell then bark some commands in a harsh language to a group of grey-clad figures. One of them was smaller than the others, pinafore reaching down past her knees.

He restrained himself from smiling at her, fiddling with his neckerchief as they sat in diminished silence. The ethereal snapped his fingers and the figures set to work, leaving the room. Kaspar seated himself at the head of the table, smiling beatifically down at the two of them. Asa managed to curve his lips up but Avery just looked angry.

"So," the black-eyed being started. "What to do with you?"

"What do you mean, sir?" Asa asked. "You said that we must fight, and we will."

"I mean," Kaspar pondered, ignoring Asa, "where are we to go?"

"We?" Avery interrupted.

"Yes." Kaspar nodded. "You didn't think that I would send you off alone? That would be unethical."

"You don't care, though." Asa wetted his lips, nervous. "You have no reason to."

"Of course I don't care about you two," Kaspar laughed. "You are correct in that aspect. Why should I come, you ask? Well, I'm not altogether immune to the thrill of the hunt; I also hope that in following you we may find my sister. I have not spoken to Gil for many a year. Maybe she could help you more than I can."

The door to the dining room swung open as a grey-uniformed woman entered. She set up the plates all around the table and began placing small pieces of mangled metal next to the green ceramic, together with blunted knives. Asa picked one of the spikier pieces up, turning it in his hand. He attempted to stab himself with it, causing small red indentations to appear in the skin. Kaspar stilled him with a scornful look and took up his own knife in his right hand and what looked like a small trident in the left.

"What are these, sir?" Asa inquired, mimicking him.

"This is a knife," The ethereal explained patiently. Asa struggled with the urge to roll his eyes. "And this is called a fork.

Do you not use cutlery behind the wall?"

"The upper classes use a foonif." A wave of nostalgia hit him, forcing him to swallow and look down at his plate. It was painful in a way. "They look like a cross between a fork and that shovel item over there."

"A spoon?" Kaspar smirked.

"Precisely," Asa asserted.

"And the lower classes?" The ethereal asked in amusement.

"Well." Asa felt uncultured, a savage eating from white tablecloths. "We used our hands."

"You're not doing that here," Kaspar's voice sharpened. "Sit up, please, and eat like a person. If you cannot eat like a human, then you will dine from a bowl on the floor like a common mutt."

The woman returned at that moment, carrying a large earthenware tray that supported what seemed to Asa to be an entire feast of food. There were thin rashers of meat, slices of vegetables, and thick patties made from potato and something that he could not quite discern. She slammed it in front of them and directed a similarly clothed man to put a pot of something else next to it. They bowed mechanically at Kaspar then left, not turning their backs on the ethereal. Asa and Avery waited, gripping their cutlery as Kaspar served himself, then noticed them.

"Are you not going to start?" he inquired, spearing a slice of ham on his fork and chewing it for a few bites. He swallowed, gesturing for them to eat. "It's not poisonous."

Avery filled both of their plates fairly, dealing each of them portions of potatoes, vegetables, and, as an afterthought, meat. He passed Asa's plate back to him and Asa thanked his friend, struggling with the unfamiliar tools. He would just be managing to get the knack of it, when a lump of potato would roll back off and splat onto the plate. He cursed under his breath each time and tried again and again, using the fork and knife in the clumsy fashion of an illiterate wielding a pen. The metal scraped against the plates with a sound that made Asa grit his teeth and wince since it was so horrible.

The food was delicious, though. Asa and Avery attacked their plates with all of their usual gusto, somehow managing to shovel it into their mouths despite the difficulties they were having with their cutlery.

Once their voracious appetites had been somewhat sated, the black-eyed man cleared his throat. Asa forced his eyes up from his emptied plate, though he knew that he mustn't stay here forever. Time ticked on as Kaspar straightened the cuffs of his coat idly and smiled at them. Asa was inclined to trust the powerful being, having heard his motives, but he saw Avery stiffen next to him as the ethereal spoke.

"I will take you to my sister by the route which I see fit. I trust that there are no problems with this?"

Avery shrugged noncommittally but Asa shook his head. The ethereal would get them there by the fastest way, and he was certain that any lack of cooperation on their part could land them in some sort of trouble down the line. He tied an extra knot on his neckerchief and licked the salt from his lips, savouring the luxurious taste of meat. He was hardly ever able to afford it at home.

"No problems on our end, sir," his voice was more strained than usual.

He coughed into his hand. Asa assumed that it was a one-time occurrence, but something was off in his throat and it settled into a painful hacking sound, into his hands. Kaspar handed him a napkin with a grimace, and Asa wiped his hands on the clean cloth, seeing with a twinge of concern that the white cloth was tinted with tones of frothy pink once he was done.

"We will be setting off soon," the ethereal said. "See to it that you have your bags with you and your swords are sharp. They should be. I tended to them myself. Our journey should finish within the realm of a week, if you are interested."

He left them in the dining room. Asa frowned at the piece

of soiled cloth, wondering where he could discard of it. He held it gingerly, glancing around until a small hand took it from his grasp.

"I'll take this, Master." It was the girl from yesterday. She made a disgusted face, scrunching her small nose up as she stuffed the damp cloth into her pinafore pocket. "My job."

"You didn't have to do that." Asa thanked her. "I didn't ask you to."

"No, I have to," she replied.

"Your knowledge is good for someone so young," Asa said appraisingly. "How old are you—seven? It cannot be your first language."

"I have ten years." She gave him a small curtsey and Avery a nervous half-wave. "My mother was teaching me."

"Your mother? Was she the lady in the grey dress?" he asked.

The child's face crumpled for the briefest of moments, and then she blinked away building tears. "No, sir. She was my nanny. Mother is dead."

"I'm so sorry," Asa said. "What was her name—what is your name?"

"I'm Alice," the child said. "My mother was named Rose."

"I'm sorry if this is rude," Asa probed, "but how did she die? She was the queen, wasn't she?"

Alice looked downcast. Her face fell, her bottom lip trembling as she dug bitten fingernails into her palms. She glanced around the room to see if it was empty, then looked up into Asa's face with her open eyes, willing him to understand. Asa leant forward until they were close, a palm-length apart.

"Nobody has parents around here," she told him. "They're gone now."

"But how?"

"The wizard came, my master. He sent his curses all over our town. He killed the warriors; he killed the mothers. We children ran off into the woods under the mountains but when we came home—" Her small hands shook as she tried to show him what happened. "They wouldn't wake up. We tried and tried but our grandparents, they pulled us off. Their eyes didn't look at us. I ran home and saw my father and mother lying in the hall. Master was next to them. He saw me. He caught me, and told me that I wasn't a princess now. He told me that I belonged to him."

"Oh." Asa was struck dumb. He racked his brains for something to say.

The child smiled at his upset. She picked up his dirtied plate and stacked the rest on top, before heading to leave. "Don't worry, sir. There's nothing wrong with being here. At least I'm at home."

Something rankled inside Asa's heart at this. His lips stretched into a vague shadow of a scowl as the small girl left the room, tottering under the heavy crockery. When the tall man re-entered with a sharp bang, he did not jump, as he usually would have. Asa kept his gaze fixed on the table in front of him. He heard Kaspar and Avery making forced conversation through his horrified stupor. He did not want to travel with a man who could inflict that sort of pain upon a child.

But no, he half-convinced himself. Kaspar was good. He was just strong, strong enough to hold his own against Erebus. In the end, could Asa complain about his choices in leadership? He had no idea how to rule a country. He had no right to contradict the ethereal. Avery was looking possessive, something clasped in his hands. There was a mulish look written across his features. Asa shook himself out of his stupor and stood unsteadily, walking around his friend to stand at his side.

"I'm keeping it," Avery said.

"It is rubbish," Kaspar retorted, holding out his hand. "It has no place with you."

"It's mine."

"It is dead!"

Avery brought his closed hands out in front of him and opened them, revealing his treasure. A flawless dried flower lay on his palms. His hazel eyes softened as he looked at it, before reaching to put it back into his bag. A hand's length away from the clasp, his arms stilled. Avery attempted to move against the invisible force that was holding him fast. His gaze darted to Kaspar, who was smirking.

"What are you doing?" Avery said.

"I told you that it was rubbish," Kaspar said. "In this house, we dispose of our waste."

He rubbed his ancient hands together for what seemed to be several lifetimes. The tanned digits of his fingers seemed at that moment to be growing visibly warmer. A strange red-orange glow surrounded the outline of his body as he muttered something under his breath. When Asa was finally convinced that they were once again in the presence of a madman, his head snapped up, white eyes fixed upon Avery. They had no pupil or colour. They were blankly horrific.

Asa's mind stumbled on this fact. The eyes had changed colours. Avery was frozen next to him, though Asa wasn't sure if he would have moved had he been able to. Though he could not hear it, he could have sworn that he could feel a crackling being emitted from the ethereal, sending shivers up his spine and making his clothes tick when he moved. There was a hush, nothing moved, no one even breathed. Then the rose on Avery's palm burst into flames.

Like a reflex, the blond's hand grabbed shut over the tongues of heat licking the crisp petals. He winced, as did Asa, and an audible hiss emitted with the unmistakable smell of burning flesh. He did not drop the flower. Kaspar glanced at Avery as his face hardened, sharp jaw growing more defined in his ire. He brought his fist up to his face and flicked open his fingers, blowing the grey ashes in the ethereal's smug face with determined misery. Asa sucked in a short breath as he saw the blisters forming on Avery's callused palm. The skin was shiny and red, stretched across the heel of his hand and below the knuckles. Charred pieces of petal were trapped beneath the skin, sealed in by the heat of the flames.

"How dare you?" Avery spat, coughing out the words in obvious pain. "She gave it to me."

"Who gave it to you?" Kaspar cocked his head, calmer than he ought to be in the circumstances.

"Lili."

"Lili who?" The black eyes challenged.

"I don't know." Avery's voice held a note of uncertainty. He wetted his lips. "She wanted me to remember her."

"And what a good job you did of it," sneered the ethereal.

Asa was growing more and more certain of the black eyes' malevolence. He grabbed hold of Avery's tense elbow, only just stopping his friend from landing a swift punch to Kaspar's stomach. Avery bared his teeth, hissing with anger.

"Asa, stop it, let me at him!"

"No," Asa regulated his voice. "We must work with him, Avery, you know that. Fighting won't help us here."

Avery snorted, resting a hand on his sword, and Asa rolled his eyes as he let him go, fully aware that his friend would never attack anyone with a blade. It may have looked confrontational, but the gesture was defensive. They exchanged tired grins, and Asa placed himself in front of his companion, just so that he would be able to stop anything from happening if the ethereal decided to push it.

The black-eyed man did not. He merely shoved a chair under the table with somewhat alarming ferocity and pulled the door open, holding it in place for them. With a jolt of astonishment, Asa saw that he did not use his hands to do so. Glancing up at Kaspar, he caught the change of his eyes from solid white to black once more. Kaspar smiled at him, revealing rows of needle-like teeth behind his thin lips. He ducked under the doorframe and, taking a deep breath, Asa and Avery followed him.

The town outside was silent, except for the mumbling footsteps of the glazed-eyed civilians, trudging rhythmically along together. They moved between the stumbling figures, pushing them aside as though they were dolls instead of real people. Asa bit his lip as he did so, feeling uneasy. How did he know that they were unaware? He didn't, but he swept civilians aside with a hand that barely hesitated. They would pause, blink stupidly, and then move on again. Kaspar trod a clear path in defiance of the stream of people, heading towards the steep peaks that emerged above the houses. Thick coats of leafy trees, which gave the impression that they were furred and rocky heads rising up into the clouds, covered the peaks. Without either Asa or Avery knowing it, the ground beneath their feet started to slope up.

Kaspar was wearing similar clothes to both of them, only without a neckerchief so that the collar of his shirt lay open against his chest. He instead had opted for a burgundy cloak, tied around his throat by wide ribbons. The excessive material swished behind him, reaching to his knees when he took a long stride. The trousers were just as tight, in the same linen material, sticking closely to his legs and emphasising how strong he had the potential to be. They reached the edge of the forest, the line between urban and wild blurring here. The ethereal smiled, and then disappeared into the foliage.

Asa had to run to keep up with his pace. It was as though he was flying over the ground, covering as much distance per step as the ethereal could in five. He could hear Avery thudding behind him, both breathless with surprise at the sudden change in tempo. Asa could only see glimpses of purplish material through the tight trees ahead as he wound through them, desperate not to get lost. They were a good few hundred metres away from the town now, and Kaspar had taken them such a convoluted route, he was sure that he would never find his way back alone. He pushed himself from tree stump to fallen log in his haste, not able to consider waiting to go around. Avery chose instead to go around, and they were side by side when finally they burst into the clearing where Kaspar was standing, waiting for them.

"That was fun," he said complacently, admiring his own tanned hands.

Asa swung his arms by his side, looking around the woods around them. No birds sang. There were no squirrels in the trees. He gave a small sigh and fixed his attention to the path in front, where he could see Kaspar's moderately broad back draped in burgundy wool.

"Thoughts?" he inquired.

Avery smiled and shook his head. "None worth speaking of."

This caught his attention. Asa turned to his friend, walking sideways in his eagerness to be told what the secret was.

"Liar." He grinned. "Tell me."

"No." Avery blushed. "I mean—no, I have nothing to say."

"Why are you lying, Avery?" Asa pouted, moving closer to his companion. "Am I not your friend?"

"'Course you are," Avery muttered.

"Then tell me!"

He punched Avery's arm. The blond moved his shoulder out of reach. Asa darted around him and began teasing him, attempting to invoke some other emotion in his friend. Avery pushed him away but he kept at it, knowing fully how irritating he was being. He enjoyed it when, after a good few taps and nudges, Avery gripped him in a headlock and held him there. He continued to walk, dragging Asa's kicking body with him by his neck. Asa struggled, playfully at first, but changing to frustration when he realised that he was not going to be able to beat his friend.

"Feeling better?" Avery ruffled Asa's hair patronisingly.

"Oh, fight me," Asa cursed.

"You don't want that."

"Please tell me."

Avery dropped Asa to the forest floor. He thudded painlessly to the mulchy substrate and rolled once before picking himself up. He sprang after his friend, tugging at the sleeve of his shirt.

"Asa, it's embarrassing," Avery pleaded.

"Embarrassing, you'll see." He paused, realising the source of the problem. "Oh."

"What?" Avery huffed.

"A pair of dark eyes?" Asa inquired. "A pretty girl who you kept a flower from?"

The blond turned crimson and rubbed his face.

"Well." Asa relished the sound. "Aren't you a romantic?"

"No!"

"You can't even remember her full name!" His tone was bordering on irritation now. He was bored. The girl was now boring. He was completely finished with that topic of conversation.

"Uh, I do," his friend said. "She is called Lili, so there."

Asa stifled a scowl. He nodded darkly as Avery spoke, a weak smile plastered over his features. The blond's eyes were lit up with a reverence Asa had never seen before. He looked completely changed as he talked, even when their thread of conversation had moved on. There was a lightness in his step that was beyond belief, given the situation that they found themselves in. Kaspar's cloak snagged on branches as they climbed farther up the incline of the mountain woods, always a few steps ahead of them. The pace was slow enough but excruciating to keep up over long periods of time, and soon Asa's feet and lungs burned with a dull pain.

It was getting dark when finally the tall figure ahead of them stopped. He turned to motion for them both to hurry up, and then lead them down a narrow mud path that had been cut between the close trees. It wound left and right for quite a long way, until Asa could hear even Avery's breathing grow heavier at the punishing pace. Eventually, it opened out into a small, clearly man-made clearing that was surrounded by trees.

It was a safe place, Asa decided, a completely safe place. The trees that lined the rectangle of grass were tightly packed; so much so that he doubted even a fox or a rat could fit through them. The only entrance that he could see was the one through which they had come, and unless they were to be attacked by eagles, the skies were blissfully clear and safe tonight.

"Sit." Kaspar gestured to some tree stumps at the edge, near a spot of scorched earth. Asa prodded his with the toe of his boot, unsure of the structural security of it. The ethereal pushed him down. "I said sit!"

"I'm sitting," Asa protested, allowing himself to sink down onto the natural stool.

The ethereal flicked a tongue of fire into the pit and swept a faggot of wood into it with his foot. Asa wasn't one hundred percent sure that the wood had been there before Kaspar was. He moved closer to the delicious warmth of the flames and allowed himself to relax. His feet ached but he couldn't bring himself to remove his boots. The night was mild enough but he was chilled, lips a delicate shade of blue as a breeze rustled the branches of the trees around them.

"We will have dried potatoes tonight," the black-eyed man stated, removing a cloth pouch from the bag and dividing the contents on a stump of wood. "It's an ancient delicacy. I'm sure that you will appreciate it. This is how meals shall work: breakfast will be high-energy honey loaf, for luncheon we shall have maybe some fruit, and supper will be a preserved dish of my choosing, based on the amount of work we will be doing the next day. I have brought some apples and lemons with me to keep our diet healthy."

He took a round yellow fruit from his bag and Avery pulled a face.

"We've had them," he groaned. "They taste dreadful."

"They will keep your little teeth from falling from your skull like icicles from a stove," Kaspar said archly, handing each of them equal portions of thin circular chips of some beige substance. "But no, if you fancy that then I won't stop you."

Asa took a potato fragment and nibbled on it as he stared at the fire. It was bland and chewy, like the apples that his mother had used to bake for him at home but without the flavour. He wasn't too hungry and only managed half of the portion that he had been allocated, before sliding the rest onto Avery's lap. His friend either didn't or chose not to notice, as he took the new number of potato slices in his stride and devoured them. Kaspar cleared his throat and raised an eyebrow at Asa's behaviour, but made no comment.

Asa blinked. It may have been a trick of the flickering firelight or his own weary eyes, but Kaspar's solid eyes seemed to glow as they stared back at him. It was hard to comprehend, glowing black, but Asa couldn't describe it any other way. His face must have betrayed his thoughts, because Kaspar laughed.

"Yes, they are rather attractive, aren't they? Moths are a problem in the summer, though."

It was fully dark now. Kaspar pointed at the ground in a condescending manner. Asa and Avery looked at him, not quite as confused as they would have liked to be.

"Um, what?" Avery inquired, somewhat cheekily.

"Sleep." The ethereal's tone left no room for comment. "I will seal our perimeters, but I expect you both to be lying there by the time I get back.

The two of them sat in solemn silence, as Kaspar walked off, then lay on the grassy ground, unused to it. Asa slipped his hand into his friend's and they were quiet before Avery broke the silence.

"Don't you think"—Avery checked behind him before continuing—"that he's a bit of a slave driver?"

"He has control issues," Asa admitted. "But what other choice do we have?"

"Run." Avery's face was alight with a manic gleam. "Leave.

Go on alone."

"That's madness," he replied. "And you know it. He'd kill us."

"Come on, Asa!"

"Go to sleep, Avery," his voice was tired, but firm. "We'll discuss this further in the morning."

Avery soon fell into an easy rest, his hand growing slack in Asa's. Yet Asa found that he was unable to do so. He felt the chill of the wind on his back, the scratchiness of the blades of grass below his body, and the bleak loneliness of their situation as he did his friend's callused palm. The night grew darker and stiller. No moon rose to light the sky, and the stars were so far away. He hoped that Kaspar was asleep as he turned onto his stomach and let out a low and despondent sigh, curled in a protective ball on the ground.

"Do you hate me, Asa Hounslow?" Kaspar spoke in the darkness, the slight glow of his eyes the only light visible to Asa, who froze and lay as still as he possibly could. "Don't just lie there. I believe that I asked you a question."

"No," Asa murmured, voice dry. "No, I don't."

"Liar," Kaspar said, amused. "I took great pleasure in the look on your face as I was torturing your pathetic friend's love-lost heart. Fighting won't help us, you said. But I knew that you were dying to let him hurt me. But you were so aware that I would have destroyed him that you merely mewed like the feeble kitten you are."

"I am no kitten," Asa's tone was steady. He turned onto his back, keeping track of those lion-like eyes as they glowed back at him.

"You're playing with the big cats now, boy," Kaspar's voice came through the gloom. "If I were you, I would watch my words. We wouldn't want to aggravate any of my wilder characteristics, would we?"

"You are quite mistaken." Asa stuck his chin up as he looked into the inky dark. "If you think that I fear you."

"Then you live a fool," the ethereal chuckled. "And you will die a wiser man."

Asa lay back down on his dry bed of grass. The oak tree that branched out over his head provided a merciful amount of shelter for which he was grateful. Yet still, even in this uncomfortable situation with a proven killer just steps from him, he was glad of the stars. They sparkled just like they had in Salatesh when he was young, only clearer here, brighter. The eternal sky reached up as far as he could ever see, no borders to its magnitude. As Asa finally managed to get to sleep, those tiny pinpricks of light were burnt into his vision, there even when his eyes were closed.

TEN

THREE DAYS PASSED. THOUGH he would never have admitted it, Asa was growing increasingly uncomfortable with the ethereal's presence. Kaspar was everything that Asa disliked. He was volatile, smug, and sadistic with a curious and sinister talent of making animals around them fall silent.

Their booted feet sank and slid on the mulchy ground, and the tree roots seemed determined to send them tumbling head over heels down the mountain. Asa could not believe that they had not managed to reach over the mountains yet, but Avery assured him that they were indeed going in the right direction. Still, neither of them would have put it past Kaspar to send them to their deaths.

The magical creature controlled every movement. When he saw them doing something of which he did not approve, he would merely freeze them in position and leave them there until their joints cramped and they groaned with stiffness and pain. Occasionally Asa and Avery would lie together at night, seeing the stars reflected in the other's eyes but unable to talk to them for fear of Kaspar. Asa was by that time convinced that their journey was hopeless. They were never going to be allowed to survive.

He coughed, wiping his hand on his tight trousers in a way that he would have proclaimed as disgusting two months ago. They were nearing the top of their current climb, which had taken them the better part of a day to complete. There were few trees and the land around them was plagued with strange dryness. The grass was dead and yellow and the streambeds dry. Asa swallowed for what seemed to be the hundredth time that day, mouth not producing quite enough saliva to cover the ache in his throat and lungs. He paused for a moment to catch his breath but found himself propelled forwards by an unstoppable force.

"Just . . . let me . . . breathe," he wheezed, tripping over his feet as he was pushed up the mountain.

"Fine." Kaspar relinquished his hold on Asa, causing him to stumble backwards at the lack of pressure. "We will eat and then press on."

Asa moved to a rock that stuck out of the ground near him and collapsed onto it, slouching as he worked to untie his bootlaces. His shoes were tighter than usual, rubbing the skin on his feet raw as they were walking. Avery sat next to him and pulled Asa's boots off, looking concerned.

"Asa?"

"Mm?" Asa grunted.

"You alright?" Avery's eyes were boring closely into his. Asa looked at his sore feet.

"Great," he intoned.

"It's time for luncheon, anyhow." Avery smiled.

The blond reached into the bag and pulled out two apples. Halfway through his portion, Asa set the apple down on his knee, nausea churning his stomach so that he did not feel he could eat even another small mouthful.

"You should eat this." he pressed the fruit into Avery's unsure hands. "I'm full."

"Poppycock." Avery took the apple, but unwillingly. "You've barely eaten."

"Yeah," Asa sighed.

"I can't eat this." Avery held the half apple of Asa's in one hand and his stem in the other. His stomach growled and Asa chuckled.

"Go on, then." he smiled. "You're hungry."

"If you say so." Avery finished off Asa's lunch, and Asa leant against his broad back, closing his eyes to try and stop his thoughts from racing. He heard Kaspar's sinister footsteps walking up to them and kept his eyes shut, refusing to give the ethereal the privilege of his gaze. His breathing evened out and his heart rate slowed, falling in time with the strong slow beats of Avery's.

"Is he dead yet?" Kaspar snickered, foot whistling less than an inch past Asa.

"That's not funny," Avery said. "He's just tired, thanks to you."

"Thanks to me?"

"If you didn't make us walk everywhere at bird flight speed, then he wouldn't be so tired."

"Oh, Avery, dear," Kaspar crooned. "That's not why he's so tired."

"Give me a good reason why, then," Avery snapped, stiffening.

"He's dying, Avery. Don't you remember?"

Avery paused for a moment, before answering. "I know."

Asa quailed at the way his voice broke on the two small words. He didn't want his friend to be sad because of him, that wasn't a good enough reason. Far greater people were dying and he, who had just one friend and no family, was not worth bothering about, let alone crying over. He heard Avery inhale and shake beneath his body and realised, with shock, that he was struggling not to cry. Now that was wrong. Avery was as tough as nails and never cried. No one could make him sob, even as a child. Why, he would sooner be hit a million times than shed one tear. Asa's heart sank as the breaths grew lighter and Avery's demeanour softened.

Kaspar stood, and as if drawn by an invisible lead, Asa and Avery stood as well, stretching their sore limbs. Kaspar walked past them and they saw him get onto the path that they were following. They trudged behind him automatically, aware that any other action on their part would result in a painful punishment from the powerful being's magic.

"Faster!" the ethereal shouted, voice caught by the wind and blown back to them. "We must cover more ground."

"Where are we even going?" Asa tossed back, hurriedly tugging his shirtsleeves down to cover his hands.

Kaspar turned to them, black eyes unreadable. "We are going to see a dear member of my family."

Asa caught up to him, curious. "Not Erebus?"

"Not everything revolves around Erebus," Kaspar snapped at him. "We are travelling to meet my sister Gil."

He shoved past Asa as they left the path and started to walk upon the dry grass, going up the slope of the mountain. The ground grew much steeper here, littered with rocks and scratchy bushes covered in flowers. Their pace increased yet again, and Asa found his feet being pushed faster than he could have, unwillingly drawn along next to Kaspar.

"Where does she live?" he asked, huffing with the exertion of their climb.

"In the mountains," Kaspar muttered.

"Really?" Asa's tone contained so much latent sarcasm that he knew that he was in for it. "How could I have guessed that?"

"Enough," Kaspar growled, stopping Asa in his tracks. "I have had quite enough from you for today."

He turned on Asa with a feral glint in his eyes. Asa swallowed, stepping away from the outstretched hands, though he knew that it would not do much good. The ethereal tensed, his unfocused gaze somewhere above Asa's right shoulder. Tingles of something sinister ran up and down his spine. He fought to move but found that he was trapped to that same spot on the ground, mutely twitching as Kaspar won control of his body. He watched, dumbfounded, as Kaspar's copper-coloured fingers closed into the man's palm. A spasm of burning pain radiated throughout his chest, holding him immobile for a moment, and then pulling back. Asa dropped to the ground, clutching at his torso. He could feel phantom pricks of fire all over himself. Looking up, he saw a polished black boot.

"Kiss it."

"What?" he spluttered indignantly. "No."

"Do as I say, Hounslow."

Averting his gaze from Avery's, Asa pressed his lips to the leather. He recoiled instantly, dragging his numb body into a standing position. He nodded, and Kaspar brushed past him as they carried on up the mountain. His feet dragged on the ground as he was pulled along, huffing with veiled anger with the ethereal. Asa could feel Avery's eyes on the back of his neck, but he just glowered into the air in front of him.

As they rounded the side of the hill, a small hut came into view. This house was smaller than the one which Asa and Avery had stayed in within the walls. It was minute, a mere room with two windows, a front door, and a smoking chimney. A wicker fence enclosed a tiny garden, overflowing with blooming flowers even in this barren landscape of dirt and scree rock. Kaspar reached the gate before either of them. He pushed it open.

There was only room for one person on the thin cobblestone slab that acted as a path. Asa and Avery leaned gingerly on the fence as the tall man rapped twice on the door. It was a strange shape, like a gravestone, a rounded-off rectangle. A brass handle was in the middle of the wood. Asa considered it for a moment. It must be impossible to open that door, he decided. You would need to be rather strong. Nonetheless, the door pulled back away from Kaspar, and they saw a flash of a black eye.

"Who is it . . . Oh, it's you. Why are you here?" a thin voice from inside demanded. "You never come to visit."

"I came to see my favourite sister," Kaspar said. "That is legal, right?"

"Favourite, hah!" the person behind the door snorted. "You'd be the one to know about legality."

"I have some visitors to see you, sister dear." The ethereal stuck his foot in the door, breaking the security chain with a snap like that of a strained rope rather than links of real metal.

"Visitors?" The person stepped back from the door. "What sort of visitors?"

"Mortals," Kaspar stated. "From Jundres."

"Ria's?"

"Yes."

"Let's see them, then."

The door opened and a tall woman emerged, her thick black hair cropped close to her head. Her skin was darker than Kaspar's—a beautiful colour the exact shade of the dark leather straps that attached Asa's sword to his leg. Avery was staring at her with undeniable interest, until Asa kicked him in the shin. The woman was wearing low-hanging loose trousers of some light cotton material and her torso was covered by a thin vest-like garment. Both of the items were dyed in vibrant blues and greens, swirls that looked like a lake in the height of summer.

"Good morning." Asa held out a hand. She took it and shook, smiling a dazzling smile at him.

"Thank you, Asa," she greeted him, before turning to his friend, eyes as white as her teeth. "And good morning to you too, Avery."

"Magic?" Avery managed to squeak out.

"Oh, yes," she said. "My magic is more holistic than my siblings'. A choice that I will never regret."

Kaspar stuck his hand in front of her. She grimaced and clasped his fingers in hers, closing her eyes. She waited for a moment, and then opened them, surprised.

"You know what I want," he growled.

"Indeed." She looked perturbed. "I don't understand, brother dearest. What if I don't want to? It's barely reversible, you know."

"Does it matter?" he snapped. "You are in my debt."

"I see," she said sadly. "Well, I guess I have no choice."

"To do what?" Asa demanded.

The female ethereal started. "Oh, how rude of me! I never told you who I am. My name is Gil."

"What's going on?" Avery asked. "Why're you both being so cryptic?"

"My brother was reminding me of a debt I must pay," Gil said. "I must be a good host to you all. How about a picnic? I know a good spot not too far from here."

"Do as you will," Kaspar sneered.

Gil's eyes flashed alabaster, and after a few muffled crashes from within the cottage, a large open basket crashed into her hands. Asa peered into it. It was filled with all manner of pleasant foods—small pies, cuts of meat, and different fruits. She took the handle and shut her front door with a definite click.

"Follow me," she chirped. "It is a lovely spot."

They went down the mountain for a while, curving around on a winding sand path that was cut into the side of the hill. The woman moved with a slight but evident limp, a dragging of her left heel across the ground. Her feet were bare, and when the hem of her trousers hitched as she trod on a stone, Asa could see a livid scar against her calf. He opened his mouth to ask her about it, but found his mouth closing again as she spun around to face them, moving backwards for two steps as they realised the beauty of their surroundings.

They were atop a high precipice, a rocky cliff. The sides were so steep that Asa could not see the bottom. It was covered in rocks, not jagged ones, but smooth—like moonstones. It was obvious that it had been cultivated by someone, evidently Gil by her proud smile at their awestruck faces.

"Lovely, is it not?"

They assured her that it was, indeed, lovely. She walked across the stones and set her basket down, sitting cross-legged with her back to the cliff. She indicated that they were to sit down and they did so, both Asa and Avery eyeing the basket of food.

"May we?" Avery asked, stomach growling.

"As you wish."

Kaspar took his meal first, filling his hands with meat as though he had never eaten it before. Gil looked smug at this and teased him about his diet, surprising Asa. He never thought of Kaspar as being anywhere near human, yet he had a sister who chatted with him as if they were not the most powerful beings in existence. Avery filled his lap whilst they were not looking, choking down food like a starved gull. Asa picked up a pie but found that he had little appetite for it, ending up just playing with the pastry.

Once they had sated their stomachs, Avery and Kaspar were quiet. Gil met Asa's eyes with her black ones.

"Yes?" Asa stared unblinkingly at her, on his guard.

"Come for a walk with me." It was not a question.

Asa followed her mutely away from the two people who he knew, and they turned around the mountain until they were out of sight and earshot.

"What do you want with me?" he asked.

"Your time is running short, little one," Gil said.

Asa swallowed. "I know."

The ethereal smiled wryly at him. "I, too, know the feeling. But you are not accepting it?"

"No," he replied. "Never. Whilst I still have breath in my lungs to say I am not dead, I will not accept it."

"You are brave." They stood under a sheer cliff of rock. She leant on it reflectively. "But bravery is not always enough."

"It will be." Asa stuck his chin up and looked her in the eyes. "I can feel it."

Gil glanced down, inhaling a breath that rang in Asa's ears.

"I have seen the runes, Asa. I know how much time you have left. Nothing you can do will change your destiny. Only others can do that, and they won't even know it."

"No. I will not discuss this." Asa shrugged. "I am sorry, but I do not wish to know my future. It is the one thing that I will eventually discover for myself."

"If you are determined then so be it." Gil did not sound in the least phased by this. She cracked her shoulders in a relaxed way and started to follow the path that they had just taken. "If you will not listen then I cannot say."

In a matter of what seemed like moments, they were back in the grove of stones that they had eaten in. Kaspar was standing close to the edge, looking in all of his mannerisms and stature irritated.

"Finally. I was beginning to wonder if you were returning, sister."

"I would never go back on a promise."

"No, I believe that of you at least," Kaspar sneered. "Always so good."

"Thank you." Gil nodded to Kaspar, then smiled at Asa and Avery. "Good luck, young ones. I can assure you, to whatever end, I will be watching."

She shuffled closer to the edge of the cliff, curling her bare toes over the rocky edge. Her eyes were lighting up with a sort of manic fire, and she shifted from foot to foot whilst staring up at the sky above.

"Wait," Asa said. "What are you doing?"

"What I've always wanted to try." She breathed, a breeze picking up her hair and tousling it. "Little brother just had to give me a push. Here I go!"

Avery leapt to his feet. "No!"

But he was too late. The black-eyed woman had taken a hop backwards, and then flung herself off the cliff. Asa froze, staring at the spot, while Kaspar snorted with laughter at their shocked expressions. Avery ran to the spot where she had jumped, peering down into the crevasse below.

"I can't believe it," Avery croaked, voice dry. "I simply can't. She was your sister."

Kaspar chuckled. "She has not died. Or have you forgotten what I told you of my brethren? We do not die. Our kind is just like wisps of cotton—so fragile, but unbreakable. You cannot break cotton by dropping it," Kaspar explained, a glint around his black eyes. "She has, for want of a better word, flown away."

"What are you made of?" Asa shook his head. "I don't understand."

"We are made of everything, Asa," Kaspar crooned. "We are the air, we are the ground. We take our forms as such for communicatory purposes, but if we willed it we could be anything. The rocks on a mountain, the grass on a field. Energy never fades, remember that. It remains when all else is gone. We are the land. We are the energy."

He seemed to fade in and out of sight before their eyes, a wavering around the edges of his surreal form that rippled through the centre of his torso. He lifted a hand to his vanishing chest with a sigh of relief. Asa narrowed his eyes.

"I will see you two again." The ethereal's black eyes were all they could see. They gleamed with the same infinite power as a roaring waterfall—natural, unquenchable energy.

And he was gone.

"I can't believe this. The utter—" Asa cursed, pacing before his friend, and tugging at his hair.

"Hush," Avery said.

"Don't you even care?" Asa exclaimed. "You stand there like an impassive tree! What in Eodem is the matter with you?"

Avery glanced up at the grey sky overhead. His eyelids were twitching as his gaze moved beneath them, and he shuffled around, pointing in one direction then the other. After thinking hard for some time, Avery opened his eyes and sighed.

"That way." He shrugged.

"You tracked our journey from the last camp, I assume?"

"Yes."

"In your head? That's a long way." He was impressed.

"Sure," the blond acknowledged. "It's not like it's hard."

Avery was smirking, the natural light casting shadows on the chiselled features that Asa might once have considered handsome. That was past, though. He had a greater responsibility now. He had to finish his quest, then he could worry about the strange thoughts he'd been having about his best friend.

Avery flashed a white smile, and Asa's his heart melted. He stepped towards his friend, eyes wide and desperate.

"Kiss me," he blurted, voice too loud for the far-reaching emptiness around them.

"What?" Avery laughed, squinting at Asa. "What did you say?"

"Kiss me," he repeated more quietly, voice steady. "Life is too short for us to mess around with this. I don't want you kissing some pretty migrants, I want you to kiss me."

Avery blushed, the roots of his hair practically strawberry blond. He ran one of his hands through it, causing it to stand on end. His face bore no disgust or repulsion, as Asa had feared, but seemed conflicted. He smiled shakily again, surveying what the effect was on Asa, who stared at him intently. They looked at each other for a long time, brown boring into hazel.

"Are you sure?" The blond was now scarlet. "I just don't want to make you do something that you don't want to."

Asa almost laughed out loud at the uncertainty in Avery's voice. He closed the distance between them in three easy strides and squared up to his friend, looking carefully at his confused face.

"Did I stutter?"

All of a sudden, Avery's strong arms pulled him closer than he had ever thought possible. He had never kissed anyone before. That thought flashed across his mind, locking his limbs stiffly as he was enveloped in Avery's arms. He was so close that he could see every single one of his friend's light eyelashes, so close that he could see the freckles across his nose. He leant forwards nervously, and their lips finally met.

It was a strangely familiar feeling, that of being so close to someone. However, he had never experienced this buzz. An undercurrent of emotion sang through Asa's body as they stood in that intimate embrace on the cliff side. It was everything that he had ever dreamed. It was terrifying, but at the same time so safe and loving that Asa forgot to be scared. For a moment in time he had stopped falling. Now he thought he could fly.

"Oh, Erebus," Avery murmured as they broke apart. "I had not expected that."

Asa kissed him briefly on the cheek, his heart racing too fast for him to even speak to his friend. Somehow, the world now seemed brighter than before. His body was relaxed, despite his nerves, and he slipped his hand into Avery's, pointing down to a thin footpath. Neither of them spoke of what had passed as they descended.

The path down the other side of the mountain was steeper than the one that they had taken before. The air was dustily dry and growing thicker the closer they drew towards the ground. It was warm and fresh, a combination of traits that Asa never thought he would consider air to be. The wind was more condensed than it had been. It ruffled their hair and tugged on their garments, as if it wanted to pull them away when it was strong enough.

The ground was soft underfoot, covered in a blanket of grass. A loch lay to their left, curling around the side of one mountain and being fed from a stream that tumbled into its depths. Trees were scattered everywhere—thin with sparse leaves that allowed dappled light to shine through. The valley was quiet, and for the first time since Kaspar had left them, Asa could hear the muffled sounds of a world beyond their own. Birds sang to each other as they darted through the branches, insects hummed beneath their feet. It was as if a muffler had been lifted from their ears and now they could hear the world living.

It wasn't long before the shadows were growing longer, though there was no sun to be seen wherever they looked. Asa knelt by the shimmering surface of the loch, drinking the water from cupped hands. It was cool and refreshing to his parched tongue. Avery was lighting a fire behind him, he could hear the strikes of flint on steel, and after a few clinks the hiss of flames catching to the kindling. The leather satchel that Avery had been carrying, Kaspar having departed with the other, was showing signs of the long journey it had taken. Its leather was cracked and peeling, worn through to cloth-like thinness in some areas. Asa saw Avery remove some of the disgusting nutritional biscuits from a cloth bag. He smiled apologetically.

"There's nothing else left."

Asa nodded, taking the biscuit and collapsing on the grass next to his friend. The stars were out again that night. They sparkled tantalisingly above them, just out of reach. Avery mouthed some words under his breath, laughing at Asa's confused glance towards him.

"What was that?" Asa inquired, chuckling unsurely. Avery indicated a star that shone only just over their heads. It was the brightest in the whole sky.

"The clouds have cleared. I just remembered that from here one can see Boreas. The star of the north." He pointed at a particularly bright star that shone in the direction that they were travelling and sighed. "Eurus. My mother loves that star. Had I been born when Eurus was in our charts, that would have been my name."

Asa squinted up at the blanket of glittering black. He could not fathom how anyone could see the difference between the tiny beads of light.

"How?" he asked. "How do you know them?"

"You don't just start off knowing them," Avery explained. "It's like reading. Where you read your letters on a page, I read the sky. If you know one constellation then you are able to map out any other that you may come across. You're a mapper, aren't you? Then this should be easy enough."

"It's called being a cartographer," Asa said. "But I don't map the skies. I draw streets, fields. It's linear work, simple enough for someone like me."

"Believe in this for one night, Asa." Avery pointed to a line of stars close together above their heads. "That's the waist of Harloziel, the warrior. See how you can trace the shape of her body? Her arm is drawing a bow. From the bow you may trace the top of her head, and then you can see her fully. And it all came from learning that her waist is made of the five king stars that I pointed out now. Learning these patterns is like learning the alphabet. It's essential if you want to see the bigger picture."

A streak of light shot across the sky in front of them. Asa twitched for his sword, safe against his leg, but Avery grabbed his arm.

"Avery!"

"It's a firefly, you paranoid idiot. Just look."

As the final vestiges of day left the sky, the air around them seemed to come to life. Tiny insects flickered in front of them, their brightness illuminating their faces in the darkness.

Asa smiled as he looked at his best friend. They were still here, despite all of the odds. He had never been so happy to be with a person, not in his whole life.

"Do you wish on fireflies?" he asked casually.

"What? No, that's shooting stars," Avery scoffed.

"What would you wish, just suppose that you could?"

"I don't know." Avery was quiet for a moment. "To go home,

see my mother again? Maybe I would start a garden and grow my own vegetables; that has always seemed like a good dream. Not for necessity or anything, just because I could. What would you wish for?"

"Something a bit more immediate." Asa's eyes were fixated on the blond's lips. "You know, in case neither of us live to see tomorrow. Life's too short. I want something that I can have right now."

"What do you mean?" Avery rolled his eyes, before Asa cut him off, pressing their lips together. "Oh."

It wasn't the hasty embarrassment that had been their first kiss, or either of the quick pecks that they had enjoyed since. Only the stars were there to watch them as they sat there, both crossing their legs so that their knees touched. The world around them seemed to have faded and slowed, nothing could matter outside of this. Erebus was nothing but a word; his influence was null and void when the two of them were together. They were unstoppable.

They reluctantly broke apart, the world shifting back into sharp focus. Asa squirmed away from Avery as he brushed a lock of hair from the nape of his neck, though neither of them said a word. They made no pretence of not linking fingers that night. The air was still warm though the wind was high, and after an indeterminably long time watching the fluttering fireflies, Asa let his eyes drift shut.

It was around the third day in the mountains that Asa fell. His stumbling walk was replaced by a swift flurry of movement as he curled up into a ball to protect his head. Once he had stopped sliding on the frozen stones, he lay there motionless, breathing shallowly through his teeth as he tried to right himself on his own. He pressed a cautious hand to his chest, which was aching badly. There seemed to be no sharp pain, no broken bones. He heard Avery's heavy footsteps thunder towards him, sending sharp shards of rock over his body.

"Asa?"

He moved in affirmation. The dust was coating his face. Asa wetted his lips with the tip of his tongue, longing for the clean rationed water. He could have drunk it all in one sitting.

"I'm fine, Avery." His voice hoarser than it had been. He coughed up some rock dust, covering his mouth with his hand. "Just took a tumble."

"No, you're bleeding," Avery argued, taking Asa's hand and gesturing to the dark droplets beaded on the palm. "We can't go on if you're injured."

Asa considered arguing that he was already dying, and that was about as injured as one could get. However, his body ached and his head was slow and useless. He shook his head.

"I didn't hit my hands."

"Well, you're bleeding anyhow," his friend said, wiping the blood off of Asa's hand with his own. "Did you get cut anywhere else?"

"I don't think—" At this, Asa started to cough again, feeling the sharp rock shards scraping at the inside of his throat. He covered his mouth in the usual reflex action and shook his head again. "No. I don't think so."

Avery caught one of his hands in his own, before Asa could wipe his on his trousers. Asa saw his face recoil for a moment in reflexive disgust, before softening into a frown.

"Asa."

"Avery, no. I'm not in the mood to discuss it."

Why wouldn't he just let it be? Of course Asa was not well. Avery had known that when they had set off. Why, then, was he now fussing like this? It would not do for Avery to fuss anymore, Asa decided. He should not be under any more stress than the situation warranted. He moved his hands away from his friend's gentle grip, wiping the blood away on his grimy trousers. No, it would not do to upset Avery.

"Asa, you cannot just ignore this," Avery said sincerely. "You know as well as I what this means."

"I can do just that," Asa declared. "It isn't over until it's done."

"Your heart won't wait for you." Asa heard a deep sadness in the usually bright tone. "Asa, we're going to have to get there sooner."

"Oh, lay off, Avery." His head hurt so much, like it was filled with mud. Asa curled in on himself on the sharp rocks. "We can camp here, can't we?"

He registered the childish impetuousness of his voice. Avery apparently did too, because he let loose a low chuckle.

"Seventeen years of age and still throwing temper tantrums? Come on, Asa, we just need to get to that outcrop over there."

He gripped Asa's cold hand in his warm one, somehow managing to pull him to his feet. Asa swayed, clutching Avery to stand straight. He tried to lift his feet, but it was as though they were made of lead. Walking was clearly out of the question.

"I—I can't," he murmured, clasping his friend even tighter as blackness started to make its way into his vision. "I just can't."

He fell backwards as Avery let go. Startled, he let out a small yelp, which he stifled as his friend's arms arrested him. Avery manoeuvred Asa until he could pick the man up in his arms. Asa lay back into the warmth, shivering at the frigid mountain air. His cheeks were wet, he realised. Why were they wet? The fierce wind bit into the exposed skin, turning what once was damp tear tracks to flushed cold skin.

"Don't drop me," he said, clutching at Avery's tunic. "I don't want to fall."

"I won't, Asa." He could feel his friend's deep voice in his chest. "I'm never going to let you go. You are the most precious thing that I have ever loved."

"You'll have to, one day," he snipped back, a fierce glint alighting and dying in his eyes.

"Today is not that day." He was taken from the warmth of Avery's arms and set on the rocky ground. He propped himself up, head spinning as Avery talked to him. "Nor is tomorrow, nor the day after."

Footsteps walked away from him, crunching in the frost. Asa tried to stand but fell back, mind clouding as he tried to form a coherent sentence over the frantic rushing of his heart. "Don't!"

"Don't what, Asa?" Avery asked, feeling his forehead. Asa didn't want to know if he had a temperature or not.

"Don't leave me here alone."

"Never," Avery swore. "I will stay with you for as long as this takes, Asa. I promise you that."

ELEVEN

CLIMBING THE FINAL PEAK was the hardest thing that Asa had ever done. His legs ached, his back hurt, and even the act of placing one foot doggedly in front of the other was enough to make him gasp and groan in protest. Avery was faring only slightly better. His boots had worn through on the soles and the bottom of his right foot had been scratched into a raw and bleeding mess. They wrapped their arms around each other's waists, not knowing if it even helped their struggle, but the simple act of feeling another warm being was enough to keep them both on their feet and moving.

They reached the top at mid-morning. The sun was still rising in the miraculously blue sky, not a cloud in sight. A thin sheen of sweat covered Asa's entire body as he squinted around for their next climb from the mountaintop. Avery had collapsed onto a small cairn of stones, picking bits of gravel out of his foot. Asa looked once, twice, and started trembling, unable to believe what he could see, or rather, what he could not. No more steep rocky slopes met his gaze. A stretch of flat land lay before them, not far in terms of length. And then all along the horizon lay something vast—shimmering and azure blue.

"Where land, sea, and sky meet," Asa mouthed, unable to believe his eyes. "The concourse."

His voice had risen to a whisper, and Avery looked up from his foot-tending duties.

"The what?" he yawned. "Speak up?"

"The concourse!" Asa's heart was pounding, whether from exhaustion or excitement he did not know. "Look, Avery."

Avery heaved himself onto his feet and limped over to where Asa was standing. As his eyes scanned the scene in front of them, a grin spread over his face, tugging at his cracked lips.

"We're here."

"Almost." Asa shrugged, trying not to show his frenzy of conflicted emotions. "Not quite."

Avery's face dropped, even his eyes showed no hint of confliction. "Asa. How're we going to get home?"

Asa shrugged. "The pendant, remember? I didn't know how Queen Ria had magic before, but I guess that it makes sense for an ethereal."

"Oh yeah, the pendant." Avery didn't look any happier.

Asa turned to him in a panic. "Wait, you still have it, don't you?"

The idea of them making the return journey was impossible, terrible. Avery nodded.

"Never took it off." He withdrew it from inside his ragged shirt. The stone glinted in the strong afternoon sun.

"Well then, why do you look like someone has slapped your mother?"

"Oh, I don't know," Avery huffed. "Tired, I guess."

"We can't afford that now." Asa took a deep breath. "Tiredness will have to wait."

He looked down the relatively steep path that led onto the marshy land. The ground was lined with small and relatively sharp stones. Avery was nursing his foot, one leg lifted as he rubbed at the sore skin. One of his fingernails caught on the wound and he flinched, falling over. Asa would have laughed if the situation had been different.

"Oh!" Avery cursed, bending in on himself.

Asa frowned, again staring at the gravel-lined path. His own boots were fine, even if they rubbed his feet. Then again, his feet seemed to have grown since they embarked all of those weeks ago. He set his resolve, and then turned to his friend.

"Get on my back," he said, bending his knees in anticipation.

Avery didn't move. "What?"

"I'll carry you down this part," Asa stated. "It'll be easier than any other way. You can barely walk."

"You're tiny," Avery laughed incredulously. "How do you think you're going to carry me so far?"

"Through sheer will and determination," Asa laughed. "Or perhaps by using my not-inconsiderable strength."

"Don't drop me," Avery warned him, "or I will kill you."

"Yeah, like you're the person who I have to worry about killing me," Asa snorted.

As Avery clambered onto his back, he saw for the first time how little his companion weighed for his height. Asa glanced back to ensure that his friend was secure, and then took a few uncertain steps to the top of the unworn path. Avery's hands gripped his shoulders as they made their first steps down the steep hillside, leaving deep-dragging footprints in their wake.

Moments stretched on into days as Asa plodded forward. His breath came in short pants, whistling through his gritted teeth. All that he could focus on was the feeling of his companion's weight on his shoulders and his sharp fingernails digging into the soft skin on the back of his neck. He strained to push them as far as he was physically able to, lungs burning with exertion.

"Thank you, Asa," Avery said, pecking him on the cheek as he tried to slide onto the ground.

Asa stopped, confused. "What?"

"For doing this." Avery made another attempt to get off his

back, but Asa held firm.

"Avery, what are you doing?"

"Asa, look." His friend unhooked his legs from around Asa's waist and landed on the ground with a thud.

There was only a step or so more of the gravelled terrain, the stones merging with fibrous grasses and soft, mossy ground. Asa smiled in relief, running the short distance in his haste for a rest. The mud was cushioned and soft compared to the rocks that they had been climbing over for days. The concourse was in front of them, he knew it. The marshy ground gave out to a low sand bank some way ahead, but the scenery beyond that was completely obscured.

"Ready?" he asked, voice unsteady and hoarse.

"Bring it."

The sun was shining on Avery's hair, bleaching it silver with its light.

Stumbling, feet struggling for purchase as they sank beneath the mud, Asa and Avery made their way towards the sandy ground with a new resolve. Gone was any inclination to stop or rest, any feeling of discomfort. The warmth of the sunlight on their backs filled them with courage, hope-filled eyes fixed on their goal. They did not lean on each other, but stood separately, arms brushing each other's occasionally with their closeness. Asa's legs were soon covered with a layer of splattered green-brown mud, reaching up to just above his boot tops. They reached the bottom of the sloping mound of sand, which was covered with wiry grass, and paused, stomachs both sinking. Each opened their mouth to say something, and then waited for the other person to. Eventually, Avery broke the silence.

"Asa, I don't know what's going to happen."

His tone was sombre, and his eyes were filled with a fear that Asa had never seen Avery have before.

"Neither." He gave a low, nervous chuckle.

"I just want you to know something." Avery shut his eyes, and then opened them again. They shone yellow as he swallowed. "You know—if I don't make it."

"Don't be ridiculous," Asa said.

"Quiet, idiot. I'm trying to say something deep. Asa, I want you to remember, whatever happens, that I love you, and that this was one of the best things that I have ever done. Adventure isn't so bad, if you can do it with a friend."

Asa was quiet for a moment.

"Thank you, Avery." He struggled with the words, though he had thought them so many times before. "I don't know where I would be without you. You've saved my life more times than I can count, yet you still act like the naïve child who was my best friend in Salatesh. You are one in a million. I am so privileged to be your friend."

Avery blinked hard. "Thank you."

His voice was choked.

"To whatever end?" Asa asked, sadness that he didn't understand filling him with trepidation.

"Sure," Avery replied, if a trifle sarcastically. "For our country, and our people."

They clambered up over the sandbank together. For a moment, all that Asa could see was a wide beach, the waters clear and blue, with clean pale sand as far as the eye could see. It was as if the world was divided into three strips, two of blue and one of white. Avery stiffened beside him, hand reaching for and withdrawing his sword. Asa followed his line of sight and had to blink the dust away from his eyes to make sure.

"Kaspar?" he breathed, eyes widening. "What are you doing here?"

The ethereal was seated on the sand, sifting the grains through his fingers in a methodical manner. He looked up as Asa and Avery appeared, smiling a strange, needle-toothed smile.

"You made it," he observed, standing up and walking towards them. The waves washed backwards and forwards over the sand.

"I was beginning to wonder."

"Where's your brother?" Avery asked, narrowing his eyes.

"I have more than one brother?" Kaspar frowned, a crease appearing between his eyebrows. "Never heard of the chap, I'm afraid."

"Are we alone here?" Avery demanded. "Where is this monster we were told to fight?"

"Ah." Kaspar paused. "That. As far as it can be understood by good children such as yourselves, I may have embellished upon the truth there. You might be reasonable in the assumption that I lied."

A nasty feeling spun in the pit of Asa's stomach. He looked around the deserted beach. There was no sound. Not even that of the waves that continued to break over the shale. His heart began to race as he and Avery were pulled over the sand dune which they had been hidden behind, drawn as if by magnetic attraction to the ethereal's feet.

"You lied?" he asked.

"There were only four siblings to begin with," Kaspar chuckled. "The four pillars of our kingdom and all of that. I thought that if you knew who I was, you would be reluctant to travel with me."

Asa reached for his sword, but Avery interrupted him.

"What do you mean?"

"Oh, you know fully well what I mean," Kaspar purred, black eyes sparkling. "The name Kaspar was such a clever little trick, such an innocent distraction to my cause. Two ethereals gone, and the third a miserable fool who locks herself in her little walled kingdom. Eodem is mine."

"You're not Kaspar . . . You're Erebus."

Asa's stomach dropped. He looked at the ethereal, who plumed himself, a smile twitching at the corners of his mouth.

"You don't know how happy it makes me to admit it."

He examined his tanned fingers, muttering a string of

incomprehensible words under his breath. Asa gripped his sword. He faced the ethereal, knowing that it would be to no avail. The dry ache in his heart told him enough. They were both going to die.

"We don't need to do this." Asa shook his head, trembling. "You can let us go away. We are no threat to you."

"But you are a threat, Asa." Erebus looked sorrowful. "You know my little secret. As if any of Ria's idiots could ever make their way home. I'm sorry, but this is going to be your final adventure."

"No!" Avery stood in front of Asa. "That's not fair. We're making our way home, and you can't stop us. You have to give us a chance—a chance to fight for our freedom!"

"Oh, little Avery. I never did like you," the immortal tutted. "Fair. On the count of three—but actually, that's no fun. Let's just say that you have until I kill you."

Erebus pushed his hands together, the crackle of electricity filling the air around them. Asa and Avery separated, each of them gripping their swords, ready to dodge, to attack. Time slowed down as the black eyes turned white, glowing with a power Asa did not understand. The ethereal chanted some words in a tongue the humans did not recognise before a jet of white light was released from the palms of his hands, pulsing away from him and hitting Avery with a crack like a thunderbolt in the centre of his chest.

The blond crumpled, falling to the ground with a sick thud.

"Avery!" Asa jolted into action, running as fast as he knew how to his friend. His legs, previously like lead, had lifted him into a stumbling sprint before he was able to form a coherent thought. He pulled his dragging body to Avery, who was lying on his side, curled in on himself. Asa threw himself down on his knees next to him, unwanted tears forming muddy streaks down his face. Avery was breathing shallowly, his face a mask of pain. His hazel eyes, at once brown and green, looked into Asa's brown ones.

"I guess this is the end of my adventure, then," he whispered, the words evaporating from parched lips. Blood was spreading through the blond hair, staining it dark.

Asa shook his head, screwing his face up. "No, it can't be. You can't die, Avery, that's not how it happens."

Avery cringed as he tried to move himself, reaching an arm out to Asa. His fingers, usually so warm, were like ice on Asa's cold arm. Asa covered the frigid fingers with his own and blew on them, as his friend had done for him so many times before.

"Hurts." Avery breathed, closing his eyes. "I didn't think it would hurt, Asa. I thought dying was supposed to be painless."

A weak hand moved to touch the wound on his head but Asa caught it in his own. He wouldn't let Avery know how bad it was, it would only go to upset him. Asa pulled the blond to him in a close embrace, feeling the wasting muscle shudder beneath his thin fingers. He rubbed smooth, calm circles into his back, letting the tears flow now he wasn't being watched.

"I love you," he croaked, the beach around him blurring. "I love you so much."

"What?" Avery stirred, breaths rattling in his chest. "What did you say?"

"I love you!" Asa sobbed, pulling him closer. "You were right, it was possible. You're my best friend and I love you."

Avery managed to pull away from the brunette until they were eye to eye, nose to nose. Asa could see how pale and translucent his friend's face was, drained and hollow.

"You mean that?" he murmured.

"Yes."

Asa could see his friend beginning to cry.

"But you don't believe in that sort of love." Avery tried to blink tears away from his eyes but they were too heavy. Asa wiped them away with his thumb.

"I believe in you," he whispered. Asa pressed cracked lips to Avery's forehead. He tasted of salt, of dusty snow, of the road they'd travelled. Avery smiled, relaxing into Asa's arms.

Asa thought for a moment, mind clinging desperately to any possibility of hope. He couldn't cure a head wound, he couldn't just bandage his friend. Something cracked inside him. He couldn't do it. Why was he so useless? Trembling fingers moved to unfasten Avery's cloak, catching on something. Asa inspected the item. It was the pendant given to them in the palace, all of those weeks ago.

"That's it!" he exclaimed, flicking the worn cord over Avery's head. "Avery, I can get you home."

"What?" his friend mumbled groggily, hazel eyes struggling to focus on Asa.

"You had the pendant all along, you idiot," Asa laughed, hysterical. "I can send you back."

Avery looked at him for a long, steady moment before speaking. "No, you can't, Asa."

"What do you mean?" Asa asked. "I have it here."

"It doesn't work." He grimaced in pain as Asa jolted his body.

"What?"

"The little girl told me, you know, when we were with *him*. You were being kept away from me and she just took it and asked what it was. I told them that we'd been given it to get us home and she said that it was just stone. It's just stone, Asa. That sort of magic doesn't exist, not out here. Queen Ria, she lied to us."

Asa numbly dropped the pendant to the sandy ground. He resumed the soothing back rub with eyes glazed. Avery began to sob, shivering with feverish cold, unaffected by Asa's whispered condolences and dropping tears.

"It's okay, Avery," Asa murmured, panicked mind telling him the opposite. "It's okay. You'll be fine. We just have to get you back home."

Avery gave a small lurch and lay more still in his arms. Asa looked hurriedly down, fearing the worst, but saw the continued rise and fall of his friend's chest.

"It doesn't hurt so much anymore," Avery commented, with a small chuckle. "Funny, eh?"

"Hilarious," Asa choked, a mixture of a sob and a laugh escaping together. "Oh God, I can't do this alone. I can't!"

"You won't have to." Avery gripped Asa's hand with his own. "I'll never let you go. You know that."

"Don't leave me here alone." Asa moved as close to Avery as he could. He could feel how cold the other's fingers were, cooling with an alarming rapidness. Avery's face was turning grey. Asa leant forwards, the sick tang of blood on his tongue. He had the sudden, unexplainable urge to pull his friend to his chest, to warm him up, he reasoned.

Avery's blond eyelashes were caked in blood. His breathing was fast and light, all in the throat. As Asa embraced him, he gave a small sigh. His lips were chapped and raw, and the sound of his tongue wetting them was like sandpaper against stone. Asa leant closer to his face, trying desperately to feel the gentle breath against his cheek. It only took a slight turn of his head for their lips to brush together, causing Asa to recoil. It was a wistful, fleeting sort of kiss, bittersweet in its finality.

"I'll always be with you, Asa," Avery tried to speak reassuringly, but his voice sounded strained and hoarse.

"No!" Asa shouted, dropping Avery's hand like it had scalded him. A new wave of tears pushed past his eyelashes. "You're going to leave me. It's all my fault, this always happens. I'm sorry. I'm so, so sorry."

"Asa." His breaths hitched. "You've got to do it. You've got to."

"But how?" Asa asked him desperately. "I—I can't."

Avery shook his head mutely, sinking backwards. His mouth opened and closed like he was trying to speak, but couldn't. An expression of fear and desperation coming over his dust-covered features. Asa pulled him close to him, feeling struggling breaths against his ear.

"You can." Avery reached up, batting Asa's hand away and touching the gash on his head, bringing his fingers close to his eyes to see the red on them.

His eyes rolled backwards and he fell limp, dropping his body weight fully upon Asa who held him with a desperate hurt deep in his chest. Avery smiled and gave a small twitch, and the light rise and fall of his chest stopped.

"No!" Asa pushed his friend's body onto the sand in front of him. "No! Avery, come on! Wake up, you idiot. Wake up!"

He slapped Avery's pale face, but no angry flush rose to meet him. He looked into the cold hazel eyes, and they were just that. Hazel. A light-brown colour. No sparks of caramel or green met his frantic gaze. They were gone. And so was Avery. Asa closed his best friend's eyes, fingers lingering on the still-damp cheeks. His tears had outlived him.

"You can," he murmured to himself. "You can and you must, Asa Hounslow."

He stood, legs weak under his slight body, managing to walk in small stuttering steps to his sword and pick it up, the weight enormous in his thin arms. He turned. Erebus was watching him, a small smile playing around the twisted features. Black soulless eyes gazed dispassionately into his own brown.

"You're dying, Asa," he said, voice as natural as the waves. It was an indescribable sound. It was the cawing of a gull, the wind in the grasses, the scrunch of sand underfoot.

"I know," Asa replied, vision swimming. He wanted to lie down next to Avery, to clasp him close and join him in peace. He wanted to be at home, in bed, with Avery bringing him a mug of tea and a plate of charcoaled toast. He didn't want to die. But he stayed standing. He had to do this.

"You're not going to kill me," the ethereal stated, standing neutrally in front of him. "You won't."

"And why not?" Asa asked, sword swaying in his hands. "Why should I not? You going to kill me first, is that it?"

"Oh, I won't kill you, Asa." He smiled. "Time will do that service for me. No, you won't kill me because your greatest fear is not death. You fear death as one would fear sleep. It's inevitable for you. Your greatest fear is . . . loneliness," he snorted.

Asa shook his head. "You're making a big mistake not fighting me."

"You wouldn't want to die alone and forgotten on some deserted beach," Erebus crooned, moving closer to him. "Killing you now would be a mercy compared to the pain that would cause you."

"I guess we're in a paradox here," he growled, barely coherent, head spinning sickeningly. "I wish to kill you, yet your death would cause me pain?"

"Quite right," Erebus agreed companionably. "I must say, I am surprised that the two of you got this far. You couldn't have done it without Avery."

"I know," Asa said. He clutched at his chest, where he could have sworn his heart had been just moments before.

"So, Asa. Will it be abandonment and cold or will it be sufferance and peace?" he asked him, smiling an indulgent smirk.

"Simple choice." Asa glared, steadying his footing on the shifting sand.

"As I thought." Erebus smirked.

"Quite," he replied, giving a terse smile whilst tightening his sweaty grip on the cotton wrapped iron. He waited for a moment, and then he lunged.

Erebus shrieked in anger as Asa made for him, his form growing sharper, truly inhuman. Asa heaved the metal up at him, swinging it as hard as he knew how. The beast was terrible in his anger. Erebus slashed and grabbed at Asa, who didn't feel the pain. He knew that blood was trickling down his back but did not stop his relentless assault on Erebus. He could do this. There was nothing that Erebus could do to make him scared now, nothing. Erebus was vulnerable.

Asa moved his sword through the air, hitting the creature on the nape of the neck. The blade sank into the ancient flesh like a knife into butter. The ethereal gave an inhuman screech as the force of the blow pushed him to his knees. There was a sickening crack, and its head dropped to the scarlet-stained sand. Asa stared at it for a moment.

"Mercy me, I did it. How in Eodem—?" Blood was dripping into his eyes, obscuring his vision. Asa wiped it off with a quivering hand, numb to the gouges carved like crevasses in the pale skin of his back.

He coughed, not bothering to cover his mouth. Raw droplets of red fell to the ground. Asa spat the revolting substance out, feeling his parched throat burn with the effort. Well, at least it was a form of warmth. The ground seemed to roll beneath him, and Asa struggled to keep his balance, wobbling on legs that should not have been able to support his weight. His feet were light now, too light to feel, but the act of taking a step proved too much. He crashed to the sand.

"Avery?" he asked, without thinking, holding a hand out. "Avery? No. He's gone now."

Asa sat up, vision fading in and out of focus. Instinctively he did not even try to stand up, electing to shuffle forwards on his hands and knees to where his best friend lay. Had he been reduced to this? The biting wind hit his wounded skin, allowing himself now to whimper at the harsh sensation. It took an age for him to reach Avery's side. He looked at the grey, still face.

"Avery," he whispered, collapsing on the cold sand next to him. "I did it."

He turned on his side to look at his friend, a hand reaching out to clasp his as they had done so many times before to get to sleep. Avery's fingers were not warm and safe now. Death had taken safety from those warm hands.

The beach around him was beginning to blur around the edges, the sounds of the gulls and waves growing louder, and yet more faded. Asa was tired. He stroked Avery's face with a numb hand, smiling. His body was feeling so warm; the pain was not a problem anymore.

"They said we couldn't, but we did." His words slurred together and he closed his eyes, feeling for the first time in forever watery sunlight warm his features. He rolled over onto his back, managing to close Avery's fingers in on his. He laughed in his own bitter triumph as he registered the pain in his lungs and in his back. Somehow the world felt like it was swinging beneath him, sending him off into a deeper sleep. He knew that the pain would be gone in time. He relaxed into the sand.

Asa's mind began ticking over faded memories from his past, like it was telling him his own story. He saw himself, a thin child with overlarge brown eyes and thick lashes. His parents were with him, piling more and more food upon his plate—wild rice and thick sauces with meats in them. He noticed, for the first time, them giving up their portions to the ravenous child, unconscious of their sacrifice. Avery came into the picture, a chubby, dirty child who bounded along behind him like some overgrown puppy. He saw his parents grow older, worn and thin, but so proud of him, so loving. He saw his own happiness, gap-toothed smiles and long limbs giving way to a sober face and lean muscle. He saw himself wake up for the first time alone in the house. He saw himself walk away from his past, leaving in the same way that his parents had done. He saw himself finally completing his adventure. Now he knew how his story would end.

The magical pendant that he had torn from around Avery's neck started to glow. Asa recognised the brightness of light from beneath closed eyelids. One hand reached out to stifle the source of it but it shone through. He grasped it hard in his hand.

The world seemed to bulge around him, everything too big, too bright. The intense colours and shapes made him smile despite himself. But how? His eyes were closed.

He exhaled, and then knew no more.

TWELVE

ASA COULDN'T SWIM. HE had never been able to. When he was younger, his dreams had been haunted by lakes over ten men deep, waves which crashed down on his head. He had never been one to partake in the swimming games that his friends had, splashing around in the freezing salt waters of Salatesh Lake. But he was swimming now. Or, to be precise, floating. Weightless. The water that surrounded his body was warm and all consuming. He wondered if that was what it was like to drown. But he did not feel the need to take a breath.

Nothing happened. His mind was curiously foggy, he could remember everything, or so he assumed; but could not quite put his finger on what he could not recollect. His thoughts were slow and languid, like he was suspended in a time that ran slower to the one he knew. But something twitched in Asa's mind; it was as if he wasn't supposed to be here. Though his body wanted to float in this infinite calmness, his mind realised that he was sinking.

He tried to strike out, to swim for the surface. His movements were clumsy but graceful. As he pushed his legs in a subdued kicking motion, he had the all-encompassing need to take a breath. He opened his mouth and inhaled as hard as he possibly could, panicking when nothing passed his lips. Asa's thoughts flashed tauntingly in front of his eyes. This was his last chance. If he was going to escape then he had to reach the surface. The waters were dark around him. He couldn't even see his hands, though he waved them in front of his face. At once a thought occurred to him. How could he possibly see with his eyes shut? With a tremendous effort, Asa pulled his eyes open, and he was wrenched from the warm comfort of the water with a painful ripping sensation.

He gasped aloud in shock, cold pain shooting through every one of his limbs, from his chest right down to his fingers. The sense of directionless drifting was gone in a flash, and he was lying on a cold stone floor with his cheek pressed into the tiles. All around him, filling the echoing room, were the sounds of people scattering, shrieking as they ran from him. His chest burned, nothing to do with the deep cuts across his back.

"Let me through," a low, commanding voice of a woman ordered. "As your queen I tell you, let me through."

Asa saw a pair of fitted leather boots over breeches, like those of an army officer's, and the hem of an expensive skirt. He couldn't move, and when he opened his mouth only a groan came through. "Asa Hounslow," the woman said, bending down to look at his face. With strong hands, she moved him onto his back so that he was facing the high ceiling of the Throne Room in Brandenbury. Asa was silent, mouth open half in pain and half in shock. "Can it truly be you?"

He twitched his head mutely in a weak combination of a shrug and a nod, eyes unable to focus on even the decorated ceiling. The woman, who he now recognised as the queen, removed her dark glasses, revealing eyes that were just as black as any other ethereal's.

"Kean," she barked, turning away so that Asa could not see her.

"Yes, my lady?"

"I need a healer." Her hand felt under Asa's chin for a pulse. "And quickly!"

Her voice was urgent. Asa could not quite figure out why. He heard footsteps running from the room, the slam of a door. Time drifted as he stared at the gilding above him, eyes open but barely recognising what he was seeing. The door opened again and he could feel a woman's hands on him, softer than the queen's. His mouth was pulled open and some herbal concoction was poured down his throat, another vial of liquid held under his nose, startling him with the vile smell of it.

He recoiled from the scent, pulling back from the healer's warm hands. The room was shifted into clearer focus, a terrible taste in his mouth. Asa shot up and started to retch, vomiting up the medicine. Once the violent coughing had subsided, he looked up to the faces of three people, two whom he recognised. The memories of what had happened flickered inside of his head and Asa's shoulders fell with the terrible pain of it. The healer put a small bottle to his lips and he swallowed the substance reflexively. It tasted of mint and of willow oil.

"That should help with the pain," she told him, wiping saliva away from his chin. Asa would have been embarrassed, but could not find it in him to care. He stared into the queen's black eyes, remembering the others of her kind whom he had met.

"Where is your companion, Asa?" she asked him, eyebrows furrowing. "Why are you alone?"

"Avery," he mumbled, slurring his words. "He's gone."

"Gone." She retained an impassive mask. "I am sorry, Asa."

"No, you're not." His desiccated lips cracked as he spoke. "You want to know if I did it."

"Yes," she ordered. "You may rest once you have told me."

Asa licked his lips with his dry tongue. "They're dead, or as close as they can be."

"Who, Asa?" she demanded. "Who is dead?"

"Erebus and Gil." Asa coughed, and then continued. "I don't know about Parlan."

"Gil," Queen Ria muttered, in shock. "All three. You know about us."

"Yes," Asa said, voice colder than he meant it. "I am sorry, My Queen."

Queen Ria did not appear to have heard him, but she pointed to the door. "Take him to the sanatorium."

Kean and the healer helped Asa to his feet. He staggered across the room and was half-dragged down another corridor, supported by the two Jundres citizens. The last thing that he remembered was the feeling of bandages wrapping tight across his grimy skin, before he fell into a deep, unconscious state. He did not dream at all that night.

"What was the point?" he was sitting up in a too-white room, staring down at alabaster sheets beneath his cleaned hands. "If your kind don't die, if you cannot be killed, then what is the point?"

Queen Ria stood a pace or two away from the edge of his bed. "The point?"

"Of our quest," Asa replied. "I believe that I deserve that much."

"The point, Asa, was that you rid Erebus of his physical body. He is weakened now; he cannot use magic and poses no threat to us. He may never retain a solid form, being merely an ill wind that kills some crops or topples a stall in a market square. You saved the world behind the walls, my kingdom. The snow would have frozen us eventually, would have starved us. Your actions broke his magic. They broke the curse. If our luck holds out then there should have been swift enough action to save the harvest. You and your companion saved our world some time, and that is worth everything."

"Not everything," Asa said.

"His death meant something." The queen's lips tightened. "You couldn't have said that if he had died, as so many have, in the salt mines. There were casualties on both sides of the war, Asa. Would Avery have wanted you to linger upon his death, or to move on?"

"How do you expect me to do that?" Asa asked.

"Stay here for today, tomorrow if you wish, then go home. We will give you enough money so that you won't have to work to maintain a comfortable existence."

"I think that you're forgetting something."

He stared into the dark glasses that the queen was wearing, seeing his gaunt face reflected back at him.

"I don't think so." She gave a knowing smile and cleared her throat. "Ahem."

The healer came out of an antechamber at the side of the room, wiping stained hands on her protective robes. She did not look altogether surprised to see Asa and the queen talking, the appointment had been settled as Asa slept the previous day, but her shrewd face was blankly confused.

"Did you mean me, my lady?"

"Yes." Queen Ria cleared her throat. "Mr. Hounslow thinks that we are to send him back to his home town in his current state."

"That will not be possible." The healer shook her head. "Not without his medicine."

"Medicine?" Asa sat up straighter. "But I was told that there was nothing that could be done."

"I am the best in my field," she chided him, bringing forth a large glass bottle filled to the brim with thousands of tiny herbal tablets. "There are few things that I cannot make. Take one of these each day mixed with boiling water."

"What're in them?" He uncorked the bottle and sniffed it. A pungent aroma came from within. "They smell revolting. Every day?"

"Yes, every day," she replied. "Foxglove for your blood,

hawthorn for your heart, and willow for the pain."

"But will it save me?" Asa asked, hardly believing his ears. "I thought it was too late."

His excitement was evidently misplaced, as the healer swallowed, shaking her head.

"No," she said quietly. "I couldn't do that. It will help with the pain, give you a better quality of life, but it won't save you. I wish that I could, child, but it's too far gone. Only a miracle could save you now."

"A miracle," he murmured. "Stranger things have happened, I guess."

"I'm sorry," she insisted. "Sometimes there are things that even magic can't fix."

"I want to leave." Asa sat up in bed, startling both of the women present. "When can I leave? I need to get back home before the roads are flooded by the thaw."

"You plan on going north, then?" The queen's sharp eyes narrowed. "Farther north than Brandenbury?"

"To Salatesh, if my lady permits it."

"That is where your parents lived, is it not?" she probed.

"Yes." Asa looked up at her again. "I, too, lived there until I was sixteen."

"We will send you on your way, then," Queen Ria decided. "But first—"

A distant tolling sounded out. At first, Asa thought that he was listening to a clock somewhere in the palace. But the sound grew louder and clearer, radiating through the walls themselves, fed through the caverns around the underground city of Jundres. A bell chimed like the one that had heralded his and Avery's departure but faster, joyous. Another joined it, and for a while it was like the whole world was ringing with excitement, the growing realisation that this was the day that had ended their fears. When the last chime fell, Asa was silent. His heart, though not erratic as it had been, was heavy in his chest.

"I will tell Avery's parents," he said, partly to himself. "They should know."

"Do you wish to leave?" Queen Ria asked him. "You are not obliged to take part in the celebrations."

"I would like that, thank you." Asa nodded. "But, my lady?"

"Yes?"

"Do you know what happened to my parents?" he asked, hope burning in his chest.

"I think that you know, Asa." The queen's eyes grew sombre. "You can't have missed the signs."

With that enigmatic phrase, she left the room. Asa stared after her in shock, wondering if that would be the last that he would ever see of her again. He shivered. The world seemed too full of goodbyes at that moment, as he prepared to once again start afresh. Kean opened the door, bowing his head so that all that Asa could see was his thin, well-oiled hair.

"My lord."

"Excuse me?" Asa snorted, a brief smile flashing across his face. "What did you call me?"

"My lord." Kean lifted his face so that Asa could see him. "That is the standard address for people who have done so much for our country, to protect those of us outside of the walls."

Asa frowned at the faith in his voice as Kean held out a hand to help him out of bed.

"No, I can get out of bed on my own, thank you."

As the blankets dropped, he realised with astonishment that he was wearing new clothes, not the worn ones that he had been given when he had truly left the walls. They were plain enough—a grey tunic over black trousers, but of such fine material that Asa found that his hands were drawn to the cloth. Beside his bed stood a pair of soft leather boots. He slipped his feet into them and grabbed the bottle of pills from the short table next to the bed, placing them into a bag that lay across the toes of the boots. Inside the bag was a package of what Asa imagined was food, a heavy bag of coins and a brown box.

He slipped the strap over his head and withdrew the wooden container curiously. It was only just bigger than a ring box, lined with maroon velvet. He prized the top open with his fingernails and examined the contents curiously. A silver badger on a black ribbon.

"Is that the badger?" Kean asked, dropping his honorific attitude and staring at the token with an intensity that made Asa feel uncomfortable.

"What's the badger?" Asa replied, closing the box with a click and shoving it back in his bag.

"It's the highest award of military courage that the country can give." Kean's face was lit up. "I wrote an essay on it when I studied our history. They give out only a few each century. It is a great honour."

"I'm sure." Asa rolled his eyes, straightening his tunic. "Are you here to escort me to the carriage?"

"Yes," Kean replied. "But no farther. I am needed here. My lady has a lot more to manage now that our enemy has been defeated. Why, we may even be able to reclaim the land inside of the walls!"

Asa paused, struck with the knowledge that this loyal servant would never know what truly lay within the borders of his own land. All of these people, who seemed so clever, so certain in their convictions, were believing a lie.

"That sounds exciting." He nodded, recognising where the battle was lost before it had even begun. "I'll listen for news of your successes."

Kean led him from the room with swift, quiet footsteps. Asa recognised the décor of the corridors from the last time that he had been in the palace. The satchel bounced against his legs, the pills rattling inside. He wondered whether or not he had to take one now, but on remembering the acrid herbal tea that he had been forced to drink with his breakfast, realised that he would not need to.

The wrought iron gate that divided the corridor was still open, twisted and foreboding. The stairs were now lit with the light of tens of candles, suspended in brackets on the walls. They smelled like his study did in Brandenbury. Kean kept pace with Asa as they climbed the stairs with respectful silence, Asa remembering his previous journey more with each step he took. At long last, they reached the close gap in the sheer wall of rock. Asa's thin body slipped through as naturally as a native-born Jundres citizen now.

The stables were busy in the mid-morning sun. Asa breathed in the fresh air with a feeling of quiet content. The ground was soft under his feet, the fields now cloaked in a coat of torn up mud. Small puddles and rivulets of water trickled over the path. As he walked along next to Kean, the stable hands fell quiet. One of them was readying a plainer carriage than the one that he had ridden there in, harnessing a stocky skewbald pony to the front.

"That can't be—Freda?" Asa asked, eyes widening in astonishment.

The horse swung her plain head around and snorted, pawing the ground beneath her large hooves. The stable hand managed to hold her fast, and Asa felt a jolt of recognition. Though he did not know her name, he knew the blond hair and harried look of the woman who had shown them the stables in the first place.

"You're alive?" she exclaimed.

"Apparently so." Asa walked to the front of the carriage and stroked the pony's nose, smiling at the recognition in the brown and electric blue eyes. She nudged him with her blocky head, though stood still for the hand to finish tightening her harness.

"We assumed the worst," the blond sighed. "When your horse returned, we all thought that it was over again. The only reason that someone new wasn't sent was because Neasa never came back. We thought that your companion had gone on. But, seeing you here, I guess that that is not the case?"

"No," Asa said, not wanting to talk about it. "But why is she now on the carriage? I can assure you, she was a beautifully steady mount."

"She was not undamaged by her journey." Freda adjusted herself as one of her front hooves was lifted. "Her tendons were torn all along her hindquarters. She will never make a competitive riding steed again, but she'll be good enough for a few more cart journeys yet."

Asa gazed lovingly at his horse, plain as she was. He thought of his welcome compared to hers. But didn't he have money now? His old house in Salatesh, though derelict and in a state of disarray, did have a meadow behind it. He stroked Freda's neck again. She was warm, healthy, and against all odds alive.

"I will pay for her," he declared, withdrawing a handful of gold coins from his bag, a small fraction of what he now owned. "Let her return with me."

"This is over twice what she is worth," the stable hand laughed. "I cannot legally accept this."

Asa thought for a moment. "Then let the excess be used to pay you for riding alongside the carriage and driver with another horse to return the carriage with. Take the money, ma'am. I do not want it."

"But—" She looked conflicted; however, she took the coins in her hand. "I will accompany you, then."

He pulled open the carriage door with a nod to the unfamiliar driver, refusing Kean's offer of assistance with exasperation. The window was open, and Asa said a simple goodbye to the shallow guide, a smile playing about the edges of his mouth. As the carriage pulled away from the stables and onto the road, Asa looked out at the muddy landscape. Water was dripping from the trees that they drove under, hitting the roof of the carriage with dull plops. Asa thought of the drama of the carriage ride to Jundres with a hollow sensation in his stomach. He closed his eyes, relaxed by the rocking motion of the carriage, the sounds of the two horses and the general atmosphere that the world around him was thawing.

THIRTEEN

THE MOONLIGHT WAS SHINING down on Asa's bed when he awoke. His back was aching again but he merely glared at the starry sky outside of his bedroom window and pulled the blankets back over his head, trying in vain to fall back asleep. He had been having the loveliest dream. However, the dull ache turned into a sharp pain the longer he stayed there. He waited for a few moments more, trapped between his own idleness and the soothing idea of a hot water bottle next to him. Eventually his imagination won over and he pulled the blanket off, climbing unsteadily out of bed.

His hands shook on the side table, tapping for a flint and steel. He found the necessary tool within a few clumsy movements and lit a small oil lamp that lay on his sideboard. The light startled his blurry vision and he tried to blink the fiery image of a flame out of his eyes for a few moments. The lamp's light threw the room into sharper relief and Asa clutched it, listening to the sounds of oil lapping at the inside of the well. He was not used to using the new appliance, and he held it with stiffened fingers, aloft, as he used to a candle. His tired eyes caught on to the absolute untidiness of the room. Books littered the floor and the surfaces were covered in half-drawn maps and old pens. On the wall opposite hung a huge completed map, illuminated in coloured ink. A map of their journey. Asa hobbled over to the drawing and caressed it. It had taken him over ten years to complete, so long ago now that even the little pen pricks of ink that he had inflicted upon himself by accident had faded from beneath his skin.

A mirror was next to it, wooden framed and simple. Asa saw his face with the same uneasy stirring in his stomach that he felt every day. His worn skin was translucent and pale, creased all over like a crumpled sheet of mapping paper. Dark-grey hair, unruly as ever, curled all over his head and fell to his collar. He lifted a veined hand to touch his lips, as dry and as fragile as a spider web. Deep brown eyes, unchanged by the years gone, gazed worriedly back at him. He wondered what had happened. Time had passed without him consciously noticing it.

"Seventy-one," he murmured. "Not too bad, I guess."

He looked appraisingly down at his body, now more fat than muscle, clad only in a soft, warm nightshirt. He shifted the collar with unsure hands, before leaving the mirror behind him and exiting the room, making for the kitchen with familiar shuffling steps. He was all alone now, no other human lived here. He was always alone.

There was the clatter of nails on stone in the kitchen, and Asa pushed the door open, hushing the large dog that bounced up to him. The animal sat on her haunches, staring at him with open black eyes. Asa patted her on the head and crossed the room to the cupboards, picking up a ceramic bottle and cork. He stoked the coals of the stove for a minute, waiting for the ever-present kettle to warm up. There was water already in it, flecked with white specks. He ignored the scaly interior and watched as the water in the pot bubbled, not much at first but rising into a full boil. Steam rose into the air like his breath had done so long ago in the cold. No snow had fallen in Salatesh since then. The dog whined and scrabbled at his ankles.

"Hush, Bramble!" Asa chided the dog in a voice that cracked and wavered in a way it hadn't before. "Be quiet, lass."

His accent had changed after all this time back home. Asa wasn't sure if it was his voice growing deeper or the long stay in the little town that did it. On a bad day, like this one, he could swear that he could hear Avery's tones mixed in with his own. He moved to the window whilst the kettle started to shriek and stared out at the stars.

Nearly fifty years had passed since their return, but he could not fail to be astounded by their glittering depths. He swung the pane of aging glass open to breathe in the fresh air. It was salty upon his tongue, like the sea air had been, a fine but chilly night.

Placing the hot water bottle on the table, Asa neglected to fill it. He glanced at the other bottle that lay there. Three tiny, dusty pills rattled at the bottom. He sighed. Deep within his bones was a restless, terrible longing. Asa shifted from side to side on his cold feet, considering. He would be mad to leave the house at this time, at this age. He would get sick. He could die.

"Well then," Asa chuckled darkly. "I guess I'm just mad, then."

He could smell it, the scent that pervaded through the entire building. Dust. Death. Despair. This did not feel like an occupied house. He didn't bother to light the candles as he passed them. He'd only have to put them out. Besides, there wasn't any wax to burn. He carried his lamp as he went over to his coat rack and pulled a thick coat over his nightshirt. As an afterthought, he also put on a pair of loose trousers and thick socks that sat in the washing basket from the previous day. He called Bramble to heel as he fiddled with the old clasp on the simple entrance to his home and tugged on a stout pair of boots.

The stars were shining above Salatesh as Asa and his dog crept out of the front door and into the deserted street. He could hear the wind whistling through the openings of the mines, the strong weather forcing him to wrap the thick wool coat around his frail frame. He held a stick in one hand, not even sure if he needed it now. The ground was damp under his booted feet, the residual smell of rain still in the air.

He checked the brightness of the growing moon without thinking about it. Satisfied, he started wandering down the paved road with a wistful sigh, tapping the stone with each step. Puddles were forming on the grey slabs. He knew where he wanted to go. His heart ached to get there, to stand alone once more.

The town was quiet at night, no carts tripping through the deserted streets. Bramble sniffed at the ground as she skipped along next to him. Asa paused and held her collar, forcing her into a calmer walk. Still she sprang along next to him as though she was a taut bow ready to be fired. Asa's feet led him along his usual route, past the shuttered shops and into the cleared market place. Skirting along the edges, Asa squinted to see the piece of newish art that had replaced the old fountain. Eyesight failing him, he walked towards it with a wistful tug in his heart.

Asa reached the centre of the square eventually, seating himself by the statue of a young boy holding a sword. It was made of a polished rock, smooth enough for him to run his delicate hands over without feeling so much as a hint of a snag. The frozen stone eyes gazed out across the empty market, dew still collected on the ridges of its eyelids. Its hair was wild and matted, clothes crumpled. Asa smiled as he stroked the embossed image of a badger on their chest.

"Of course they'd get the age wrong." He shook his head, breath fogging on the lonely figure.

His mouth tightened as he saw the plaque again, a simple brass plate on the front of the pedestal. He cleared away some of the moss from it with a careless hand and frowned at the words engraved in clear letters, even after all these months of rain.

In eternal gratitude to
Asa Hounslow.
Through his deeds we live on.

Asa withdrew the knife from his pocket as carefully as his trembling fingers could. He laughed. He had spent two weeks being frozen, two being desiccated, and yet a simple cold night could reduce him to shivers now. He placed it on the metal, praying that no one would hear him in the still night. The screech that the metal made from its abuse was deafening to his ears, but he continued to work away at it, adding his own line to the plaque. Avery's name, scarred into the tarnished metal.

"There," he breathed, barely moving his lips. The dog started to whimper, and Asa looked at it with a sense of curiosity. Bramble backed away, sat herself at the other side of the courtyard, and began to howl. Asa flinched at the loud noise and covered his sensitive ears until the dog quieted and lay down.

Eventually, he straightened up, sure that the night was getting to his weakened state. He finished the amendment to the plaque in a matter of moments, but a tremor flickered through his body, making his hands twitch. Asa's first instinct was to protect his work, reflexes kicking in as he shielded the straight letters that he had carved. The knife bit a tiny cut into his index finger.

Asa hummed in irritation as blood beaded on the small wound. However, he just licked it, retrieving his knife from the wet ground. Scattered moonlight glinted on the sharp blade. He slipped it back into his pocket. He looked up at the sky, tracing the stars that Avery had taught him. He didn't know them all yet, but he would, one day. He swore it.

A pensive smile on his face, Asa stroked the face of the youthful soldier, so unlike either of the pair. He pressed a chaste kiss to the stone locks and his brown eyes softened. Maybe he could see a similarity or two. If only those curls were blond.

"I know that you'd want to be with me today," he whispered. "I know that I want to be with you."

Asa shook his head, determined not to think those thoughts. He looked into the open face of the boy who had been his best friend. He had moved here to be closer to him, and it had worked for the most part.

"In their looks," he muttered, "and in their mannerisms, all I see is you, Avery. I can't force myself to stay here any longer. I have to move on."

The air grew colder and somehow thicker as he strode towards that side of town. Asa leant on his cane, limping with each step. It was barely noticeable, a dragging of the toes of his left foot. He licked his dry lips with a parched tongue, feeling them stick for a moment. His dog licked at the hand clutching the cane in a plaintive fashion, whining. Asa wondered why she was being so attentive to him all of a sudden. She had quite discarded the soft aloofness that she usually treated him with. Not unwelcome to her affection, he caressed her soft ears, directing himself towards the grown-over slagheap that lay next to the mines, an immense artificial hill.

As he began to climb the short distance, weight pushing the point of his stick into the mud, Asa thought back over his adventure. His one adventure. It was not enough; he wasn't sure that it ever would have been. If only he had had more time. Bramble rubbed encouragingly against the backs of his legs, forcing him to struggle up the steep incline. After a while of hauling his body weight up the slagheap, Asa at last stood on top of it, staring at the flat countryside which surrounded him. To the northeast he could see the clear peaks of the Moving Mountains.

He sat himself on the grass more carefully than maybe he once would, feeling his joints crack and ache as he bent down. A lush garden of flowers and mosses was growing here, over the mounds of waste stone and rubbish that had been thrown away. Asa picked a white blossom and stuck it into his lapel pin, as if it was a lover's corsage. The dog gave a light huff and flopped down next to him, head lying in Asa's lap. She gazed up at him, dewy eyes filled with an ancient, primal loyalty. Asa ran his aged fingers over her soft coat. The sky seemed in that instant to be closer than he had ever seen it, a canvas painted only just above his head. He was overcome with a sudden urge to sleep.

Asa laid back, eyes half-shut, watching the movement of the skies above him. Time seemed to slow with the skies as he fell into a state of deep relaxation, warmth spreading throughout his body despite the chill of the wind coming over the mountains. He sighed, a barely audible sound, breath visible as clouds against the dark sky. He knew in his heart of hearts that he would never again climb those peaks. The age of that sort of adventure was passing, along with him.

He lifted a weary hand to his eyes, half expecting to see it young and smooth once again, the hand of a youthful aristocrat. Asa did not feel surprised at the sight of such weathered digits, bringing his fingers to his mouth in a grim mockery of a kiss. Chapped lips against his creased skin. He chuckled, the sound not leaving his mouth. He was half aware of what was happening but his mind was dashing between the present and the past, blurring the lines between the two. For the first time in over half a century, Asa could feel the burning of hazel eyes on the back of his neck. He rolled over, sensing his companion.

"Avery," he breathed. "You're still here, aren't you?"

His desperate voice was silent in the quiet night, but another one came to him, not with the wind but within his own head. And although its tone was his own, the accent his own, the words were not.

I couldn't leave you, Asa.

ACKNOWLEDGMENTS

Whilst I would love to claim full responsibility for every aspect of this work, it is a simple fact that no book is published by just one person—especially not a sixteen year old.

I would firstly like to say a big thank you to the wonderful people at Koehler Books: to Dean Robertson for initially believing in my idea; to John Koehler for actually making my pipe dream a reality; to Joe Coccaro and Esther Keane for their hard work in editing my book; and to many others who have also worked to give me such a pleasant publishing experience. An additional wave of gratitude must also go to Shari Stauch, without whose guidance with the publicity I would be completely lost.

Closer to home, I would like to thank my mother and father, even though they said that I would never get published. After all, they taught me to read and write, and together with my brother, Edmund, have supported me in all of my current endeavours. Thank you also to Amy Grant-Moreland, Catherine and Gemma King, Alice Norrington, Lucy Kean, Nessa Blackmore, and Vasu Prasad for being patient with my non-existent social life. One day, I will have time to spend with you all.

Finally, I must thank all of my teachers through my GCSE and A-level years for not murdering me over the sheer amount of homework that I have never handed in.

It was for a good cause, I promise.